REBEL FIRE

Also by Ann Sei Lin

Rebel Skies

REBEL FIRE

ANN SEI LIN

tundra

Library and Archives Canada Cataloguing in Publication

Title: Rebel fire / Ann Sei Lin.
Names: Sei Lin, Ann, author.
Description: Series statement: Rebel skies ; 2
Identifiers: Canadiana (print) 20230557988 | Canadiana (ebook) 20230557996 |
ISBN 9781774884010 (hardcover) | ISBN 9781774884027 (EPUB)
Subjects: LCGFT: Fantasy fiction. | LCGFT: Novels.
Classification: LCC PZ7.1.S475 Ref 2024 | DDC j823/.92—dc23

Published simultaneously in the United States of America by Tundra Books of
Northern New York, an imprint of Tundra Book Group, a division of Penguin
Random House of Canada Limited

Library of Congress Control Number: 2023947953

Printed in Canada

www.penguinrandomhouse.ca

1 2 3 4 5   28 27 26 25 24

tundra   Penguin
Random House
TUNDRA BOOKS

When this flesh withers
Throw my soul unto the flames
And forge me anew

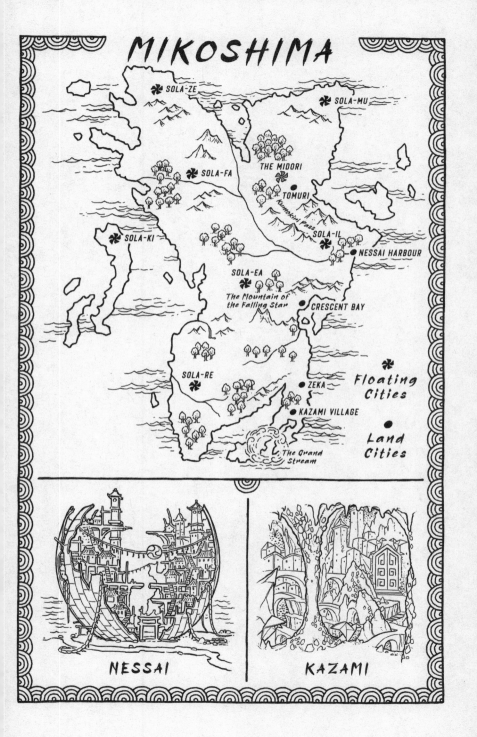

PROLOGUE

ON Princess Tsukimi's seventh birthday, her father set fire to a god.

The snow-white stag was taller than the cherry trees that lined the royal courtyard. Its antlers shook the blossoms from their branches as it was pinned down and wrapped in chains. Blank eyes rolled in fear. Hooves beat the ground, thrashing, bucking, as her father approached it with a flaming torch in hand.

Something in Princess Tsukimi's blood trembled, though she could not tell if it was awe or anger that made her heart pound.

Members of the royal court cheered her father on as he boldly approached the stag. It was all a sideshow. A display of strength. Even as a child, Tsukimi knew how performance was tied to power; how looking like you were strong was halfway toward making people *believe* that you were strong.

The stag lunged at her father. Its mouth opened to crush the Emperor's skull between its teeth, but the chains held it back. In that moment, Tsukimi got a glimpse of its white teeth, its snowy tongue, the folds of paper that made up the muscles of its jaw. The stag was a marvel of crimp folds; its hooves made from box pleats, its tail a twist of paper, its fur a series of ripple-creases that patterned its hide.

Once her father was a foot away from the shikigami, he tossed the torch at its feet. Living paper became a living pyre as fire licked up the creature's body. The stag screamed, but the flames were merciless, devouring the beast in a thrashing mass of heat and light while the royal court applauded.

"Good riddance," her brother, ever the oaf, muttered. "One more shikigami we don't have to worry about."

Cherry blossoms burned to cinders as they fell upon the flames, but Tsukimi could not tear her eyes away. Something in her blood sang to her, whispering that what she already knew inside herself was true, that what she was witnessing was in fact the death of a god. A tingle of electricity ran through her fingertips.

The stag looked at her as the flames licked up its body. When their eyes met, a thunderclap rolled through her heart.

She was sure that she would never see anything so beautiful ever again.

"That concludes the report, Your Imperial Highness."

Tsukimi blinked. She glanced around the ruined throne

room, her eyes traveling from the cracked tiles and broken statues that littered the floor to the messenger prostrating himself before her.

Ah yes, the report. She was supposed to be listening to the soldier's account of the damage to the sky city, not daydreaming of the past.

She sighed. Why should she care whether the locals were blaming her for the destruction of their precious city? A lion had more important things to worry about than the feelings of the ants beneath its feet. *She* had more important things to worry about.

It had been three days.

Three days since the dragon shikigami had burst from the underbelly of Sola-Il. Three days since her summer palace had been reduced to ruins and her library of precious books burned to ash. Worst of all, it had been three days since those shikigami children had escaped her.

Yet she was still here, stuck on this floating rock with a city in need of repair, bodies to bury, and angry locals on the verge of rioting over something that was not even her fault. Yes, she was trying to make her own shikigami. And yes, she had experimented on humans—orphans and beggars no one would miss—but the dragon that had attacked the city had nothing to do with her. Despite the Sorabito's accusations, she did not know where the dragon had come from and, frankly, she did not care. Not when there were more important things preying upon her mind.

She had heard nothing from the men that she had ordered to chase after the children. Even Fujiwa, her prized imperial Crafter, had sent back no reports. Did he not understand the importance of his mission? Did he not realize how rare and precious such shikigami were?

Incompetence! Tsukimi was surrounded by it! Irritation clawed at the back of her throat. Like a scavenger spotting the glint of a buried treasure chest, her fingers itched with the urge to get her hands on those children and take them apart.

The messenger coughed. "Your Imperial Highness, it would be helpful if you were to attend the funerals at least. The local Sorabito are also unhappy with—"

The doors to the throne room burst open.

A soldier entered, smartly dressed in a black uniform trimmed with gold. The moment Princess Tsukimi saw him she knew that he was not one of her troops: he walked with the confident swagger of a man who had not yet learned how to fear her.

"Your Imperial Highness, Princess Tsukimi!" He bowed only as low as required. Even his voice was reedy and irritating. "Your father, the Lord Emperor, sends his greetings. And his disappointment."

Tsukimi's mood plummeted. She knew exactly what was coming next.

"Due to the . . . disaster that has occurred here, he has decided to personally visit Sola-Il and ensure that order is restored. The Lord Emperor has heard the troubling rumors regarding your behaviour here. Rumors of your attempts to create shikigami. Rumors that you are conducting godless human experiments. The Lord Emperor orders you to remain in Sola-Il until he arrives. You must—"

A sigh escaped Tsukimi's lips. Her father was a chore to deal with even on the best of days. She would rather be flung into the darkest corner of Yomi than stay here and listen to his squawking.

"It's been three days since Sola-Il was attacked, and yet he only sends me this message now?"

The soldier frowned. "The Lord Emperor sent me to Sola-Il as soon as he heard what had happened. This was as fast as I could get here, Your Highness."

"He could have sent a mechanical bird instead."

"The Lord Emperor wanted to be certain you would receive his message."

"And how will he know if I have received it?"

The soldier looked at her in confusion. "Because I will report back to him, Your Highness."

Princess Tsukimi laughed. She disliked stupid men. "Will you now? And what makes you so sure?"

At last, he caught on. "P–Princess!" The blood drained from the soldier's face.

There. That was better. That was the look all men should wear in her presence.

She rose to her feet. With a cry of alarm, the man stumbled backward, tripped, and fell onto a pile of rubble. Tsukimi's smile was as thin and sharp as a knife.

"Why don't you stay here and wait for my father? I've even left you a friend." She gestured to the messenger who remained in the room, clutching his report and probably wishing he were elsewhere. "You can even take it in turns to sit on my throne while I'm gone."

"G–gone?" squeaked the man.

"Hunting," she said, sweetly. "I'm going hunting."

ONE

SILVER fish cut through the clear water. Each glimmering scale was bathed in the soft glow of dusk. Kurara peered over the edge of the stream, watching her reflection ripple beneath the splash of a fish tail. Strands of black hair, growing just past her shoulders now, skimmed across the surface of the water. Her hands—one as white as fresh snow, the other utterly unremarkable—clutched at the tufts of grass that grew on the riverbank. Her nails sank into the dirt.

A pond skater landed on the water. The fish surged towards it, mouths open. As they broke through the surface of the stream, Kurara's left arm suddenly snapped off at her elbow.

The limb crumbled into a hundred tiny squares of paper that circled around her like asteroids in orbit. A single piece of paper darted away from the others to slice through the air, impaling one of the fish through the middle with more force than an arrow. Its companions fled as a drop of blood bloomed across the water's surface. Kurara clicked her fingers, and the piece of paper brought the fish to her.

"Got one!" She pulled out the sharpened bolt of paper and tossed her catch to the boy sitting by the campfire.

Haru's hands fumbled over the slippery scales. He paled as his gaze slid down to the fish's bulging eyes and dead, gaping mouth. Thrusting it away from him, he cried, "OK, good job. Now take it back, Rara! It's looking at me!"

The empty sleeve of Kurara's kimono fluttered against her stump of an elbow. Paper danced through the air in a slow, confetti parade. As they circled her, they merged together again, each tiny square combining with the next, stretching and hardening until they formed a smooth, marble-white arm.

The paper limb reattached itself to her elbow. Kurara gave it an experimental swing. The weight felt good. Though it looked nothing like a real, human limb, it was as solid as muscle and as supple as flesh. She took the fish from Haru's nervous hands and settled down near a dead tree stump to gut and prepare it.

Maybe this body isn't so bad after all, she thought, as the tips of her paper fingers turned knife-sharp.

She did not look anything like the snow-white, origami creatures that people usually thought of when they pictured a shikigami, but she had to accept what she was. Her insides were filled with bloodless, paper organs and string-like muscles. A paper core instead of a heart lay suspended inside the cavity of her chest. Denying the truth of her body was pointless.

Besides, she had more important things to worry about.

The moment Kurara had met Tsukimi, she knew that neither she nor Haru would be able to escape without a fight. She remembered the way Princess Tsukimi had looked at Haru. The way Tsukimi had looked at *her*. There was no doubt the princess had sent men after them. Perhaps they were even already here, in this forest. Every rustling bush could be the sound of a soldier approaching. The rumble of thunder might be the growl of a hovercraft engine.

"Did you hear footsteps?" Kurara looked up as the tree branches whispered and knocked together in the wind.

Haru circled the edges of their small, makeshift camp-site. They were surrounded by bushes and trees that pressed in upon them from every side. An amber sky wheeled far above the tangled branches, the dim light casting murky shadows that made it difficult to see beyond the clearing.

"I'm sure it's just your imagination, Rara. *Again.*"

"I thought I heard voices too."

Haru sighed. "Come on, Rara, relax. Why don't you show me more of what you've learned since I've been away?"

"Away." That was what Haru called the period of time he had spent as nothing more than a tatty ball of paper in Kurara's pocket. As if he had not burned alive in that forest after the *Midori* came crashing down, leaving nothing but his core behind. As if there had been no doubt that he would come back.

Kurara wondered if he called it "away" for her benefit or his own. She wondered a lot of things about Haru these days. After he had told her that he had always known they were shikigami, after he had told her that he remembered all the things she did not, there were cracks all over their relationship—hairline fractures that she knew they both felt, even though they were pretending nothing was different. Fissures that she was scared would become rifts.

"I'll show you when Tomoe and Sayo come back."

"Ooh, you're going to give us a proper demonstration then?"

Haru's eyes lit up with joy. Kurara had not realized how much she had missed his smile until she was faced with its impossible brightness. He was just as she remembered, right down to the boyish angles of his face and the curls of ink-black hair falling into his eyes. Princess Tsukimi had done many terrible things, but at least she had done a good job recreating his physical form.

"Sure. When they get back." Kurara tensed. "Didn't they only go looking for firewood?"

Tomoe and Sayo had been gone for a while now. How long could it take to gather some sticks? They were in a forest. There was wood everywhere!

Haru opened his mouth to reply, then suddenly jerked his head towards the south side of the camp.

"Did you just hear something?"

"What?"

"I thought I heard twigs snapping."

"Oh, so it's OK for *you* to hear strange sounds in the forest, but if *I* hear something I'm being paranoid?"

"I'm being serious, Rara!"

Kurara snapped her mouth shut. A thousand awful possibilities circled her thoughts.

"Keep your ofuda out and ready." Haru stepped closer.

"My ofuda is always ready. I'm made of it, remember?"

Haru nodded. "There's something—"

"Heeeey!"

Kurara jumped. She pulled a piece of ofuda from her arm and flung it in the direction of the sound. The paper square cut through the air like a throwing star, slicing through several tree branches.

"Whoa, Rara!" Tomoe leapt clear as the branches came crashing down in front of her feet.

"Sorry!" Kurara paled. She had not meant to do that. Well, she had, but only because she thought they might be something dangerous.

Tomoe pushed her way into the clearing. Like all Sorabito, she was tall and willowy, her steps light as she hopped over the fallen branches. In one hand she held an armful of mushrooms cradled to her chest like a particularly ugly baby. Sayo trailed behind her, empty-handed and sullen.

"Look before you throw!" Sayo scowled at her. "Or have you lost your mind already?"

Kurara sucked in a sharp breath. That was a low blow. A reminder that she was not human, that she was a shikigami without a master, and that beings like her usually went mad when they were not bonded to Crafters. That Tomoe and Sayo made a living hunting her kind.

"Sayo!" Tomoe scolded her. "I thought we agreed not to mention the shikigami thing!"

Had they? Kurara flushed, annoyed that they were treating being a shikigami like some kind of awkward condition that should not be brought up in polite company.

Haru quickly switched the subject. "I see you found

18

a mushroom patch. Did you get those for me because I'm a fun-*guy*?" Pointing to Tomoe's arms, he grinned. "Get it? Because mushrooms are a kind of fungus."

Sayo pinched the bridge of her nose. "Dear skies, you think you're funny."

"I'm *hilarious*! Right, Rara? Rara?"

"Don't worry, Haru, *I* think you're funny!" Tomoe looped her free arm around Haru's shoulders.

"Did you spend all this time picking mushrooms? What about the firewood?" As glad as Kurara was for the food, she could not help but notice how the sun had dipped farther below the horizon. They would have to eat quickly and sleep immediately afterward if they wanted to set off first thing tomorrow.

"Actually, we found something amazing!" Tomoe grinned.

"Will this amazing thing help us shake Princess Tsukimi's soldiers off our tail, get us out of the forest and back to the skies?" Kurara wanted to add *and teach us about all the mysteries of shikigami blood bonds*, but she reckoned only she cared about that. "No, but it's something just as good!"

TWO

"*BEHOLD*, a roof!" Tomoe stood before the ruins of an old, run-down temple. It was not clear why anyone had thought it was a good idea to build a temple in the middle of the forest, or how long it had been left abandoned, but the cracked flagstones of the courtyard were overrun with weeds and the rotting wooden porch was crawling with ants. Fallen leaves and twigs gathered over the top of an old stone well next to an offering box that housed nothing but spiders and dust.

Kurara jerked away as something with far too many legs crawled out of the box. Besides a few moths and the odd stowaway ant, insects were not something she had to deal with in the skies.

Tomoe danced gleefully across a stone path half-buried beneath weeds and dirt. "Finally, somewhere out of the wind! I'm tired of waking up with leaves in my hair. All this ground is unnatural, I tell you. I'll need to purify myself when we get back to the sky!"

Kurara peered at the top of the building. Clouds, dyed in the bruised-pink glow of sunset, brushed over the sagging roof. A long time ago, the temple had likely been a magnificent sight to behold, but now the paint on the wooden walls had lost its color and the pillars that held up the overhang were rotting and buckled. It was impossible to tell what the statues lining the courtyard were meant to be. Lions, perhaps? Or maybe some sort of cat-headed fish?

"It's late. We might as well take shelter somewhere cool and dry for the night. Dry-*ish*," said Haru, eyeing the holes in the roof.

"Exactly! Look at the sky! Look at those clouds! It's going to pour tonight, and the last thing we want is to get sick from sleeping in wet clothes. All the mosquitoes will be out! My hair is going to curl! I'm going to stink!" Tomoe grabbed her long red braid and waved it in front of her nose. Though the tips remained the same dark crimson, it was beginning to look brown at the roots.

"I suppose it will do us no harm to stay one night; it doesn't look like anyone's been here for a long time. As long as we leave at first light," said Sayo.

"I don't know . . ." Kurara hesitated. "It looks . . ."

Ancient. Haunted. The kind of place where people disappeared and were never seen again. She was not sure if Sorabito had ghost stories similar to the groundling tales Kurara used to hear on the *Midori*, but the temple seemed like the perfect location for a horror story about vengeful monks and bloodthirsty yōkai.

Yet Tomoe was already climbing the rickety steps to the porch and the others were making their way toward the front doors. Well, Kurara supposed, the clouds *were* darkening. Even if it did not rain, the temple promised shade from the heat and humidity of late summer.

Reluctantly, she followed the others up the creaking steps. As she reached the warped threshold of the temple entrance, she swore that she heard a voice singing.

"A dying star fell from the heavens."

She froze, heart pounding, ears straining. That sound had come from somewhere inside her own head and echoed against the walls of her skull. It almost sounded like . . .

Kurara shook her head. She was just hearing things. The temple had her nerves on edge, that was all.

Taking a deep breath, she followed the others inside.

―――――――o―――――――

The interior of the temple was far larger than it had seemed when viewed from outside. Light filtered through the cracks in the walls and the corridors were blocked by vast cobwebs hanging over every path like heavy drapes. Kurara crept over the rotting floorboards, testing them first before entrusting them with her weight as she followed the others past empty rooms with battered, lopsided doors.

The dry air sucked the moisture from her mouth. Rotting floorboards and decrepit walls stank of rot and mold. The acoustics were strange too, contorting even the slightest noise so that, even though Haru was walking beside her, the sound of his footsteps seemed to come from somewhere miles away.

Kurara tried not to think of it as evidence that the temple was haunted.

They found food in what was once the kitchen—a small sack of rice and some jars of pickled vegetables in remarkably good condition—along with some old clay bowls and an iron pot.

"There was a well outside, I think. There might be water in it still," said Haru. "We could light the cooking pit and have a proper meal."

"We can make some okayu!" Tomoe crouched in front of the hearth. Kurara gave the girl a wide berth as she grabbed the bits of charcoal and dead wood scattered among the ashes. Ever since the day the *Midori* crashed—the day soldiers had set Haru's body alight—fire made her nervous.

Once the food was prepared, the four of them sat down to eat. The rice was on the mushy side, the mushrooms were a bit burnt and they had nothing to season Kurara's fish with, but it was good, hearty food. Kurara could feel it slide down her throat and settle in her paper stomach, warm and heavy.

"We'll head out at first light," Sayo said again, swirling an old wooden spoon through her steaming rice. As the *Orihime*'s navigator, and the only person who could tell that they were not walking in circles, she was in charge of setting their pace. "We're about a week away from Nessai Harbor. Once we reach Nessai, we can take an airship as far south as we can. As close to the Grand Stream as possible."

"A week!" Tomoe groaned. "Everything is so slow when you have to walk!"

"Well, if *someone* could fly us out of the forest like Himura . . ."

Kurara glowered at the mention of Himura. "He never taught me how to fly. And even if he did, I could carry one, perhaps two people, but all four of us is far too big a strain!"

She did not know how to describe the bone-deep exhaustion that came from overusing her ofuda; how it felt like someone sticking their hands in her head and pulling her brain in different directions. Even the giant paper ball she had created to save everyone when they had fallen from Sola-Il had been difficult to hold together.

"Hear that, Sayo? If Kurara flies us out of the forest on her ofuda, we'd have to leave you behind." Tomoe nudged her.

Swatting the girl away, Sayo muttered something under her breath.

Kurara had seen Himura's paper creations, of course. She had once marveled at the way his ofuda folded together to create such intricate beasts—box pleats turning into fur, curling paper becoming horns and fangs, and folds cascading into limbs. She had seen Himura fly on a paper falcon larger than a horse, but she had never seen him carry anyone else on the bird's back.

Still, a part of her wondered if she could do more. If she were better at controlling ofuda, perhaps they could have left the ground behind by now.

"It's not your fault, Rara. I bet the best Crafter in the world couldn't manage flying with four people." Haru pulled

24

a bunch of mushrooms from their skewers and slid them into her bowl.

Kurara startled. She had forgotten how perceptive Haru could be. She was no longer used to having someone so closely attuned to her moods, someone who could read every furrow of her brow and twitch of her lips with pinpoint accuracy. How strange it was to be so known.

Especially when she was just discovering that she did not know Haru that well at all.

"So we go to Nessai. Then from Nessai we go to the Grand Stream. And what if the *Orihime* isn't there when we arrive?" said Tomoe.

"It'll be there," Sayo insisted. There was no room for doubt.

"But what if it's not? What do we do about Suzaku?"

"Suzaku? You're going to *hunt* Suzaku?" Haru jerked his head up so suddenly he almost stabbed himself on a mushroom skewer. "I thought your crew only hunted shikigami that were a danger to others. Suzaku's not doing anything! It never leaves the Grand Stream."

Staying in one place was part of the problem, thought Kurara. The phoenix shikigami that ruled over the Grand Stream was known to tear apart any ship that flew too close. People said that the beat of its wings was the source of the violent winds that created the Grand Stream. For years, it had remained hovering around the southern tip of Mikoshima: an immovable, untouchable monster that none could destroy. No one could pass through the winds, and plenty of people died when their ships sailed too close to the currents.

"Oh, Suzaku's killed plenty of people!" said Tomoe. "It's a nuisance! Fortunately, Captain Sakurai's got a foolproof plan. And when we're done, we'll be famous throughout the empire! Not to mention rich."

Haru frowned. He did not look upset, but Kurara knew him well enough to tell when he was troubled.

"Let's concentrate on getting to Nessai Harbor first," said Sayo. "We'll need to keep a low profile. I bet Princess Tsukimi has soldiers waiting for us there too."

"Why do you say that?" Kurara's core felt as though it had dropped into her stomach.

"Because that's the only big city close to Sola-Il, and if we don't want to walk all the way to the Grand Stream, that's where we need to go to get an airship back to the skies. I know it. Princess Tsukimi knows it. She'll have someone waiting there for us, you can bet on it."

Great. It was not as if Kurara needed more things to be anxious about.

Her skin tingled, but not the way it did when she was near a Crafter. Perhaps it was just her imagination, but Kurara could not help but feel an odd pressure on the back of her neck—the strange, hair-raising sensation of being watched.

THREE

THAT night, Kurara lay awake listening to insects scuttle across the floor. While the others slept near the corners of the empty prayer room, she lay on top of the frayed tatami, unable to close her eyes.

Even if the temple was not haunted, it made all sorts of eerie noises. The floor creaked each time she rolled onto her side. The sound of tree branches scraping against the temple made her think of the man-eating yōkai from old folktales tap-tapping their spindly fingers against the roof as they beckoned to be allowed inside.

"*A dying star . . .*" someone sang with a voice like the wind through the trees.

Kurara sat bolt upright.

Her gaze swung across the rest of the empty, sagging room. Moonlight crept through the broken windows and played across the splintered floor, bright enough for her to pick out Tomoe and Sayo sleeping near the opposite wall, huddled together despite the heat. As usual, her instinct was to reach out for Haru, but when she searched for a familiar mop of jet-black curls she found him missing.

Panic slammed into her with the force of a speeding qipak. Where was Haru? What if he was in danger? His core . . .

No, she forced her swirling thoughts to a complete halt. Haru was fine. She was not going to lose him, not again.

I am a lotus. I am a lotus floating upon the calm water. Nothing troubles me. I rise above the mud to bloom upon the surface of a silent lake.

Kurara held her breath and waited for the dread to ebb away. Once she felt calmer, she slipped out of the prayer room and into the dusty corridor.

The shrine was just as haunting at night as it had been during the day. A warm draft blew through the rickety walls, making the thick cobwebs flutter.

Kurara thought she heard the voice again, but perhaps it was just the wood squeaking under her feet. The temple was built in a way that played on her hearing. Sounds were swallowed up and tossed aside. Things that were close sounded far away, and things that should have been far away felt as though they were right next to her. Even the echo of her footsteps was distant and warped.

As she approached another set of battered shoji, the voice faded into silence. Sliding the doors open, she found herself inside another prayer room. The floor was covered in the same worn tatami. Broken statues of six-armed gods lined the cracked walls, staring at her with stony displeasure, but Kurara's gaze was only for the person in the middle of the room.

Haru sat cross-legged beneath a large hole in the ceiling where the moonlight streamed down and bathed him in silver light. His head was tilted back, his expression inscrutable.

"There you are, Haru! Don't disappear like that!"

Haru swiveled around to face her. "Oh, hey, Rara."

"Don't 'hey Rara' me! What are you doing here?" Kurara gave him an exasperated look. She was used to him disappearing from their quarters on the *Midori*, usually to steal food from the kitchens or play a prank on the entertainers, but sneaking around here—when Kurara did not know whether one of Tsukimi's soldiers might pop out of the shadows at any moment—was different.

"Couldn't sleep." Haru grabbed his ankles and rocked back and forth restlessly.

"Why not? Did you have that nightmare about being chased by a giant salmon again?"

"Once! I had a nightmare about salmon once, and now you never let it go!"

"You wet yourself."

"Once!"

"If not giant salmon, what's keeping you up?" Kurara sat down next to him. This was not the first time she had stayed up with Haru through the dead of night. On the *Midori*, they would often soothe one another through nightmares and bad days and Madam Ito's beatings. Sometimes, they would sit together with Kurara's pieces of origami between them, and she would make the paper animals dance for his entertainment. Kurara did not miss the *Midori*, but a part of her did long for those secret moments together when she could pretend that there was no one else in the world but the two of them.

Haru pressed his lips into a thin line. "When we fell from Sola-Il, I asked you what you wanted. Heading back to the skies, finding the *Orihime* again, hunting Suzaku . . . is this really what you want to do?" he asked.

"Is that what's really keeping you up?"

"You don't get to answer a question with a question, Rara." Haru made a face at her. She could not distract him so easily. He knew all her tricks.

"Of course there are other things I want."

Kurara was full of nothing but wants, each one growing tangled and vine-like until she could not tell where one desire began and the other ended. She wanted Princess Tsukimi to disappear from her life. She wanted to punch Himura in the face. She wanted to know more about shikigami and about herself, too. She wanted some way for shikigami to live without needing a bond with a Crafter. She wanted them to have real freedom.

Want and need were two different things though, and right now they needed to get out of the forest. She *needed* to find the *Orihime*, if only to make sure Tomoe and Sayo would be safe. And perhaps to deliver that punch.

"I made a promise. I said that I would help the *Orihime* hunt Suzaku."

"That's still not an answer." Haru was annoyingly stubborn.

Kurara groaned. "*Fine.* If I could wish for anything in the world, it would be for shikigami to be free. *Really* free. No need for a blood bond. No fear of going mad."

No matter how hard she tried, she still could not forget the adoring look Akane gave Himura whenever he was near.

She could not forget the look in Himura's eyes when he told her that shikigami were nothing but tools.

"Really?" said Haru. "*That's* what you'd wish for, Rara? Not 'I wish that Haru and I will always stay together' or 'I wish everyone in the world would recognize how funny and smart and handsome Haru is'? I'm hurt!"

"Oh, don't be so full of it!" She laughed even as she delivered a swift jab to his ribs.

Haru squirmed out of the way, chuckling, but the moment of levity was short-lived. It was hard to be cheerful in such a somber place.

"If I could wish for anything, it would be for you to tell me everything you're keeping from me," she said.

Haru's smile disappeared.

Kurara sighed. She knew the situation with her past-self, with Aki, was complicated. She was the one who had asked Haru to wipe her memory, then made him swear not to tell her anything. She did not want to push him or punish him for something that was her fault, but it was frustrating to know that there were parts of herself that she was missing. Parts that had been taken from her.

"I asked you not to tell me, but I can change my mind, can't I?"

Haru sighed. "I can't just break my promise to you—to Aki—but . . . I need to think about it, OK?"

"But what if there's something in my memory that could help the shikigami? I can't just let them live like this," she said. "It's just not right. But we know so little about them! How are shikigami made? Why do they lose their minds if they don't bond with a Crafter? *Is* there a way for them to live freely without going mad? If I knew more about them, if I knew more about myself, perhaps I could do something to help!"

But no one knew how to make shikigami anymore. At least, that was what Himura had told her. Princess Tsukimi could make a shikigami body, but she did not know how to create a core. That knowledge had been lost to time.

Kurara got to her feet and began pacing around the room. Crafters—humans—might not know how to create shikigami, but what about shikigami themselves? What about those ancient, fearsome ones that ships like the *Orihime* hunted? Perhaps there was still something, some information, that she could squeeze from one of them.

"Haru, if you know something . . ."

"If I knew a way for shikigami to live without needing a bond, I'd tell you, Rara."

Kurara opened her mouth when a sudden, sickening thought crossed her mind.

On Sola-II, one of Princess Tsukimi's imperial Crafters had formed a blood bond with Haru. It was a tether that forced a shikigami to obey their master. To love them. It was a sick and twisted thing.

"If I killed Fujiwa . . ." she said, darkly.

Haru laughed as if the thought of her killing anyone was absurd. Kurara was not sure whether to feel flattered or insulted.

"If you kill Master Fujiwa, would I lose my mind? Is that what you're thinking? No. You and I are different. We can live without a blood bond. Although I *do* feel the pull of it, I feel something inside me that yearns to return to my master's side."

Before Kurara could reply, she heard the faint sound of someone singing.

"A dying star fell from the heavens . . ."

"Do you hear that?" Kurara glanced around the empty room, but she still could not tell where the voice was coming from.

Suddenly something cracked beneath her heel. Before she could take another step, the floor collapsed, crumbling into a sinkhole beneath her feet.

"Rara!" Haru lunged for her. Their hands barely missed each other as she fell through the floorboards and into the darkness.

Into the jaws of a giant beast waiting below.

FOUR

KURARA did not realize that she had landed inside the thing's mouth until she saw teeth closing around her. Hardening her paper arm, she jammed her limb between its white fangs to stop it from crushing her but, to her surprise, the beast did not bite down. In a shower of dirt and splintered wood, it thrust its head through the floorboards and into the prayer room, gagging as it spat Kurara out of its mouth like a piece of spoiled fish.

She landed right on top of Haru just as the paper doors slammed open and Tomoe and Sayo skidded inside.

"What in the blue sky is going on?" shrieked Tomoe.

Kurara rolled to her feet. As the dust settled, her gaze locked on a pair of marble-white eyes and the beginning of a massive, dirt-stained muzzle.

The beast was enormous. Only the front of its body could fit inside the room while the rest of it was hidden somewhere beneath the floorboards; its head brushed against the ceiling, its front paws gouged long trenches into the floor. Though it was covered in dirt, Kurara could clearly make out the line of folds along its origami body, the reverse pleats that patterned its fur, the crimps along its snout.

A bear. Kurara's breath caught in her throat. *No, a shikigami.*

Without warning, the bear brought a giant paw crashing down against the ground. Pieces of tatami split apart upon impact.

"Move!" Sayo yanked Kurara out of the way just as the bear's claws swung inches from her face.

As Kurara stumbled back, Tomoe drew the tanto that she kept tied to her obi and charged. The edge of the knife flashed in the moonlight.

"Sayo, keep it distracted!" she yelled as she ducked beneath the bear's paws, moving with a graceful precision she had picked up from years of hunting shikigami. The room shook from the strain as the bear braced its front paws against the floor and pushed.

It was trying to haul itself up. Kurara dreaded to think how big the bear would be when the bottom half of its body was out of the ground. Surely, its head would go right through the roof.

"*Humans,*" it growled. Its white gums were pulled back over chipped and ancient teeth. "*What have you come here for?*"

Like all shikigami, its voice echoed inside the heads of everyone close by. Kurara winced as its rumbling voice beat against the walls of her skull. The bear was as hulking and intimidating as an ancient forest god, but she did not think it had lost its mind yet. There was understanding and intelligence in its gaze. Its shouts were not the mad ramblings of a crazed beast.

Sayo charged toward the shikigami and leapt onto its trunk-like forepaw. With a furious yell, she wrapped her legs around the limb and climbed up to its shoulder. The bear screamed and shook itself furiously but Sayo clung on, yelling, "Stab it, Tomoe!"

"STOP!"

Kurara's paper arm crumbled. Her ofuda swirled through the air—a hurricane of paper butterflies.

To her surprise, everyone froze.

"Stop, just stop!" Taking a deep breath, Kurara glanced at the shikigami and held her hands up in a pacifying gesture. "You're not mad, are you? You understand what I'm saying, right? There's no need to fight. We just wanted a place to sleep. We're not here to hurt you. In fact, I'm a shikigami too. Like you. Look."

She pulled back her empty sleeve to reveal her paper limb. In the moonlight, the arm looked almost silver. Kurara lifted the stump of her elbow to show the hollow cavity inside her body and the paper strings that acted as muscles.

The bear leaned down, peering inside her empty arm before rearing back in shock. *A shikigami human! But I thought . . ."*

"Hey, I'm a shikigami too!" Haru, who had spent the entire fight avoiding falling roof tiles, scurried around the holes in the floor to stand beside her. "I'm Haru. And this is Kurara."

Sitting up a little straighter, the bear waved a massive paw. *"Banri. I am and will always be Banri."*

Sayo slipped off the bear and retreated to a safe corner of the room, though the floor was littered with splintered wood and broken tatami, and pieces of the roof were coming down. "You don't have a master anymore, do you? Are you *going* mad? Is that why you were trying to kill us?"

"I was not trying to kill anyone," Banri snorted, affronted. *"I was merely defending myself. Shikigami lose themselves and attack people. But humans need no such excuses to hurt others."*

Sayo muttered something unpleasant beneath her breath, but she seemed content to stand next to Tomoe and let Kurara do the talking—a role Kurara was more than happy to fill.

"Banri, what are you doing here?" she asked as her ofuda returned to her, transforming back into her paper arm. She took a step forward. Shikigami were fearsome and marvelous beings: snow-white creatures that felt as ancient as the stars. It was hard to believe that she and Haru were just like them when they looked nothing alike.

The shikigami visibly drooped. *"My master and I were traveling when he died. Our home is a long way away. I tried to return, but . . ."* It shuffled its paws, nervously. *"I kept running into . . . people. Villagers screamed at my very presence. Hunters tried to burn me. The nights were dark and full of wriggling, creeping things. I had never been on my own before and it was scary without Master to guide me.*

"Then I felt my mind slipping. I did not think I would make it home, so when I found this abandoned temple, I buried myself beneath it, where no one would bother me. Where I could be at peace."

"And we disturbed your rest. I suppose we should apologize for that." Tomoe sat down on a broken wooden beam. Sayo hurriedly shushed her, as if she thought Tomoe might be in danger simply by talking to the shikigami.

Banri shook its head sadly. *"It is a shame you are not a Crafter, even though you can control paper. If you were, we could form a bond."*

Kurara hissed. "You *want* a bond?"

The shikigami's claws scratched at the ground, leaving long gouges in the floor. *"To bond with someone is painful, but losing one's mind is painful as well. If you knew how frightening it is to feel your own mind slipping away from you, piece by piece, you would want the same."*

Kurara and Haru glanced at one another. Guilt churned through her gut. She and Haru did not have to worry about bonds or losing their minds, but for so many shikigami their only options were an eternity of servitude or a slow, agonizing madness. It felt wrong. Like she had cheated at life somehow and was now enjoying a reward she did not deserve. Why was she different? If she could live without a bond, there had to be a way for other shikigami to do the same.

Uncomfortable silence festered inside the ruined prayer room.

"It cannot be helped. Leave me to my solitude." Banri began to sink back into its hole.

"Wait!" cried Kurara. "There has to be something we can do to help! Do you really want to spend the rest of your life down here, alone in your own tomb, just waiting to lose your mind?"

It was too cruel, too awful. When was the last time Banri

had felt the sunlight on its back? Or the breeze rustling through its fur? When had it last spoken to other people like this?

The bear's ears perked up. Its hopeful expression was rather endearing.

"I would like to go home. My master had a student. Another Crafter named Oda. If I could reach her . . . If I could only form another bond . . ."

Again, the shikigami spoke of tethering itself to a Crafter. How could Kurara agree to something that would end with Banri becoming a puppet? How could she help the shikigami chain itself to a Crafter who might not even care about Banri's thoughts and wishes? That was the complete opposite of what she wanted!

Yet, what other choice did Banri have right now? As much as Kurara despised the idea, if this was what the bear truly wanted then who was she to deny it? A shikigami had its own thoughts and wishes. Desires that should be respected, even if Kurara did not agree with them.

"Why not come with us then?"

"You're joking," said Sayo.

"Where is your home? We can . . . we can help you get there." Kurara reached out a hand toward the bear's snout, ignoring the way Sayo was glaring daggers at her.

Banri shuffled a little farther away from Sayo. Despite its size, it seemed to find the navigator particularly menacing.

"We lived far, far south, in a village called Kazami."

Kurara could not help but notice Haru flinch.

"I have bad news for you then. Kazami doesn't exist anymore. It was destroyed years and years ago," he said.

"It was an old Crafter village. Now it is nothing but ruins, yes. But Master's student should still be there. They moved in long after Kazami was destroyed. We all lived in the ruins together," said Banri.

"A Crafter village?" Kurara's imagination ran wild with the things she might discover there. Perhaps she would find clues about how to create shikigami. Or something that would help her understand how blood bonds worked.

Was she starting to sound like Himura? She feared that she might be.

"Kazami is dangerous. The place will be falling apart," said Haru.

"You heard him," said Sayo. "Besides, the *Orihime* will be waiting for us at the Grand Stream. We don't have time for detours."

That was right. They had to go to the Grand Stream. They had to hunt Suzaku. Sayo and Tomoe wanted to return to their ship, to their crew, and their way of life. Yet the more time Kurara spent on the ground, the more she felt her wants and desires pulling her away from them.

She tried not to dwell on it. She did not want to part with her friends, but she did not know how much longer she could stay with them when her heart was leading her down other paths.

Tomoe jumped down from the wooden beam. "I have an idea! You said this Kazami place is in the south, right? And so is the Grand Stream. We're all going the same way so why not travel together? When you were alone, people kept attacking you, right, Banri? Well, people won't attack you if they think you're controlled by a Crafter. If Banri carries us, we'll cover a lot more ground. So, Banri gives us a ride and Kurara can pretend to be its master. It's a win-win relationship!"

"You're only saying that because Kurara wants the shikigami to come with us." Sayo scowled.

"I'm suggesting it because it's a good idea. Do you doubt my genius, Sayo?" said Tomoe.

It *was* a good idea, Kurara thought. Simple yet efficient.

"No, you always take *her* side!" hissed Sayo. "Even on the *Orihime*, you would always hang around her like she was some shiny new toy! And then during the Festival of the Seventh Star, you ditched me to—"

Sayo suddenly clamped her mouth shut as if someone had cut the chords of her throat. Kurara had not thought it possible, but the girl's face reddened even more and her cheeks puffed out like she was swallowing a pickled plum.

"I did what?"

Sayo threw up her hands. "Nothing! Fine, let's go! Bring the bloody bear! Bring the whole forest for all I care!"

Banri nudged its nose against Kurara's side. *"If you will have me, I will go with you."*

In the corner of her eye, Kurara noticed Haru turn away to hide the gloomy look on his face. She frowned, wondering what danger he saw in her decision.

FIVE

"*I love you, Master.*"

Himura awoke with a start.

The sound of pounding hammers echoed through the thin walls of his room. The ceiling shook in time with the banging. Heavy footsteps raced past his door. Something crashed to the ground, followed by alarmed shouts. For the hundredth time that day, the water pipes gurgled.

He sat up, groggily, and peeled his eyes open. His head throbbed. Dawn was creeping at the corners of his window, beams of soft gray light brushing against the faded tatami of his quarters and over the pillow of his futon.

His room was the same as always, except for the additional heavy, leather-bound tomes he'd added to the stack that sat in the corner next to piles of blank paper. He tried to tell himself there was nothing different about today compared to the hundreds of other times he had woken up bathed in the cool light of the morning, and yet, when he gazed at the books, he felt a certain heaviness hang from his shoulders.

"I love you, Master."

The echoes of a dream clung to his thoughts: a dream where Akane leapt into the flames of Princess Tsukimi's library as fire twisted around the fox's body. Those flames then turned into Kurara, who looked at him with a gaze that burned harsher than wildfire.

Himura scrubbed his hands over his face. What had happened inside the sky city should not bother him so much. Akane was just a shikigami. Kurara was just a student.

A student, his mind supplied, *but also a shikigami—one that deceived and lied to you.*

He was used to losing things: his family, his village, comrades he had once considered friends. He could get another shikigami. He could find another student.

It should not bother him.

The water pipes rumbled louder than an earthquake.

The *Orihime* had been forced to flee from Sola-Il so quickly they'd had no time for repairs; the crew was doing all the maintenance work while in flight. The past few days had been noisy enough to wake the dead. He sighed and clutched his pounding head. He just wanted one night of restful slumber.

If he had that, perhaps his dreams would not be filled with the smell of smoke and the sound of crackling flames.

Himura stepped out of his quarters, throwing open the door and slamming it shut behind him.

———————o———————

The *Orihime*'s hangar was an inferno of noise. Every single sound that traveled through the ship—the clash of hammers, the buzz of a drill—echoed through the cavernous room. Metal walls vibrated beneath the strain of the engines. The heavy whirr of fans hummed through the air.

Himura's boots clattered on the first step of the steel staircase as he picked his way down to the landing. Dangling orange lamps gently swayed to and fro, providing just enough light for him to see where he was going. Behind him, an engineer—the only crewman Himura had managed to wrangle away from repairs—mirrored his steps.

"I'm telling you, Mr. Himura, the pipes will be fixed once we've finished the hull!" The boy's lilting Sorabito accent was not as pleasant as Tomoe's, but nevertheless rang across the walls like a melody—a single note of birdsong carrying over the sound of thrashing engines and gurgling levistone boilers.

"You'll fix it now if you know what's good for you. The crew can't sleep in this racket!" Himura did not say anything about his own fractured sleep, but he was sure the boy understood the real reason he was complaining. In fact, he had the irritating feeling that the engineer was trying to be kind to him.

Ever since Sola-Il, he had noticed the way the crew tiptoed around him. Whenever he ventured from his quarters he saw their pitying looks, their consoling nods. They mourned the loss of Akane and worried over their missing comrades. As both Kurara's teacher and Akane's master, they expected Himura to share those feelings.

They did not know Himura had betrayed his student.

They did not know that he had ordered his shikigami into the flames.

As if to confirm his suspicions, the engineer said, "I'm sure Miss Kurara and the others will be back soon. There's no reason to lose sleep over it. Miss Kurara will make sure everyone returns in one piece; she's a Crafter after all."

A Crafter, the boy had said. Himura reminded himself that he was the only one on the ship who knew that Kurara was actually a shikigami. He knew that he should at the very least tell Sakurai the truth, but that would mean telling the captain exactly what had happened at Princess Tsukimi's summer palace, and how Himura had treated Kurara. How he had ruined everything for her.

"Forget about her and concentrate on fixing the pipes." Himura led the way to a small metal door to the side of the hangar. When he stepped inside the boiler room, nothing seemed amiss. The egg-shaped furnaces were exactly where they should be. The pipes that covered the walls were silent.

"Look—" the engineer began, but the moment he entered Himura shoved him aside.

"Stay back!" He drew a square of ofuda from his bracelet and threw it at the furnaces. The piece of paper whistled through the air and buried itself in the metal wall.

Right above the head of the man crouching behind the boiler.

Himura stiffened. The figure hiding in the shadows was no crew member. How had this intruder made his way onto the *Orihime*? How long had he been here? Himura's headache was getting worse. Of all the times to pick up a hitchhiker, it had to be now, when the crew was stretched to breaking.

"Go and get Captain Sakurai," he ordered the engineer.

The boy did not need telling twice. Turning on his heel, he ran out of the room to fetch the ship's captain.

"Come out!" Himura shouted at the huddled figure. "I can see you."

There was a beat of silence. Then, slowly, a pair of raised hands emerged from behind the boiler. Next was a head—a perfect oval sitting upon a thin, brittle neck. The man stood up, wrapped in a ragged cloak and a dirty kimono. His tall, lean frame left no room for doubt: he was a Sorabito.

"Who are you?"

The man grinned. He moved faster than Himura anticipated. One moment he was standing behind the boiler, the next he was right in front of him, pulling something out from the sleeve of his kimono.

Himura jumped back on instinct. His bracelet broke from his wrist and his ofuda separated into a dozen squares of paper that moved to shroud him in a defensive swarm.

The man threw himself to the ground and reached into his sleeve. Pulling out a small shuriken, he hurled it at Himura's neck.

Himura knocked it away with a hardened piece of paper. The weapon spun off-course, clattering somewhere among the furnaces. Before the man could retaliate, Himura's ofuda crashed into him like a tidal wave, pushing him backward and throwing him into the wall. Paper shackles locked around his wrists and ankles, keeping him from moving.

"What is the meaning of this?" cried Himura. "Who are you?"

The man laughed. "You don't know who I am, but I know

46

who you are. My daughter mentions you all the time in those stupid letters she sends to her mother."

"Your daughter?"

There was something distantly familiar about the man's expression. Himura's mind flicked through the faces of the crew until he found an answer.

"Tomoe?"

Himura could see it now. That broad nose. Those sharp eyes. The way their smile could eviscerate everyone in the room.

"My daughter." The man nodded. "Don't worry, she didn't betray you. I think she believes me dead."

"Who are you?" Himura was not used to asking twice.

The man smiled. "My name is Kazeno Rei."

SIX

THOUGH there were only a few hours left before sunrise, the group snatched what little sleep they could and woke with the dawn, ready to set off before the summer heat made traveling unbearable. After a hurried breakfast of mushrooms and the rest of the temple's rice, they filled up some old gourds with water from the well and gathered outside.

A chorus of chirping cicadas greeted them, along with the morning mosquitoes that were up bright and early for their first meal of the day. Haru delighted in watching them land on his arms, trying to suck out the blood he did not have.

"I like to imagine their disappointment." He cackled as he watched one fly away from him with an irritated whine.

He seemed to be in a better mood than he had been

last night when Banri had mentioned the ruins of Kazami village, though Kurara knew better than to assume anything. One did not survive on the *Midori* for years without learning how to put your feelings away in little boxes while you dealt with the rest of the world. And if Haru really did not want to go to Kazami, Kurara wanted to know why.

First, however, they had to help Banri out of the temple. A shower of dirt cascaded from the bear's paper fur as they pulled the shikigami out of its hole and into the harsh morning light. When it stood on all fours, its head was level with the temple roof, and if it reared back onto its hind legs it could peer over the tops of the pine trees.

The outside world seemed to stun it. It glanced at the rocks dotted with shiny white mushrooms and the tangled thickets with the look of a man facing the ocean for the first time. There was awe in its gaze. And trepidation.

"Is something wrong?" Kurara tried to remember how she had felt the first time she had left the *Midori*; the terror of facing an unknown world.

"There are a lot of cicadas." Banri flinched as one flew right past its nose.

"Of course there are cicadas! It's the forest!" said Sayo.

"I do not remember there being this many." The bear shrank from her withering disdain much like a giant wolfhound cowering before a particularly unimpressed cat.

Sayo's eye twitched.

"Banri! Pick me up!" Tomoe held her arms out to the bear like a toddler demanding attention.

"Tomoe," Sayo warned. "Don't get too cozy. You can't trust a shikigami without a master."

49

"Sayo," Tomoe countered in exactly the same, flat tone. "Don't look at me like that! We made a deal, now get on board!"

Before Sayo could protest, Banri seized the back of Tomoe's clothes and lifted her into the air. Sayo gave an alarmed squawk, reaching for a weapon she did not have, as the bear tossed Tomoe over its shoulder, placing her on its back.

The girl landed with a surprised *oomph*. Tomoe blinked, as though she could not quite remember how she had got there. Then, she began to laugh.

"Woo! This is amazing! I'm as tall as the trees!" She squealed with delight, rocking back and forth and stretching out her hand as if she could gather up pieces of the sky.

Without warning, Banri nipped at Kurara's kimono and hauled her into the air too. She yelped. Her legs kicked out in panic as the ground fell away. Banri twisted its head around as far as it could manage and dropped her between its shoulder blades. Kurara grabbed handfuls of Banri's paper fur to steady herself while Banri picked up Haru next and then—very gingerly—Sayo.

Once everyone was on its back, the shikigami marched forward, brushing against the trees. Its lumbering body swayed from side to side like a boat rocking upon the tide. Bushes rustled as creatures scurried out of its path.

"Woohoo! This is great, isn't it?" Tomoe's grin was as wide as her face.

"As long as the bear knows how to keep on course." Sayo grabbed the back of Tomoe's kimono to keep her from falling off. "If we're to catch up with the *Orihime*, we need to reach

Nessai in five days. From there, we'll take an airship south."

The tops of the trees felt so very close. The air was cooler and the sky brighter from up here. Kurara tilted her face toward the sky and let the sun bathe her face in light. A grin tugged at her lips. Riding on Banri's back was like being carried by the wind. With a single stride, the bear covered more ground than Kurara could dream of.

Excited chatter drowned out the chirping chorus of cicadas. Kurara let her paper arm crumble away and spin around her, transforming into a small origami dog, then a cat, then a crane.

Finally! Now they were *really* moving!

When they eventually stopped for dinner, the sun was going down. The others scattered to fill up the water gourds and forage for more edible plants. Kurara was about to join the others in the search for food when Banri nipped at the back of her kimono.

"What's wrong?" she asked.

"*Nothing,*" the bear said, sheepishly. "*Just . . . it is getting dark and you are all going far away.*"

Kurara stared at the shikigami. The others were no more than six feet away, searching through the thickets for mushrooms and berries, and the sun was still out, even if it was momentarily hidden by clouds. Surely it had been darker beneath the temple, in Banri's makeshift lair.

"Do you . . . want me to stay with you?"

"*Please.*" Banri suddenly jerked its head away to avoid

a cricket hopping past. The bear whimpered. *"I would rather not be alone. There are bugs."*

There must have been bugs beneath the temple too, thought Kurara, but she held her tongue.

"How are you feeling, Banri?"

"Perfectly fine. I am a shikigami after all. I have no need for food or sleep."

"I wish I didn't have to rest either. I don't understand why I have to when other shikigami don't get tired. It's inconvenient." Kurara sighed. How much closer to Nessai would they be if they did not have to stop to eat and sleep all the time? Not to mention that having the necessary plumbing needed for digestion meant that toilet breaks were a thing too.

Banri chuckled. *"But I have seen humans eat. They seem to always enjoy themselves when they do."*

Kurara could not think of anything enjoyable about the last few meals she had eaten. There were only so many different ways one could cook a mushroom.

"In order to appreciate the good, you have to put up with the bad. Maybe that is why your body is as it is. To be as human as possible. I admit, I am jealous. We normal shikigami were made for war. We were made to be useful to our masters."

"What do you mean?" asked Kurara. She could not help but remember how Himura had called shikigami nothing but tools.

Banri looked at her in confusion. *"Do you not remember the war?"*

"The war? I . . . I'm not sure . . ." She glanced over to the other side of the camp where Haru and Sayo were discussing

52

something. From the way he was waving his arms, Haru was either trying to explain the difference in edible flora or replicating the mating dance of a red-crowned crane. Perhaps Haru would know what Banri was talking about.

"*It is fine to not remember.*" Banri mistook her uncertainty for forgetfulness. "*Memories are like drops of water in a bucket. There are only so many drops the bucket can hold and, over time, it begins to overflow. There are many things that I have forgotten too.*

"*I was created near the end of the war, but my master at the time told me how it started. When this country was still young it was ruled by Crafters, by clans that split the land into pieces. Those clans fought one another for control over the entire country, and they created us to help them in those battles.*"

"I think I've heard of that." The entertainers on the *Midori* sometimes performed plays about the beginning of what would become the Mikoshiman Empire. In those plays, there was always something or other about how the age of Crafters was over and the dawn of a new, enlightened era had begun, or some similar patriotic fluff like that.

"*When you first revealed yourself to me, I could hardly believe it. I did not think there were any like you left. You are an old type of shikigami—one that was not made to simply fight.*"

Banri's words made Kurara queasy. She disliked the thought of living for so long when she remembered none of it; the idea that perhaps she and Haru were the last of a particular type of shikigami that no one knew how to make anymore.

"But what makes us so different? You said that you were made for war and I wasn't. But what does that *mean*?

What's the difference between how you were made and how I was made?"

"Why do you wish to know these things?"

"Because I want to find a way for shikigami like you to live without a bond! Don't you want to be free?"

"Free? Oh, I would not know anything about that. It would make me nervous." Banri shuffled its paws like a schoolchild afraid of giving the wrong answer.

"But no one would be able to force you to do something you didn't want to do. You could do whatever you liked!"

"You mean, I could spend my days sleeping in the sun?" Banri's voice slipped into a whisper. *"I could lie around all day until birds landed on my back and no one would try to burn me or yell at me?"*

"Of course!"

"And if I wanted to sing, no one would tell me to be quiet?"

"You could sing as much as you wanted!"

Banri stared at her in awe. *"That sounds wonderful!"*

Kurara ruffled the bear's fur, although given its size she could only reach its leg. How strange, she thought, that such an old shikigami could feel so young.

"I just need to figure out what exactly makes us so different. If I knew that, then . . ."

Then perhaps she could understand how to free the shikigami from their bonds without the risk of losing their minds.

"You could try asking Oda when we reach Kazami. Master always said that Miss Oda was a good student. Perhaps she will share her secrets with you."

Himura had said that everything regarding how to make

shikigami cores was lost to time. She was not sure how much a Crafter could tell her these days, but Kurara smiled regardless.

"Oda is the name of the person you want to meet, isn't it? That's a good idea. Thank you, Banri."

The bear beamed at her. *"And when I bond with Miss Oda, perhaps she will let me continue traveling with you. It would be all right to stay with you, would it not?"*

The edges of Kurara's smile tightened. She thought of the bond: how it compelled shikigami to love their masters; how it made them want to stay close. Would Banri say the same thing once it was tied to someone?

"Of course," she said. "You can do whatever you want."

SEVEN

THERE was an easy rhythm to traveling with Banri. As Tomoe had predicted, riding upon the bear's giant back was far better than traveling on foot. Although Banri tended to freeze whenever it spotted a spider, they were still covering ground much faster than before. With each day that passed, the forest no longer seemed like such an impossible, endless maze.

The summer sun hung high in the afternoon sky, beating down with a relentless ferocity. Despite the heat, Haru and Tomoe sat between Banri's shoulders, jabbing at one another and bickering over who got the privilege of sitting on the bear's head. "Move over, Tomoe, you sat on Banri's head yesterday!"

"Ha! Just try and overthrow me, you weasel!" Tomoe shot back.

"See this, Rara?" cried Haru. "This is the audacity of humanity."

"Children," snapped Sayo, "could you stop that?"

They did not stop. Sayo silently implored Kurara for back-up, but Kurara only had experience reining in Haru's mischief. She had no idea what to do with *two* troublemakers. Besides, there were more important things occupying her mind: things like the war Banri had mentioned, and wondering when they would finally reach Nessai Harbor.

Things like Kazami village.

She flexed her paper fingers and transformed them into different types of claws—cats' and bears' and the talons of an eagle. The pointed paper edges were as hard and sharp as a blade. As the trees thinned, the land sloped downward and into open fields of knee-high grass tangled with bushes and flowers in full bloom. The distant rise of mountains outlined the horizon.

"A dying star fell from the heavens, and from that star grew a tree," Banri warbled, off-key.

"A dying star fell from the heavens!" Tomoe shouted more than sang.

"And from that star grew a treeeeee!" Haru joined in.

"Someone shoot me!" Sayo groaned.

"The people of the village—"

The bear ground to a halt. The movement was so sudden Tomoe would have fallen off Banri's head if Sayo had not caught her in time.

"The people . . . People . . ."

"Banri?"

In the corner of her eye, Kurara noticed Tomoe reach for her tanto. She held up a hand, silently begging the girl to wait.

"*To . . . to . . .*" Banri shook its head, forcing Tomoe and Sayo to slip down from its shoulders to the safety of its lower back.

The shikigami's claws dug into the earth. Banri shivered and twitched as if trying to hold back something explosive inside itself. Kurara scrambled to its neck and ran a soothing hand over the side of Banri's face, her fingers combing through the paper fur of its cheek and down its snout.

"A dying star fell from the heavens and from that star grew a tree," she sang softly as her hand continued to massage calming patterns into the bear's fur.

The others held their breath and waited. Slowly, gently, Kurara coaxed the bear back from wherever its mind had flown to.

After a moment—a long and agonizing moment—Banri blinked.

"*I apologize. I am feeling better now. Thank you, it will not happen again.*" The shikigami hung its head low.

When Sayo opened her mouth to say something scathing, Kurara shot her a hard look. Now was not the time.

Haru glanced from one taut expression to the other. The tension was heavy enough to club a sky whale to death.

"Maybe we should take a break. It's almost dinnertime, isn't it?" he said, smoothly.

"Great idea!" Kurara tried not to sound too relieved. If Haru had not intervened, she might have broken into song and dance just to distract everyone. "Let's all, er, do stuff! Sayo, Tomoe, why don't you two collect some firewood? Banri, you can go with them and make sure they don't get lost. And Haru . . ."

She paused. If Haru was truly one of the first shikigami ever created, maybe he knew of some way to help Banri.

"Haru, you can pick some mushrooms with me." Perhaps he would be more willing to talk if they were alone.

"Sure! I can teach you which ones are edible and which aren't."

As the others dismounted and scattered, Kurara gave Banri's flank a gentle pat.

"I'll be back soon," she reassured the shikigami, before pulling Haru away.

As they moved farther into the thickets, Kurara let her smile drop. Here, the forest grew back in a tangle of gnarled pines and broad oaks that let through so little light she couldn't help but feel rather hopeless. The dense, humid air weighed heavily on her shoulders. Every breath was like drinking in soup. The sooner they could get out of here the better.

"Look at this, Rara. Can you tell me whether it's poisonous or not?" Haru pointed to a small group of mushrooms peppering the side of a dead tree. They were dark yellow on top, the color of burnished gold, white beneath, their heads shaped like flattened umbrellas, their stalks thin.

"Haru." Kurara did not really want to talk about fungi. They both knew that.

"Wrong! It's poisonous. Very poisonous. You should be able to tell by the coloring. This shade of yellow is several tones darker than the shade you find on edible mushrooms. Some villagers call it fool's gold, you know. Because fools see its pretty color and try to eat it. And then they die. Painfully."

"Haru, I don't care about mushrooms. I'm not going to

ask you to tell me about myself or Aki either. I know that you won't. I know that you made a promise, and I respect that, but if you know about shikigami, if you have any information that might help, I want you to tell me. You saw what's happening to Banri. Even as we speak, there are probably shikigami all over the empire slowly losing their minds, attacking people, hurting themselves. Isn't there something we could do to help?"

"I've told you before, Rara, I don't know how to grant the shikigami their freedom. Frankly, it's not something that interests me, either. Isn't it enough that you and I are together again? Can't we just enjoy that?"

Kurara stared at Haru in shock. What did he mean he wasn't interested? Did he believe that there was nothing wrong with the way that Crafters treated their shikigami?

"H–how can you say that?"

Haru shook his head. He pointed to another group of mushrooms. They were small and shiny, growing together in one large lump; a dozen tiny cap-like heads bursting up from the ground like boils. "Poisonous or edible? Come on, Rara, this one is easy."

"Haru!"

He looked contrite. "Well, what's the point of torturing yourself over something that can't be changed? What's the point of wasting time trying to find a way to free the shikigami when it's impossible? You might as well try teaching wolves how to eat vegetables or asking humans not to go to war. Meeting the *Orihime*, rejoining your ship, those are things that we *can* do. Those are things we should be spending our energy on."

You sound like Sayo, Kurara wanted to snap. Sayo was the practical one of the bunch. Haru was meant to be the optimist who saw nothing as impossible. He was meant to always be on her side.

"If we go to Kazami and meet this Crafter that Banri wants to bond with, maybe she'll know a way to help shikigami!"

Haru poked at the soft caps of another group of mushrooms. There was something childish about the way he jabbed his finger at them so the heads bounced back and forth. "And what do you think this Crafter can tell you? What do you think she knows that could possibly be of any help?"

"Well, I won't know until I get there, will I?" Kurara snapped. "But whatever she knows, I bet this Crafter person will be far more helpful than *you*! Why don't *we* need a bond? Why don't *we* lose our minds? What makes us different? Can't you at least tell me that?"

Haru did not answer right away. After a moment, he stood up, brushing the grass and leaves from his clothes.

"It's our cores."

"What about them?" Kurara was shocked that he had answered. Perhaps her words had struck a nerve somewhere.

"Do you remember what mine looked like?"

"Not exactly." She remembered how surprisingly solid Haru's core was; how it had felt more like polished bone than paper. She recalled the dent from an injury long ago—an injury that had stolen his ability to use ofuda like she could—and the strange patterns written along the core in dried blood.

"In order to live, shikigami need to be tied to a Crafter, to someone who can act as an anchor, which stops them from losing their minds. All shikigami need a bond of some sorts. Us included."

"What do you mean?"

Haru placed a hand over his chest. "I mean, we also have a bond. It's just that we're not bonded to a Crafter."

"Then who are we bonded to?"

"Not who, *what*. The stars. The patterns on our cores are written with the blood of the stars."

"The blood . . . of the stars." Kurara could not help but snort. It sounded like something out of a fairy tale. "And what exactly is that? Stars aren't living things, Haru. They don't even have blood!"

She turned away from Haru and headed back through the thicket, scowling. It all sounded ridiculous. Nothing but a bald-faced lie. Did he really not know what made them different or was this just another thing Haru was keeping from her?

No, if he wanted to keep the truth from her, he would have chosen something more believable. Haru had always been an excellent storyteller—a trait he had picked up on the *Midori* by shirking his duties to watch the entertainers in the banquet halls. If he wanted, he could spin a tale that had even the head cook eating out of the palm of his hand.

Kurara's paper fingers turned to claws that dug into her own palm as she made her way back to Banri's side.

EIGHT

CAPTAIN Sakurai's room was full of birds. A dozen pairs of glass eyes stared down at Himura in silent judgement as he waited for the captain to speak. Mechanical birds roosted on the wooden pegs jutting out from the walls, each too motionless to be real. Their bodies gleamed in shades of bronze, copper and silver, color-coded by speed. Stained-glass feathers reflected the dim sunshine that struggled through the skylight. Coming face to face with so many unblinking stares was as awe-inspiring as it was unsettling. It made him feel as though he were on trial.

Sakurai was unremarkable for a Sorabito: his tall, willowy figure was typical for a person of the sky, but he had a way of commanding attention no matter where he was. The captain sat cross-legged at his writing desk, surrounded by a number of cushions of different colors and sizes.

Mismatched lacquer cups were stacked in the middle of the table, next to a pitcher of watered-down sake.

"All right." He selected a cup and filled it with sake. "Explain."

Explain. Himura hated that word. Explanation always sounded like an admittance of failure. Still, he took a deep breath and did as he was ordered.

". . . and then *he*"—Himura pointed to the man next to him as he relayed what had happened in the ship's hangar—"said that he wanted to see *you*."

Sakurai's smile was sharp as he took in the intruder. "How long have you been on my ship?"

He was angry—something one would never be able to tell unless they knew him as well as Himura did. Sakurai's smile never left his face, but behind those sharp, white teeth he was biting back a storm.

"Since you fled Sola-Il. I hitched a ride during the chaos."

Kazeno Rei was slender and bird-like. He stood proudly despite the smell of engine oil and three-day-old sweat that clung to his rumpled kimono.

What arrogance, thought Himura. This was certainly no way for a captive to behave. A captive was meant to grovel, to beg in terror, to do the opposite of everything Kazeno Rei was doing right now.

As if in agreement, a large, bronze owl hooted disdainfully from its perch and soared upward to roost in the rafters. It moved quietly, like a real owl, but for the tiniest tinkle of metal on metal.

"He's Tomoe's father," said Himura, beneath the weight of the birds' lingering stares.

Sakurai lowered his cup and raised an eyebrow. "Really? So you're the leader of Sohma."

"Tomoe told you about me?" said Rei.

"I know everything about my crew."

Not everything, Himura stopped himself from saying. Sakurai did not know that Kurara was a shikigami. He did not know what Himura had done to her. What he had done to Akane.

Why did he have to feel guilty? He wasn't guilty. The memory of his actions on Sola-Il should not curdle in his gut the way they did. Akane had been a . . . miscalculation, an accident; none of it was his fault. There was no reason to fear Sakurai's judgement, or to feel bad about what he had done. Shaking off his thoughts, he turned his attention back to the problem at hand.

"What were you doing at Sola-Il?" asked Sakurai. "Are you the reason I'm missing three members of my crew?"

"Why would you think I'm to blame?" asked Rei.

"Because one of the missing crew is your daughter."

"Oh, I saw Tomoe. We had a nice family catch-up, but after that I don't know what happened to her. It's hardly my fault you can't look after your own people."

No, it was Himura's fault. At least, he was responsible for Kurara's disappearance. He did not know about Sayo and Tomoe, but he could guess that the three had somehow ended up tangled together in some mess. A mess that Himura had created through his betrayal.

Again, he thought of smoke and fire and the smell of burning paper. It wasn't his fault. How was he supposed to have known that things would end so disastrously?

"You—" Sakurai set down his cup. The sound of the base clacking against the table jolted Himura from his thoughts—"are awfully bold for someone in your position. Do you know what would happen to my ship and crew if someone discovered that we were harboring a Sohma rebel? What is it exactly that you want?"

"A ride," said Rei. "To Zeka."

Sakurai lifted an eyebrow. "Zeka? That's a groundling city on the coast. Don't you want to return to a sky city?"

Rei shrugged. "I've been listening to your crew talk. I know about your repair problems. And your money problems. My people can help you. I have men on the ground. Take me to the port town of Zeka, and my people will refuel and repair your ship free of charge."

It was a tempting offer. The *Orihime* was low on everything: fuel, food, money and morale. Sohma had a vast network of rebels. They had people everywhere in every trade. It would not be hard for Rei to gather some funds.

Or perhaps we could just kick him off the ship now and let him tumble all the way to the ground, thought Himura. The man was poison, plain and simple. If they let him stay on board, he would infect the rest of the crew.

"Captain, let me turn him in at the Patriots Office. The reward we'll get for handing in a member of Sohma will be just as good as anything this rat might pay us." Himura did not call Sakurai by his title often, but he could not bear to stand and listen to this snake try to wriggle his way to freedom.

Rei glared at him. "A Patriots Office? And where will you find one all the way in the middle of the sky?"

"I can fly to the nearest office and be back within a week," said Himura. "Let me get rid of this louse. The rest of the crew are busy with repairs, but I have nothing to do until we reach the Grand Stream. Let me go."

Rei's only reaction was to sigh. He did not seem furious or terrified at all, but rather as if he had merely stepped out of a shop without an umbrella just as it had begun to rain.

It was an act; it had to be, thought Himura. The man was just trying to unnerve them by acting as if he did not care.

But what if . . . something in Himura's gut whispered. *What if he really does know something we don't?*

"I was trying to be generous. Because this is a Sorabito ship and I am fond of my own people, I thought I would be kind in offering to pay for your ship's repairs in return for a ride. See now how you spit in the face of my generosity? Very well, take me to the Patriots Office if you wish. Turn me in. But what about Tomoe?"

"What *about* Tomoe?" Sakurai's eyes narrowed.

"My daughter is part of your ship. The groundlings don't know about our connection. You've probably faked her identification papers, haven't you? I'm sure they're enough to pass a standard inspection, but if you hand me in and I'm questioned, I'm sure everything will come to light. Who I am. What I've done. And my connections, too. My *family.* How will the military feel when they find out that the daughter of a notorious member of Sohma works for you? They might get awfully suspicious."

Himura sucked in a sharp breath. His ofuda circled him like a swarm of angry wasps. "Tomoe has nothing to do with Sohma."

Rei shrugged. "I know that. You know that. The question is, will that matter to the military? Deep down, you know how they'll react, don't you? You know you've done nothing wrong and yet you also know that it doesn't matter if you're innocent. You know what the military will do to you—we're all dirty sky rats to them. That's why you gave my daughter forged papers in the first place."

He laughed. "Don't you see how pathetic that is? You do business with the military, you sell them cores, you work hard and risk your lives hunting shikigami for them, and yet you're still so afraid of them! You call me the terrorist, but who is really terrorizing who, hmm?"

He was right. Himura could endure many things, but the fact that Kazeno Rei had a point was perhaps the most unforgivable insult of them all.

Sakurai slammed his cup against the table. The sake in the pitcher sloshed over the rim, spilling alcohol all over the polished wood.

"Fine!" He seethed, like a man trying to crush boulders with his teeth. "But I'm not keeping you on the ship. Himura will take you to Zeka. We'll let you go free there. Himura, take this snake to where he wants to go and then meet us at the Grand Stream."

Himura's hands shook. The only thing on his tongue was the iron tang of defeat.

Rei smiled like an animal baring its teeth. "That would be perfect."

Interlude

I am a flower
Nourished by my mother's blood
One day I will bloom
Into a crimson demon
That shall devour the world

—Written by a Crafter of Unknown Origin
(from the personal library
of the Imperial Princess)

Princess Tsukimi would have to ditch the airship soon. The *Jurojin* was a beautiful vessel, all sleek curves and silver birch floorboards that cut through the clouds like a blade through silk. Lovingly crafted by the finest Sorabito shipwrights in the seven sky cities, her father had taken it, renamed it, and gifted it to her during her coming-of-age ceremony. A Sorabito newspaper—back when her father had allowed such things to exist—had called it "the greatest insult inflicted upon the people of the sky."

Tsukimi did not want to part with the ship, but it drew

too much attention. Her father was already angry with her. She did not want him tracking her down and dragging her back to Sola-Il—not when she had other places to be. For now, she sat back against one of the many plush armchairs in the captain's cabin and let the ship ferry her away from the sky city.

Somewhere out there, those shikigami children awaited her. Tsukimi tapped a finger against the wooden armrest. Patience was not her strong suit. With a click of her fingers, she could have the finest delicacies, the rarest jewels and richest silks from around the empire. Chasing after someone else in order to get what she wanted was a novelty, and not one that Tsukimi appreciated.

Her imperial Crafters and their shikigami took up position around the cabin: ever-watchful guard dogs armed with enough paper to bring down a sky whale. To Tsukimi's left, Goro—a large, bald man—and his crow shikigami inspected the vine-like decorations running along the corners of the cabin. To her right, Tamada—a slight young woman—stood near the door. Her wolf shikigami paced by her side.

The regular soldiers in her entourage stood around the edge of the room like men who had suddenly been forced into a cage with a pack of very hungry tigers. It was tradition that each member of the royal household should have four imperial Crafters to serve as bodyguards. Without Fujiwa by her side to complete the number, Princess Tsukimi felt rather diminished.

And of course, Inui was missing.

Tsukimi was sure the old crone was dead, killed in the attack on Sola-Il, perhaps. She had never liked that cackling hag, but it was a pain to find a replacement.

"Would you care for a game, Your Imperial Highness?"

Goro sat down opposite Tsukimi. He took out a deck of cards and began to shuffle them. They were expensive paper cards printed with the image of a snow-white crane. Tsukimi plucked one from the top and flipped it over. The face revealed a moon over a field of susuki grass.

"Beware, beware! Master Goro cheats!" his shikigami cackled.

"Be quiet, Yui!" Goro scolded his crow.

"No, let it speak." The way the shikigami's voice echoed through her head was always a delight. She patted the armrest like a mother beckoning to her child. "Yui, come here."

"Go to Her Imperial Highness." Goro nodded.

The white crow fluttered its paper wings and landed on the spot Tsukimi had indicated, but the princess could not help but dwell on how it had not moved until its master had told it to.

One hand flipped the moon card between her fingers while her other hand stroked the crow's wings. If *she* had a shikigami, it would obey her without hesitation.

Her grip on the crow's feathers tightened, though if the shikigami felt any pain it did not show it. Annoyed, Tsukimi released the bird.

"Actually, I think I'll go for a walk."

Sensing her foul mood, Goro looked away. Tamada, standing near the door, stopped glancing around the cabin

and took a sudden interest in her feet. Their reactions only served to annoy Tsukimi farther. Why were they acting like that? Didn't all Crafters love her?

She waved off the guards who tried to accompany her. There was nothing but tiresome people on board this ship. She wanted to be alone.

The *Jurojin*'s wide, white corridors and ornate doors led to rooms fashioned in the latest Western styles. Tsukimi did not have a particular destination in mind when she left the cabin, but her feet took her to the library. The heavy leather tomes on the *Jurojin* were gifts from her father—tedious books on statecraft and the history of the empire—but she found their presence soothing nonetheless.

The Mikoshiman flag was pinned across the back wall, overlooking a large reading table covered in maps of the empire. Two soldiers stood huddled around the table with their backs to her, so deep in discussion that they did not hear her footsteps.

"Her Imperial Highness has ordered us to stop at Nessai. We'll leave the airship once we reach the Harbor." The first—a tall, thin man with an impressively bushy moustache—tapped a gloved finger against a point on the map. "We should be there in three days."

"Thank the gods! I don't think I can take this much longer—I'm tired of being around these monsters!" The second man was almost as wide as he was tall, with fingers that reminded Tsukimi of the sausages a foreign diplomat had once gifted to her father. His belt had a few extra notches in the leather, and the man's weapons—a katana

and a standard-issue pistol—lay on one side of the table. She moved closer.

"You mean the shikigami?" The first soldier smoothed his fingers across his voluminous mustache.

"And the Crafters! I know it's tradition for the imperial family to have Crafters as bodyguards, but those people aren't . . . well, they're not right! With that devil magic and those paper monsters, I don't know if you could really call them human! Why is the princess so obsessed with them?" Sausage-fingers had a voice that boomed across the library and rattled the bookcases. His companion winced at the sound.

"Yes, well . . . But of course, you wouldn't know. The only people who know are the servants who worked in the imperial palace when Princess Tsukimi was born."

Sausage-fingers raised a curious eyebrow. "Know what?"

His companion looked at him coyly. "You know how Princess Tsukimi and Prince Ugetsu have different mothers? Well"—he leaned closer to the man—"the rumor is that Princess Tsukimi's mother was a *Crafter*."

"My, and *all* the servants in the imperial palace know this, do they?" Tsukimi marched forward.

That was a lot of people she would have to get rid of.

Both men jumped as if their very souls were being yanked from their bodies. Mustache's knees trembled. Sausage-fingers stood very straight and very still, as if he thought she would not see him if he did not move a muscle.

"Y–Your Imperial Highness! Forgive us, I was . . . We were—"

Princess Tsukimi took a step closer, bringing her face just a few inches away from the man's. There was something churning inside her stomach. She thought about the way the soldiers had whispered as if her mother was something dirty that could only be spoken about in hushed tones.

Allowing an insult to go unchallenged was a sign of weakness, and Princess Tsukimi would not allow herself to be weak. She was angry, but in the right hands, everything could be a weapon. Her rage was no different.

"I have been insulted. How dare a lowly soldier such as yourself speak of me in such a manner! Do you go to the shrine and gossip about the gods too?"

Tsukimi took a moment to bask in the men's fear. Yes, this was how things were supposed to be. Worshippers would build shrines just to beg the gods not to destroy them. *She* was a god—it was only right that men should beg her for forgiveness.

"You." She pointed to the mustachioed man. "I wonder where you heard such things? Soldiers with loose tongues are better off without them. Or, better yet, without their heads."

The man's mouth opened but no sound came out.

Sausage-fingers stumbled backward, knocking his weapon off the table. His katana tumbled to Tsukimi's feet. "Princess, please, I wasn't—I didn't say anything! I don't believe those rumors! Of course not! There's no way you are anything but of pure, royal blood! I know that your mother was a most gracious and honorable noble lady. She was not some filthy Crafter! Why, the very thought—"

Before he could finish his sentence, Tsukimi had picked

up the man's katana and held the blade to his neck. She heard his sharp intake of breath, noticed how his throat bobbed nervously as the fierce edge brushed against the hairs on his skin.

"My mother was a Crafter, it's true. My father tried to keep it a secret, but it seems there will always be rats wherever you go. He has not done enough to stop their squeaking. I shall do a better job."

She did not look behind her even when she heard the click of the library door opening or the soft pad of footsteps. When Tamada and her wolf shikigami stepped into her periphery, she could sense her bodyguard's nerves.

"Your Imperial Highness, the ship's pilot would like a word with you about our flight path." Tamada kept her gaze lowered and her head bowed as she spoke.

"Very well." She stepped away. "In the meantime, be a dear and have your shikigami get rid of these two pests for me."

"Yes, Your Imperial Highness." Tamada bowed.

Spluttering all sorts of apologies, the men fell to their knees.

With a cheery wave, Tsukimi closed the library door behind her, shutting out the screams and the wet, crunching sound of bones breaking.

She drew out the playing card she had taken from Goro. The full moon shone brightly against a red-ink sky. Tsukimi stared at the card in her hand until the image burned itself into her eyes.

Fold. Turn into a crane, she ordered.

Her hands shook. The card remained still.

With a grunt of frustration, Tsukimi crushed it and hurled the crumpled card at the far wall. Why not her? She had a Crafter for a mother—a woman her father only spoke of in whispers at night when he thought no one was around to hear. A woman Tsukimi hardly remembered.

Why had she not become a Crafter too? What was it that she was missing?

Well, if no one would give her what she wanted, she would just take it.

NINE

BANRI continued to plod on as the sun plunged below the horizon, traveling through the evening and well into the night in order to reach Nessai. No one brought up the incident of Banri's stuttering mind and, after a few days of travel, the event seemed truly forgotten. The bear sang as it moved through the dark forest, drowning out the sound of chirping crickets and the wind whispering through the branches.

The others were asleep, sprawled out in various positions along Banri's back, while Kurara remained on watch. She fought against the gentle sway of the shikigami's back, lulling her to sleep.

"A dying star fell from the heavens," Banri warbled as her thoughts swam around her head.

A dying star . . . The blood of the stars was a silly, ridiculous thing, but the more Kurara thought about it the more she wondered if there really was some truth to the words. After all, she could sever a man's head from his neck with a single piece of paper. Who was she to decide what was too ridiculous to be real or not?

"And from that star grew a tree . . ." Banri's voice seemed to fade away as her eyelids became heavier.

For the first time since she had fallen from Sola-Il, sleep came easily.

Kurara dreamed of the heavy flap of wings and the rustle of paper. At first, nothing felt amiss, but as the sound grew louder the edges of her dream sharpened into focus.

It was too dark to tell where she was, but the stillness in the air and the feeling of floating beneath clear waves felt strangely familiar. It was similar to her dreams of Haru and Aki—the sensation of walking through a dream. Or rather, a memory.

Suddenly something crashed onto the ground behind her. A shikigami. It spread its wings wide as it glowered and screamed at her.

"Aki! Aki, what have you done to me? What have you done to us all?" There was no mistaking its incandescent rage.

Kurara opened her mouth to speak, but what came out did not feel like her own voice. Someone else was speaking with her tongue, yelling awful things at the shikigami, who in turn screeched a thousand curses back at her.

"Aki!" The sound of flapping wings grew louder. *"You will never be forgiven!"*

Before Kurara could figure out what was going on, a roar jolted her out of the dream.

"Master, do not leave me alone!"

Kurara sat bolt upright just as Banri tossed her from its back. Her ofuda formed a cushion, catching her and then the others as they too were thrown off. Banri's claws gouged the earth as it screamed.

"Kill me, kill me! Please do not ask anything more from me!"

The others scrambled to their feet. Birds fled from the trees, their caws of alarm filling the normally quiet night air as the bear roared.

"I will not lead anyone to their deaths! Please, no more, Master! Do not ask me to bring them to you!"

"It's losing its mind!" snapped Sayo. "See? This is why I didn't want to—"

"Banri!"

Kurara scrambled to her feet. She ran toward the shikigami as it thrashed from side to side. Trees crashed to the ground as the bear bashed into them, ripping out roots and splintering trunks in half.

"Don't leave me, Master! I don't want to be alone!"

"Banri, you're not alone! I'm here! We're all here!" Kurara reached out to grab its leg, but the bear jerked away from her touch and began to stomp through the trees, just like the mindless shikigami that terrorized towns and flattened villages.

"Tomoe, light a fire!" Kurara heard Sayo say.

"No!" shouted Kurara. "Wait! Just . . . just give me a minute!"

"You want us to wait for it to crush us like bugs?" cried Sayo.

"Give her a minute!" Haru grabbed her shoulder, only for the girl to shove him away.

"Sayo, let Kurara handle this," said Tomoe.

Sayo whipped around in outrage. "She'll get us all killed. She'll get *you*—"

"Then protect me." Tomoe grabbed onto Sayo's sleeve, pulling the girl away from the thrashing bear. "Stay with me."

Sayo's expression softened, but Kurara had no time to appreciate Tomoe's intervention. If she did not get Banri under control, someone would get hurt. She tore off her left arm. It crumbled in her hand, turning into a dozen squares of paper that orbited around her like a stream of comets.

With a roar, the bear lunged again, catching Haru by the back of his clothes. Haru screamed as Banri shook him like a ragdoll before tossing him into the forest somewhere.

"Banri, stop this!" Kurara fought the urge to run after him, to make sure that he was OK.

Her ofuda merged together into a long paper rope. With a click of her fingers, the rope shot toward the shikigami, racing past the bushes, darting between trees, until it wrapped around the bear's rear foot and pulled itself taut.

The bear fell with a groan, crashing into the dirt. Kurara quickly hurried to its side while the rope wrapped around the rest of its limbs, binding the shikigami in knots.

Kurara placed a hand on the bear's snout as it snarled and snapped at her. "Banri, listen to me!"

"Please, please, Master!" the bear howled and sobbed.

"A dying star fell from the heavens and from that star grew a tree," Kurara sang softly, slowly, the way a parent would calm their wailing child.

Banri's snarling ceased. Its huge, colorless eyes blinked once, twice. Slowly, it raised its head and turned to look at Kurara, then at the others, who were staring at it with caution.

"Oh."

The silence that followed was as taut as a koto string. There were many things Kurara wanted to say, but she had no room for them next to her horror and grief. How close had Sayo and Tomoe come to destroying Banri? And if the shikigami had not snapped out of it, she could not have blamed them.

"W–what do you mean, 'Oh'?" Sayo spluttered, outraged. "Is that all you have to say? This isn't—you're—you're losing it!"

"Did I . . . hurt any of you?" Banri was ashamed. Afraid. Its voice trembled as it spoke. "I apologize. I did not mean to—I just—I thought I was feeling better. Traveling with you, my head has been clearer than it has been in years. I did not think this would happen."

Kurara opened her mouth when a strangled shout suddenly emerged from the bushes.

"I'm fine too, thanks for asking!" cried Haru. "I'm fine, but, er . . . maybe you should all come and see this?"

Kurara exchanged a confused glance with the others before hurrying in the direction of Haru's voice. The bushes gave way to tangled grass and then opened into wide, rolling hills. As she broke through the thickets, Kurara found herself looking down across fields of long grass and farmland. Her breath stopped short. She hardly noticed Haru beside her, or Banri and the others following just behind.

When she cleared her throat, her voice was a strangled mess.

"What in the seven hells is that?"

TEN

TWO rivers snaked toward the sea: twin trails of dark blue glittering beneath the dawning sun. In the middle of the shore stood what looked like a giant black egg, which had split neatly down the middle. Between the two halves of the sphere, a city sat as if newly hatched.

When she squinted, Kurara could see that the broken sphere was actually made of hundreds of metal plates that gleamed in the early morning light. Bits of unfinished scaffolding waved in the wind. The locals had built inside the egg, on platforms that reminded her of the way the building stacks on Sola-Il would wend their way toward the sky. Houses made of paper and wood swayed in the breeze. From a distance, they looked like trinkets stacked upon shelves, connected by winding wooden stairs that seemed dangerously brittle.

"That's Nessai, the empire's largest port town," said Sayo.

"It was meant to be the site for another sky city, but then a shikigami attacked and all the builders ran off. Even after the hunters took care of things, the workmen refused to come back, leaving a half-built sky city stranded on the shore. It was a waste to just let it sit there, so people decided to start living inside it, turning the scraps left behind into buildings."

"It's amazing," said Kurara.

"Pfft. Nessai is just a poor man's version of a sky city!" Tomoe scoffed.

Kurara marveled at how both girls could remain so staunchly unimpressed. Nessai was a dizzying mishmash of old and new: electric lights strung from building to building beside run-down Kabuki theaters. The scream of a steam train whistled on a rail track that cut through unpaved dirt roads.

Sayo muttered something about how groundlings were living off Sorabito scraps like a bunch of pack rats, but when Kurara looked at the broken sphere she saw only ingenuity and determination—the kind that urged the grass to grow in the aftermath of a fire. The kind that made lotus flowers rise from the mud.

The sight of such a marvel opened something aching and wondrous inside her chest. It filled her with excitement at the prospect of what else she would see on this journey, and a hollow fear that she had already missed out on so much. Haru grabbed her hand. She did not need to look at him to know that he was caught in the same sense of breathless wonder.

"Haven't you been to Nessai before?" asked Kurara.

Haru shook his head. His awe reminded her of the same

bright, curious boy he had been on the *Midori*, dreaming of traveling across the empire and eager to see all the sights the land had to offer.

"*A town.*" Apprehension colored Banri's voice. "*People. Noise and crowds and bright lights.*"

"We're not taking this lug into Nessai with us, are we? It just tried to kill us!" Sayo turned to scowl at the bear.

Banri withered beneath her gaze. "*I apologize. I—I never meant to—*"

"It's not your fault. No one blames you," said Kurara.

"*I* blame it!" cried Sayo, throwing her hands into the air in exasperation. "Are we seriously going to keep traveling with this thing, knowing it might blow up in our faces at any moment?"

"Banri isn't a bomb!"

"No, bombs only go off once."

Faced with Sayo's ire, Kurara squared her shoulders and refused to back down. "I'm not leaving Banri behind! We're going to get that airship and we're all going to fly south together."

"*I have to return to Kazami. When I am home, Miss Oda— Master's student—will be there. Once I have a bond, everything will be better. Then I will make things up to you, I promise. I will be good. Helpful,*" the bear whimpered, miserably.

The pain in Banri's voice shook Kurara to her core. It was all so horribly unfair that the only way to help the shikigami was to tie it to someone who would have complete control over its mind.

Right now, they did not have much of a choice. They had to get to Kazami and quickly. Kurara knew she should be thinking about the Grand Stream, about the *Orihime* waiting for them there, but the more time she spent with Banri, the less it became a priority and the more she found herself thinking about the ruined village—and the Crafter who lived there.

"How about this," said Haru. "Rara and I will find an airship that will take all of us south. Meanwhile, you two Nessai-haters can stay here and keep an eye on Banri."

Kurara grudgingly accepted his suggestion. Tomoe was fond of Banri, and Sayo would not do anything that would upset Tomoe.

"Great idea!" Tomoe chirped. "I need my beauty sleep. Besides, I doubt we *dirty Sorabito* will be welcome in Nessai. And if a groundling so much as looked at Sayo the wrong way, she'd cause an incident."

"What? No, I wouldn't!" Sayo sounded affronted.

"Remember the Patriots Office in Sola-Fa? You almost punched an officer in the face," said Tomoe.

"That's because he said your hair was the color of bean jam." Sayo crossed her arms over her chest in defence, as if food-related insults were perfect cause for violence.

Kurara stepped between them before the conversation could continue and rolled up her sleeves. The fingers on her left hand crumbled into paper squares and she sent a stream of ofuda through the air like a miniature firework. "If I need your help, I'll send out a signal like this. If you see it, come running."

"And if your shikigami friend starts turning violent in the meantime . . ."

"*If I feel myself slipping, I will be sure to warn you,*"

Banri assured her. An undercurrent of shame threaded its words together.

"Relax!" Tomoe elbowed her way between them. "Go on. Sayo and I will babysit your little shikigami. Or, at least, Sayo will. I want a nap."

The black sphere that formed Nessai hurt to look at for too long. Light bouncing against the metal plates seared Kurara's eyes. Though most of the city sat between the two pieces of broken shell, scarecrow power lines connected the two halves together. Zigzagging stairs led up the sides of the city, connecting one building to the next, but there were no guardrails or banisters, nothing to stop anyone falling off the edge at any moment.

Kurara could not look at the stairs without feeling dizzy. She kept her head down and concentrated on the path in front of her even as Haru clung to her arm with a grin too wide for his face and cried, "Rara, look at that! There are people up there! Rara, I saw a train! Hey, did you hear that steam whistle, Rara? Ooh, do you smell fried tofu?"

Kurara kept her paper arm hidden in the wide sleeve of her kimono while she tried to contain Haru's excitement. This was a groundling city full of soldiers. They shouldn't draw too much attention to themselves.

The streets were awash with shoppers. She was jostled this way and that as the crowds fought her for space. Vendors shouted at them from behind stalls laden with tanks full of freshwater crabs and fish. A sea breeze, heavy with the sound of people's voices, carried the smell of fried octopus across the air.

An airship to the south, she repeated to herself over and over as she battled her way to the harbor, where a line of ships bobbed upon the waves. Part of the port was cordoned off for airships, but Kurara did not think she could ever get used to the sight of them sitting in the water like a bunch of flightless ducks. Their angled masts and propellers were the only hint that they were made to sail through the clouds.

While Haru ooh-ed and ahh-ed at the wooden ships, Kurara was not so impressed. These airships were clearly groundling-made; their large bulky hulls and blocky prows were downright ugly next to the sleek, brightly colored Sorabito ships she had seen on Sola-II.

Perhaps her disdain was in solidarity with the *Orihime*'s crew. Maybe she had become a skyship snob. Either way, it was with reluctance that she dragged herself over to the man standing nearby.

Before she could even open her mouth, the man cut her off with a brusque, "We're not flying."

"But sir," Haru protested. "We are but poor orphan—"

"Are there rocks in your ears or summat? We're not flying 'cause we can't, and no amount of wheedling or batting your pretty eyelashes will change that!" he growled.

"You can't fly?" said Kurara.

"The Sorabito!" The man spat the word like a curse. "They're kicking up a fuss for some reason or other and they're refusing to transport levistone. No levistone means no flying, you got that?"

Kurara was certain she knew why the Sorabito were

angry. A shikigami had attacked and wrecked Sola-Il after all. A shikigami that everyone believed the princess had been experimenting on.

Were tensions really that bad in the sky cities? If she were on the *Orihime*, Kurara would have access to the reports other airships sent the crew, to messages from mechanical birds warning them of the empire's latest movements. Here on the ground, Kurara could only guess what kind of trouble was brewing above their heads.

"But you must have a *little* levistone left for emergency flights? Couldn't we—?"

"What part of 'no' dontcha understand? Now scram before I call the military police on yer!" The man spat at Kurara's feet.

Defeated, she pulled Haru away. "Let's go back to the others. We shouldn't keep them waiting." This was a disaster. How were they going to reach the Grand Stream now?

How was she going to reach Kazami?

"We could find some other way south. Like a boat?" suggested Haru.

"You're just saying that because you want to ride on one." Kurara followed his gaze to the naval ships on the other side of the port.

The harbor was bustling with men unloading their goods onto land. Small fishing ships and giant, oil-stained carriers competed for space at the dock. Boats laden with the day's catch bobbed between large silk and spice carriers, freight ships and passenger ferries. Near the other end of the harbor, where the sea level was lower, women sat on the banks washing and tending to children playing on the pebbles.

"Well, that too," said Haru, "but we don't have much choice, do we? We need to make our way south somehow. A boat might be the only way to the Grand Stream."

"I suppose . . ."

"Good, because I think I just spotted our ticket south!"

Before Kurara could stop him, Haru headed toward a group of sailors drinking by the pier, close to the front of a large steamship encrusted with barnacles.

"Excuse me, good sirs!" he shouted.

The sailors looked up, none too pleased by his interruption. They were shirtless, grizzled men who had probably spent more time at sea than they had on land. Empty sake bottles littered the ground around the crates they were using as makeshift card tables. A bolt of fear sent Kurara scrambling to Haru's side. The men did not seem the type who took kindly to strangers.

"Greetings! We were looking for someone to take us south. As far south as you can. Could you let us on board your fine vessel?" Haru asked with oblivious cheer. A rabbit wandering into a den of wolves.

Fine vessel. Kurara glanced up at the sailors' ship. It looked like something out of a ghost story. The sails were yellow and the hull had been patched up with iron bands. She opened her mouth to protest, then quickly clamped it shut.

"This ain't no pleasure cruiser, boy." A man—the captain, judging from his cap—turned to pin them in his glare. Calloused hands fiddled with the revolver at his waist. He was gruff, with silver in his hair and a map of scars across his arms and face.

He was also very, very drunk if the redness in his cheeks or the slight tremor in his hands was anything to go by. Kurara tensed. Years of work on the *Midori* had taught her that drunken men were not to be trusted. They could be cheery one moment and blind with rage the next, and this man did not seem inclined to be cheery.

"We can pay you, sir," Haru persisted.

"Oh? And with what money?"

"How much do you want?"

"Ten thousand ko." The captain's face twisted into an ugly smirk. His men sniggered. Kurara did not know anything about boats, but ten thousand ko was an eye-watering amount. She could buy a fancy manor in the capital city for the same amount of money.

Haru, however, did not miss a beat. With a gracious nod and a smile that charmed everyone he met, he said, "All right then."

The captain glanced at his men. There was a moment of bewildered silence before they burst into laughter.

Kurara was tempted to hit them all. Perhaps if she knocked them out she and Haru could steal their steamship and be out at sea before anyone caught on.

The captain looked Haru up and down with a vicious grin. "You've got ten thousand ko on you, do ya?"

"We don't have the money right now, but we'll win it off you."

Kurara sucked in a sharp breath. She was sure the sailors would reach for their weapons at any moment, but the captain merely laughed.

"The cheek! You've got guts, boy, I'll give ya that! But what do I get if I win?"

"You get two very capable servants who will work for you for the rest of your life!"

"Haru!" Kurara hissed.

"The girl don't look like much." The captain took a long swig from a dark brown bottle. Kurara scowled at him. Not much! She had polished a thousand floors, cleaned at least ten thousand plates, served at dozens of banquets, and poured wine for hundreds of men all without breaking something or punching someone. If that was not dedication to her duty, she did not know what was.

"Don't underestimate us, good sir. We used to work for the *Midori*, we're top-tier servants ready to attend to your every need!" said Haru.

The man chuckled. Even from a distance, Kurara could smell the foul stench of alcohol on his breath. "Very well then," he said. "Let's play!"

Haru gave an apologetic smile. "I don't really understand the rules to complicated card games though. Can we play Menko?"

The captain snorted. The rules of Menko were simple: two cards were placed on the table and each person would try to flip them over by throwing their own cards at them. It was a child's game.

"Have it your way, boy." The captain hiccupped and threw down a pack of cards.

Haru grinned, all swagger and with a smile that could rival the sun. There was fire in his eyes, fueled by the thrill of a risky gamble, and Kurara was reminded of how he would lure sky fish into the *Midori* and set them free inside the bathrooms.

"Rara, give me a hug for good luck!" He wrapped an arm around her shoulders, catching her by surprise. As he pulled her close, he lowered his voice and whispered, "You can sense it, can't you Rara? Those cheap cards are more paper than cardboard. You can flip them easily, can't you?"

"You want me to cheat?" she hissed.

Haru grinned at her.

"Let's play, then." The captain gestured for him to take a seat on one of the barrels.

As Haru sat down, Kurara took a deep breath and got ready to swindle their way to victory.

ELEVEN

IF Kurara concentrated, she could feel the playing cards made out of small, stiff rectangles of cardboard. They were heavier than ofuda and not as easy to manipulate, but she could move them well enough for this little scam to work.

There was no way she could lose.

"I'll go first. I ain't got to tell you not to cheat now, do I?" The captain grabbed an open bottle of sake and drained its contents in one, long gulp.

Haru gave a theatrical gasp. "Cheat? We would never!"

The man pinned them with a narrow stare. Was it her imagination or was there something knowing in his eyes? Kurara kept her head down so that her hair partially curtained her expression, in case it betrayed her.

Flipping cards was not challenging. She had made fluttering sparrows out of paper and fought an imperial Crafter with ofuda sharper than any blade. The real difficulty was in flipping the playing cards without looking like she was the one doing it. Himura had never taught her subtlety.

The captain held a playing card between his thumb and forefinger and took careful aim. With a sharp exhale, he threw it at his target.

It was a direct hit. The opposing card jumped. Reaching out with her mind, Kurara slammed it back down before it could flip over. The gaggle of onlooking sailors groaned as the captain frowned, his brow creasing in confusion.

"Ooh, so close!" Haru slapped a hand over his eyes. "I was so sure you had that one! So sure!"

Stop milking it so much, Kurara wanted to snap. She wondered if he knew how much this game was making her sweat.

Picking up his own card, Haru flung it at the cards spread across the crate. It barely glanced against the edge of his target. Kurara pointedly looked away as she reached out for the card Haru had been aiming at and flipped it in the air.

Howls of disbelief echoed around her. She closed her eyes for a second, and when she opened them again she found the ship's captain frowning at her. Did he know? Did he suspect something?

"That's round one to me!" Haru's triumphant cry gave her an excuse to break eye contact.

The captain hissed at him.

Again, Kurara stopped the man from flipping the cards over, and again she made sure that Haru's attempts ended in his victory. She even made sure his cards hit their targets when he threw them a little too far from the mark, moving them through the air with as much finesse as she could manage. As the points racked up in their favor, the sailors' grumbling grew louder and louder until they began booing every time Haru reached for another card.

"Ha! I'm undefeatable! The gods themselves bless me!" Haru slapped a hand against his chest. Kurara smoldered. All he did was strut about and boast while she did all the work!

Haru tossed his card at his target. Kurara turned her head away, letting the card veer off without hitting its mark.

A jeer rippled through the crowd of sailors as Haru's face fell in disbelief.

"Where are your gods now?" the captain crowed.

"I'll win the next round. Won't I, Rara?"

Kurara averted her eyes. "Don't look at me," she grumbled.

Haru and the captain traded barbs like two peacocks jabbing each other with their beaks. Kurara stubbornly kept the matches from becoming too one-sided, but in the end the points were always in their favor, and after a few more rounds of back and forth, she allowed Haru the victory blow.

"And that makes ten thousand ko!" Haru grinned as the last card was flipped over.

The captain sat opposite him with a look of pure disbelief. Behind him, his men roared and shouted.

"That's not fair!"

"You cheated somehow!"

"How in the bloody seas did you do that?"

The captain silenced their cries with a wave of his hand. With a solemn look, he approached Kurara. His lips curled back to reveal several golden teeth. It was not quite a smile; it was far too vicious for that.

"I know you cheated. I don't know how, but you definitely cheated." He stared at her as though she were some sort of suspicious creature he had just pulled out from the end of a fishing hook. A potentially poisonous one.

"Cheated? Sir, I was the one playing you, not Rara. And I happen to be very good at Menko. The reigning champion in my village, in fact. You shouldn't feel bad about losing to me. I used to practice three hours every day," said Haru. "Though, I'm sure if we had played some other game I would have lost. If anything, it was your kindness in agreeing to a game of Menko that allowed me to win."

The captain did not look mollified at all. In fact, he looked as though Haru had just suggested he should eat horse manure. "The name's Morita. Captain Morita. And I suppose I should welcome you to the *Kuroi Kame*."

Kurara opened her mouth to reply when she felt lightning lance down her spine. Electricity buzzed through her nerves. It was a familiar sensation—the crash of power meeting power. It meant a Crafter was nearby.

"Rara!" Haru suddenly grabbed hold of her sleeve. His eyes were wide with panic. "He's here!"

She did not need to ask who "he" was. The moment Haru spoke, a giant white spear shot out from the market crowd and flew toward her. The blade whizzed past her face—so close she felt the wind slice her cheek—and buried itself in the ground by her feet. The people around the harbor stalls screamed and scattered.

When she turned around, Fujiwa was standing in the middle of the now-deserted harbor. The black haori tied over his kimono fluttered in the wind.

"Halt!" he shouted at her. "By order of Her Imperial Highness, you're under arrest!"

TWELVE

FUJIWA was perilously close. They had to run. They had to escape. But they could not leave without Banri and the others.

She did not have the luxury of debating the best course of action. With no more than a flick of his fingers, Fujiwa pulled the spear from the ground. The paper weapon flew back to his hand, leaving behind a large gash in the stone harbor.

As he prepared for another attack, Kurara lifted her left arm to the sky. Her paper fingers twisted together, merging into a single point that stretched far above her head. Her arm inflated like a balloon, swelling outward until it burst with a thunderous bang that sent a handful of ofuda flying into the air—and everyone within ten feet of her fleeing for their lives.

That was the signal she had shown Tomoe and Sayo; the sign that would bring them running. Sure enough, Kurara soon heard people screaming in the distance as Banri hurtled down the street with Sayo and Tomoe riding atop its back.

"Get out of the waaaay!" Tomoe screamed as people scrambled for safety. The bear careened into stalls and smashed against the corners of local teashops, sending crates of fruit and glass tanks full of fish crashing to the ground as it ran.

As Banri entered the harbor, Fujiwa spun around and sent his paper spear flying at the bear's flank. Banri jumped, avoiding the blow at the very last moment, and bounded past.

"Pull anchor!" Haru turned to Captain Morita. "Set sail!"

Morita jumped. "Whatever you've done, this is your fight! I'll have no part in it!"

"If you don't start moving, we're all going to be in a lot of trouble!" Haru pushed the captain toward the barnacle-encrusted ship.

The captain looked as though he were swallowing a lemon, but he bellowed at his men, "Let's haul out of here!"

The sailors jumped at his order. Before Kurara knew what was happening, the ship was suddenly alive with men hoisting the sails, preparing the engines, moving crates back onto the deck, and rolling up the gangway.

While the sailors readied the ship, another spear flew toward the hull. Before it could strike the *Kuroi Kame*, Kurara transformed her arm into a chain of ofuda and knocked it out of the air.

"Haru, stop!" Fujiwa ordered as he marched forward.

With a jolt, Haru froze.

"Get on!" bellowed Banri as it charged toward her. Tomoe leaned down to offer her hand. Kurara grabbed it and swung

herself up onto Banri's back. The bear lowered its head and scooped a frozen Haru up in its mouth as it continued to hurtle toward the end of the harbor.

Where's Ruki? A sudden, horrifying thought struck Kurara. She had never seen Fujiwa without his shikigami at his side. The giant paper tiger was far too protective of its master to let Fujiwa fight alone.

Her answer came a beat later. As Kurara deflected another of Fujiwa's spears, Ruki came bursting down the market street and into the harbor, catching up to Banri in a few strides of its large, trunk-like legs.

The *Kuroi Kame's* horn sounded as the ship began to pull out of the harbor, drifting farther and farther away.

"Faster, Banri!" Kurara urged the bear on. They would make it. They had to.

As they reached the edge of the harbor, where water met the stone docks, Banri leapt.

So did Ruki.

The tiger's jaws snapped down on Banri's hind leg, tearing it clean off. The bear spat Haru onto the deck as it gave an awful roar and landed with a heavy thump against the side of the *Kuroi Kame*.

Its front paws clung to the edge of the ship while its one remaining back leg scrambled for purchase. Kurara climbed up Banri's back and jumped from its head onto the deck. As soon as her feet hit solid ground, she whirled around and tried to haul the massive bear onto the ship. Sayo and Tomoe quickly clambered onto the deck to help and, together, they managed to pull Banri to safety.

Fujiwa ran after them to the very end of the harbor. No

sooner were they all on board when yet another spear struck the side of the hull with enough force that the whole ship rocked. As Fujiwa pulled his ofuda back, water gushed in where the weapon had pierced the wood. Sailors scrambled to plug the leak.

"Haru!" Fujiwa bellowed. "Come to me!"

"Hold him down!" Kurara hissed as Haru's body jerked to attention.

Before he could move, Tomoe grabbed him and pinned him to the deck.

"Kurara!" Sayo's call dragged her attention to something on the deck behind her.

Barrels of levistone. Even sealed, the tell-tale smell of blood and wet earth leaked from the wooden drums. The man by the airships had said that levistone was in short supply, yet when Sayo kicked one of the barrels the metal gave a solid thunk. It was full.

Fujiwa remained at the water's edge, next to Ruki. Though the ship was putting as much distance as it could between itself and the land, they were not far enough yet to be out of Fujiwa's range. With a flick of his hand, the Crafter sent his weapon flying toward them once more. As it reached the ship, the spear split into several smaller blades. They pelted the hull again, causing more leaks. One hit the mast, bringing the sails crashing down.

With all the strength she could muster, Kurara shoved a wedge of paper beneath the levistone barrel and catapulted it into the air. With another handful of paper, she made a hardened lump of ofuda and knocked the barrel toward the harbor.

"You!" she shouted at the captain. "Shoot it!"

"No way! That's levistone! Do you know how expensive that is now that the Sorabito aren't—?"

He did not have the chance to finish. Sayo grabbed the pistol from him and fired.

Eyes widening in horror, Fujiwa grabbed hold of his shikigami and scrambled out of the way. The barrel exploded against the edge of the harbor, setting alight the nearby ships and blowing up part of the pier.

Kurara turned away and squeezed her eyes shut against the sudden burst of heat and light that curled through the air. When she looked back, all that remained was a large crater in the harbor littered with chunks of rock.

The *Kuroi Kame* put out to open sea. Alarm bells echoed. The sound of ringing hammers and shouting filled the air. Men hauled up what remained of the mast and plugged the holes in the hull left by Fujiwa's spears. Fujiwa and Ruki had disappeared, escaping the explosion, and there was now enough distance between the harbor and the ship that Kurara was sure Fujiwa would not be able to follow them— not for a while at least. Though knowing that did not help her to relax.

"Are you all right?" she asked Haru as Tomoe released him.

"Never better," muttered Haru, though his cheeks were flushed with embarrassment.

"You! A fine mess you've got us tangled in!" The captain marched forward with fury in his eyes. "Men, grab 'em and throw the lot overboard!"

A few sailors attempted to approach her. Some of the men drew their weapons.

"Stay back!" Kurara's left arm turned into a blade.

"What in the bloody seas is *that*?" barked the captain.

"A prosthetic," Tomoe lied. "A fake arm. Kurara here is a Crafter, as you can probably tell. And her favorite party trick is turning her arm into all sorts of things. Including knives."

"Y–you! You're Sorabito!" Morita paled. Now that he had the chance to really look at Tomoe and Sayo, it was plain as day. Even if their clothes had not given them away, their accents were too soft and rhythmical to belong to a groundling.

The crew muttered, darkly. They too knew about the trouble the Sorabito were causing in the skies. Morita silenced them with a harsh look.

"That's it! We're turning right around and I'm handing you over to that Crafter," he growled.

"You can't go back to the harbor," Kurara warned him. "I know Fujiwa. He will do anything to protect Princess Tsukimi. And that includes getting rid of pesky sailors who just happened to be at the wrong place at the wrong time. Pesky sailors who might tell other people about the time an imperial Crafter showed up to hunt down a bunch of children. If you're lucky, he'll have you and your crew locked up for the rest of your life. If you're not . . ." She let her silence feed the captain's imagination.

"You were already going south, right? We're not even asking you to go out of your way!" said Haru.

"Or I can always take over and toss the lot of you overboard," said Kurara.

Haru slapped a hand over her mouth.

"Joking! She was only joking!" He gave a nervous chuckle

as the captain's eyes narrowed. "We'll be quieter than mice. You won't hear a squeak from us! Besides, what about our bet? We did win after all. It would be dishonorable to throw us overboard now!"

"You cheated!" Morita shrieked. His face was bright red. He looked as though he was going to burst a vein.

"You can't go back to the harbor. I saw a school of blood-red sky fish pass by just now," said Tomoe.

The captain's demeanor suddenly shifted. Gone was his anger, his baffled fury. He stared not at Kurara and Haru but at Tomoe. "They only turn that color when the air pressure drops. That means a storm is coming," he muttered.

Tomoe's lips curled like an animal baring its teeth.

Morita scowled.

"A bet is a bet. There's a port at the city of Zeka. I'll take you there and no farther."

The crew voiced their objections, but Captain Morita cut them off with a sharp look and barked an order that sent them scrambling to prepare for the long voyage and move the remaining levistone barrels below deck.

"What was all that about?" asked Sayo once they were sure they were no longer in danger of being tossed into the sea.

Tomoe looked at her with a grin that did not quite reach her eyes. "Our dear Captain Morita is a Sorabito. And a particularly nasty one at that."

Kurara raised her eyebrows in surprise. A Sorabito? But Morita looked like nothing of the sort. There was none of the willowy grace, no bounce to his step—even his accent was nothing like Tomoe's or Sayo's, whose vowels rolled into one another like birdsong.

"How can you tell?"

"Well," said Tomoe, "he can't quite hide the way he trills his Rs. If you listen carefully, you can tell he still has a bit of a Sorabito accent."

"And what was all that stuff about bloody sky fish and storms?" asked Sayo.

Tomoe's smile faded. "It's a code. It's how members of Sohma find each other."

Sayo made a sound as though she were choking on a rock. "And how do you know that?"

"Because my father is their leader."

THIRTEEN

THE smell was Himura's first clue that he was close to Zeka. As his paper falcon soared onward, it crossed over a land riddled with the scars of industry. Mining huts and levistone deposits were no more than brown thumbprints in the distance, but there was something in the air that brought a metallic tang to his tongue and filled his nostrils with the smell of smoke. He wrapped a paper scarf around the bottom half of his face and tried not to breathe in the harsh fumes as he dived toward the port.

Zeka was a city of stairs, with wooden residences and impressive bath houses built onto floating plateaus kept suspended in the air by levistone burners. Winding staircases connected one platform to the next, curling around buildings and spiraling along the edges of the stone hills on which the theaters and temples were built. Cable cars swung through the air, leading toward the harbor.

The water was a darkish gray around the mouth of the city port, stained with sewage.

Why had Rei asked to bring him here? Why had he not asked to stop at Sola-Ea or Sola-Re or any of the sky cities? Zeka was a groundling city. Everyone from the military police to the waitresses would be hostile to him.

Himura's falcon circled above the city, safely hidden behind a screen of thin clouds. If he peered over the side of the bird's wing, he could make out the highest floating platforms decked with trees and vines trailing toward the ground. Strange, how groundlings always sneered at the Sorabito and yet their largest cities were the ones that copied the kind of architecture one could find in the skies.

"Aren't you going to bring us down?" an annoying voice rasped in his ear.

Kazeno Rei was nothing but an unwelcome weight, sitting at the back of his falcon and constantly making snide remarks.

I could always push him off right now. The thought was tempting, but as much as Himura fantasized about letting the man plunge to his doom, he had promised Sakurai he would deliver Rei to Zeka. Hadn't he betrayed enough people already? There were only so many promises he could break, only so many people he could disappoint, before it began eating away at him. Besides, he had never actually murdered anyone, and he wasn't about to start now.

Except Akane, his mind unhelpfully supplied. Did Akane even count? A shikigami was nothing more than moving paper. They weren't *alive,* not in the same way humans were. Yet the memory of Akane would not leave him. Memories of the library. Of flames consuming the shikigami's core.

Directing the falcon to carry them to the outskirts of the city, Himura landed beneath a copse of maple trees and slid off the bird.

Before Rei could dismount as well, he clicked his fingers and his ofuda crumbled into hundreds of paper squares. The man hit the ground hard and rolled across the grass.

Was that petty? Yes. Did it make Himura smile? Also yes.

"As promised, I've taken you where we agreed. I hope our business is now concluded," he said as Rei picked himself up.

"Not quite." The man brushed a hand over his ragged kimono as if he had merely stumbled upon a rock. "You said you would take me to Zeka. If I'm not mistaken, we are just outside the city."

Himura tried not to bristle. A normal human should be cowed by his abilities, by his status as a Crafter. Where was the fear? The awe? He was not used to being treated like any old person one might pass on a busy market street. Like he was not capable of slicing through Rei's throat with a handful of confetti.

He was sick and tired of Kazeno Rei. Under normal circumstances, controlling his paper falcon took most of Himura's concentration, and the added weight had made flying harder and slower. He had wasted so much time in the skies with nothing but this foul man for company—he wanted to return to the *Orihime* already.

Rei smiled at him like a cat teasing its prey. Perhaps it gave him a rush of power to toy with a Crafter, knowing what Himura could do.

"You promised your captain you would take me to Zeka, didn't you? I want to show you something."

"I'm not interested," said Himura.

"Now, now, if you come with me, I'll tell you everything I know about shikigami. About Princess Tsukimi's hidden workshops."

"There is nothing that you could teach me that I don't already know," Himura replied, coldly. He certainly did not need to be told about his own powers from a *Sorabito*, and a member of Sohma no less.

"I've seen the inside of one of Princess Tsukimi's famous workshops. There were cores all over the floor. And ashes. Human ashes mixed with bits of bone. There were rumors that she kidnapped orphans and burned them to try to make shikigami. Perhaps the ashes belonged to those children."

At the mention of ashes, Himura thought of Akane burning and the phantom smell of smoke. The look on Akane's face as it said, *"I love you, Master."*

"Fine!" He made his way down the hill and along a small stream leading into the city. "Speak."

Rei's grin was as vicious as a blade in the dark. "That eagle you fought outside Sola-Il was one of her creations, but it was broken. Defective. It wouldn't obey anyone, but it looked the part, didn't it? It looked just like a real shikigami."

Himura sucked in a sharp breath. He remembered the eagle that had attacked them outside Sola-Il. Princess Tsukimi had been *that* close to making a shikigami? Fear and outrage stormed through his chest. Fear, for what the princess might do with such knowledge. Outrage, because how *dare* someone who was not even a Crafter achieve what he and his people had strived to accomplish for so many years? The empire had banned all the books about their past, then turned around and allowed Princess Tsukimi to study from the very same texts and ancient writings that had been stolen from his people.

It was unforgivable.

"You know," said Rei as the tall stairs and floating platforms of the city loomed ever closer, "I dislike groundlings."

"The shock of the century," said Himura, dryly.

Rei's smile turned into a sneer. "I dislike groundlings, but I don't hate them the way I *hate* Crafters. You people once ruled the land, and what did you do? You squandered everything, went to war and tore each other apart like barbarians. You Crafters have so much power, and yet you either join the military or run away to live in the mountains like hermits. All your kind ever does is complain about what you want, but you never act. *That* is what I hate. If you have the means, you should step forward and take what you desire!"

Himura wanted to punch the man so badly his hands trembled. He *had* stepped forward. He *had* taken what he desired. And where did that leave him? With a dead shikigami and a student who probably hated him. In his travel sack, he carried the red leather book that Akane had died for. Sometimes, he thought he could feel it burning against his back as if it carried the flames from the library with it.

As they walked, the dirt paths turned to proper, paved roads. Himura stopped. The famous stairs of Zeka loomed above him, curving upward in tightly coiled spirals that connected to floating gardens hanging in midair. Himura had heard that the sky gardens of Zeka were wondrous enclosures full of vibrant flowers and evergreens, but from below, they were nothing more than flat panels of wood embedded with levistone that blocked out the sun.

"Here. I'll be leaving you now," he said, but Rei was not paying him any mind.

The man put a hand to his ear. "Do you hear that?"

"What?"

It took a moment for Himura to realize that the fervor in the air was not the usual buzz of harried shoppers and impatient tradespeople. No, there was an anxiousness among the townsfolk, a sense of coiled tension ready to erupt into something much darker. On the corner of the main road, a man stood on a wooden crate yelling at the people who had gathered around him to listen.

" . . . and slit our throats in our sleep!" he cried, animated by a sort of frantic zeal that made his eyes bulge and his chest heave like bellows. "We have been nothing but kind to the Sorabito, and this is how they repay our generosity? The only reason we're in charge of their cities is because those flying rats can't govern themselves! Just look at Sola-Il! The Sorabito fail to protect their city from shikigami and that's meant to be *our* fault? Our towns and cities are attacked by shikigami too, but we don't throw a hissy fit about it!"

His rant was met with cries of agreement. Several people shouted out, "What have the Sorabito ever achieved?" and "All they ever do is complain!"

Himura stared at the crowd gathering several feet away. The relationship between groundlings and the Sorabito had always been tense, but to see such open hostility was unusual. Just what was happening in the skies to cause this?

"Did you know this was happening?" he snapped at Rei, but the man was already making his way to the town square, where the shouting was getting louder.

Biting back a curse, Himura followed. Was this the reason Rei had wanted to come to Zeka? What did he know that Himura did not?

When they reached the city square, Rei suddenly stopped and raised his eyes to a tall, official-looking building that loomed above them.

The town hall was missing chunks of wall, and the Patriots Office next to it was a broken tooth of a building, burned down to its jagged foundations. Wood and scraps of cloth lay scattered over the cracked slabs of the town square, stained by scorch marks and shattered stone. Someone had painted something onto the ground in large, angry red characters.

BLOOD IN THE SKIES
SHALL RAIN TO THE GROUND

Those words . . . Himura knew those words. One did not live and work on a Sorabito hunting ship without knowing what they meant: it was a threat, a warning that any violence done to the sky cities or the Sorabito would be met with retaliation.

"Is this your doing?" Hot indignation burned in Himura's gut.

Angry crowds surged around the ruins, shouting insults and working each other up into a rage. The atmosphere was a powder keg ready to explode; even the smallest of sparks would set the town alight.

They were lucky that there were so many people that no one looked at them twice—though Rei was not dressed like a Sorabito, his height and his accent might give him away. If that happened, Himura had no doubt that the crowds would tear him apart.

"Why are you glaring at me like that? This 'blood in the skies' business has nothing to do with me. I've been with you the entire time," said Rei, though he was grinning in that infuriating way that said he knew far more than he was letting on.

"This is the work of your Sohma buddies, isn't it?"

"Have you no sympathy for the plight of the Sorabito? Not even when you live among them? You want me to politely protest about injustice like a good second-class citizen? I do what I must, what I have to, in order to help my people. Surely you understand that."

"I asked you a question. That wasn't an answer."

Meeting Himura's gaze, Rei said, "So what if my comrades are responsible? All we did was egg on what was already festering in people's hearts. And what will you do, anyway—hand me in to the Patriots Office?"

The voices of the crowd melted together into a buzz of frustration and anger. The military police posted around the wreckage were doing a half-hearted job of keeping everyone calm. In fact, Himura was sure he saw a few officers helping to whip the crowd into a frenzy.

"So now the groundlings hate Sorabito even more. How does that help you? How does that bring the sky cities closer to independence?" Himura could not understand what was going on in that arrogant head of Rei's. If he wanted Sorabito independence, wouldn't it be better to make the groundlings like them?

"It unites the Sorabito." Rei's eyes were alight with a malicious fervor now, all his coolness gone. "The more the groundlings hate us, the more Sorabito are won over to our cause. The more violent groundlings are toward us, the better!"

"And this is the only way you can win people over? By fueling the flames of division? You could have dedicated your life to building bridges between the groundlings and the Sorabito. You could have tried to foster common understanding."

The way Rei's face contorted told Himura exactly what Rei thought of that. "And you really think that would work?"

Himura shrugged. "I don't know. Have you tried?"

"I don't have to try. I know groundlings are too arrogant and too comfortable in their positions of power to ever want to treat us as equals. Besides, who wants equality? The Sorabito mastered the skies and built homes in the clouds, closer to the gods. Why should we suffer equality when we are clearly superior?

"Ships like the *Orihime* that work for the groundlings; ships that suck up to our oppressors will be destroyed for the traitors they are. But, I am generous, and I do so hate to see Sorabito blood spilled. Your ship could work for Sohma. Go back to your captain and your precious crew and tell them what you saw here. It's not too late for them. They can still be on the winning side."

Himura stared at the man in disbelief. In the distance, a clock tower began to ring alarm bells, its chimes warning of an imminent curfew. He glanced up at its scorched face, surprised to see it was working even though it had been damaged.

As the city folk began to disperse, Himura suddenly realized that Rei had disappeared. That damned weasel had brought him here just to flaunt his knowledge and then disappeared before Himura could get any meaningful information from him.

Himura swore beneath his breath and glanced around, but the crowd heaved around him like a storm upon the sea.

"Let's burn down their cities!"

"Show them sky rats what for!"

Perhaps he ought to leave too. Nothing good came from dwelling on the ground for too long, and he had delivered Rei to the city as promised.

If only he could shake the feeling that he had done something terrible by letting Rei go—something akin to releasing a calamity upon the world.

He shook his head. The Sorabito and groundlings could squabble all they liked. It did not matter to him. He should leave.

"You! Hey, pssst! You! Over here, in the alley."

Himura stiffened. A quiet voice bounced against the walls of his skull. A shikigami's voice.

Glancing around furtively, he hurried toward a narrow alleyway, away from the furious sounds of the swelling mob. Something rustled among the piles of garbage heaped against the walls.

"*Yes, you. Stop there, Crafter,*" said a voice.

Himura did not breathe.

A snow-white python peeked out from the wet cardboard boxes and bags of rotting cabbages, its flat head raised just above the refuse pile. Its body was as thick as Himura's arm and at least three feet long, though it was difficult to tell with its scales bunched up.

The snake flicked its white tongue at him.

"*Well, hello there, child,*" it hissed. "*I have been looking for someone like you.*"

FOURTEEN

"*SOHMA?*" Sayo hissed the name like a curse. "Your father is the head of *Sohma*?"

Kurara sucked in a sharp breath. She might not have the same visceral reaction to Sohma's name, but she had been part of the *Orihime* for long enough to know who they were.

"Sohma!" Sayo's face was turning redder by the minute.

Banri shuffled back, cowed by Sayo's anger. Despite its size, it looked like a child standing helplessly in the middle of an argument between two parents. Kurara placed a comforting hand on the bear's snout and concentrated on healing the bear's missing leg. Her ofuda wrapped around the hollow stump, stretching thin as it formed a new paw and set of claws.

"Are you OK?" she whispered.

The bear shuddered.

"Banri?"

It blinked. The cloudy look in its eyes cleared. *"What? Oh, yes, I am fine, little one. It hurt, but I am fine now."* The shikigami put on a brave face, but Kurara worried at her bottom lip. How long would Banri's mind hold together? Would the shikigami last the journey south?

Kurara stroked its leg. She wanted to say something, but everything she could think of felt like nothing more than empty consolation.

"And you kept this from us? From me? Who else knew?" Sayo was scowling.

Tomoe looked at her the way one would eye a wild thing. "Only Captain Sakurai. He had to forge my identification documents. On my papers, my father is a perfectly respectable cloth merchant."

She told them about Kazeno Rei and his involvement in the attack on Sola-Il, how her father had released the dragon into the city in an attempt to kill Princess Tsukimi.

If only he hadn't failed. Kurara squashed the thought as soon as it fluttered through her mind. She did not want to sympathize with terrorists.

"Unbelievable!" Sayo threw her hands in the air. "Do you know how much trouble the ship will be in if the military find out about what really happened on Sola-Il? If they find out that you were involved, that you *talked* with a member of Sohma? And he's your *father!*"

Anger flashed across Tomoe's face, causing both Kurara and Banri to shrink. Kurara had never seen Tomoe so livid—not like this, without a mask of sharp wit and an eviscerating tongue to back her up. She had nothing smart or cutting to say. There was only hot indignation layered over a thin veneer of hurt.

"And I tried to stop him! It's not like I *wanted* him to unleash some crazy shikigami in the middle of Sola-II. Doesn't that count for something?"

"That's not the point," Sayo hissed, keeping her voice low. "You know what this'll look like to the groundlings—"

"The groundlings can all go eat a buncha worms!" Tomoe's nostrils flared. "I'm good at my job; that's why Sakurai keeps me on the *Orihime*. I don't have anything to do with my father and I don't have any control over what he does; it's not fair that I should be made to feel like my very existence is a liability to the ship!"

"It's not fair, but since when have groundlings cared about fairness? You know this, Tomoe."

"Why can't you just comfort me?" Tomoe cried with such fury that even Sayo flinched. "For once in your stupid life, do you have to be so damn cold about everything? Just tell me, 'I'm sorry to hear that, Tomoe. Your father's a real piece of work, and you don't deserve this.' That's *all* I want from you!"

The heavy silence that followed could have crushed a sky whale. Kurara wished she could melt into the deck and disappear. She'd rather go downstairs and help the sailors plug the holes in the hull than stand here and witness this any longer.

"All right, that's enough. L–let's not fight," she said, weakly.

"You're the worst, Sayo." Tomoe's eyes were red-rimmed and furious.

Sayo looked devastated. She spluttered as she tried to

apologize and defend herself in the same breath, but Tomoe's glare only darkened.

By the blue skies, Kurara wanted someone to blow something up right now. Anything to distract them from the awkwardness of the moment. Besides, there were other things to worry about. Things like whether Fujiwa was chasing after them across the sea, and how long the sailors would tolerate their presence on board. Things like bringing Banri back to Kazami village.

"Is there any point fighting about something we can't change?" said Haru, his voice bright and far too loud. "Captain Morita said he'll drop us off at Zeka. That's the southernmost port in all of Mikoshima. We're on course to reach the Grand Stream and meet up with that airship of yours. What's the use in worrying about anything else?"

Kurara shot him a grateful look.

"When we arrive at Zeka, do you think you'll recognize the way home, Banri?" She turned to the bear.

The shikigami said nothing. It stared out to sea with a faraway look in its eyes.

"Banri?"

The bear jumped. *"Oh? Ah, yes, I think so. Maybe."*

"Is that a yes or a no?" hissed Sayo.

Banri hung its head, ears drooping, eyes downcast.

"If you're not feeling well, just say so," said Kurara, gently.

"I am fine, little one! Look!" With a deck-shaking thump, the bear hopped from one leg to another.

Haru sighed. Kurara's eyes darted to his face. Was he injured? Did he look slightly paler than before? Haru noticed her silently fretting.

"I'm *fine*, Rara. I just feel a bit out of sorts after listening to Master Fujiwa's orders. When I'm given an order, I do it because it feels like I *want* to, but when the moment passes I wonder why I ever believed that. It's like I'm not myself for a moment and it's tiring."

"That feeling will fade over time. The longer you remain with your master, the less you will notice the difference between your master's will and your own. That is why Crafters keep their shikigami close—because proximity keeps the bond strong."

The bond. More like mind control, Kurara wanted to scoff.

"I know. It's a good thing I never stuck around after my bonding. When Master Fujiwa's not around, it feels like his influence over me wanes." Haru grinned, but Kurara could tell that he was not as untroubled by the bond as he seemed. She opened her mouth to speak when a loud bang from inside the ship sent Banri scurrying toward Kurara for protection.

Captain Morita threw open the deck-hatch and clambered out. He glanced furtively across the ship, as if checking for spies. Satisfied, he took two long, quick strides toward them. If Tomoe had not said that he was a Sorabito, Kurara would never have guessed. When he spoke, his accent was rough and his vowels flat, falling like stones between his teeth.

"So, you're Sohma too, huh? By the skies, I didn't realize we recruited so young." As Morita's gaze settled on Tomoe, he scrunched up his face, as if trying to place where he had seen her before. "You look familiar . . ."

"How are things in the cities?" Sayo interrupted.

When the captain grinned, the gold fillings in his teeth shone, flecked with spittle. "You haven't heard? There have been riots, and not just in Sola-Il, in all the other sky cities too! It's downright atrocious what Princess Tsukimi did to our city! It was her creature that broke free, and everyone knows it. Just like everyone knows about the godless experiments she's been doing. People've gone missing you know. Orphans. Beggars. She's been kidnapping 'em and cutting them up into shikigami!"

Kurara bowed her head, deep in thought. If everyone believed that Tsukimi was responsible, hopefully the unrest would keep the princess busy and off their tail.

Then again, Princess Tsukimi had plenty of people she could send after them in her stead. People like Fujiwa.

"The situation in the sky cities grows worse each day. Finally, our people are waking up and realizing they need to fight back! Sometimes we have to give them a little push, but—"

"Push? What do you mean by push?" asked Kurara, sharply.

Morita glared at her. "And what's a paper devil doing with Sohma?"

"Special mission." Tomoe lied as easily as she breathed. "But what do you mean by push?"

The captain grinned darkly. "You know, a shattered window here, a scorched building there. Some broken bones. Some blood. Sometimes people need a little convincing to get really angry. Sometimes they want to try *talking* first or some such nonsense. That's why we need to push them. To make sure they don't waste their time with such foolishness."

The way Morita spoke—in a hushed, excited tone like a boy stealing dessert from the kitchens—filled Kurara with disgust. It was as if violence was not just ideal but something to be celebrated. As if he and the other members of Sohma were doing everyone a favor by making things worse.

"So you've been playing both sides, getting them angry at each other," said Kurara.

"Exactly!" Morita grinned. "For years, groundlings have treated us like dirt. There can be no peace between us, it would be foolish to even try! Besides, look at our airships! Look at our cities and compare them to the dirty, dreary little towns and villages the groundlings live in! Look at everything we Sorabito have built and tell me that we're not the superior people!"

"Those are some grand ideals, but it sounds to me like other members of Sohma are doing all the work while you're down here on this miserable little boat doing nothing." Kurara struggled to hold her anger in check.

Morita's face turned the color of a pickled plum. "I'm an informant! I pass on information. I keep our members connected and organize the reports that come to me every day. It's an important job!"

The paper in Kurara's left arm rustled with the urge to break away and strangle the man. She settled for letting her hand transform into a dragon-like claw, each curled talon longer than a knife and as thick as three fingers. Morita took a step back, his expression mutinous.

"I don't need to tell you that you should keep all this a secret from my crew, do I? They don't need to know any of this."

"What would we possibly gain from selling you out to your crew?" said Tomoe.

Morita's shoulders relaxed. "Yes. Yes, of course, you're right."

"And how do you explain why you have so much levistone?" asked Sayo.

The captain's expression soured. "Those are the few barrels we managed to buy before the Sorabito stopped trading. We were heading to another port town to earn a small fortune from them. Until your comrade here got us tangled in this mess with an imperial Crafter and then blew up a barrel! I'll have you know that every ko this ship loses hurts Sohma's funds!"

Good, thought Kurara.

"We'll pay you back later," Tomoe lied through her teeth.

Though he seemed none too happy about their presence, Morita let them remain on deck. As he left, he shot a glare at Kurara and Banri. The shikigami recoiled. Kurara moved to shield the bear from Morita's scowl with her body.

Tomoe threw her hands in the air. "Crud on a cloud, I can't even walk on the ground without running into bloody Sohma!"

Sayo stood beside her, a silent but solid and comforting presence, their argument forgotten. Their shoulders barely touched, but when Kurara looked at them she could not help but feel like she was intruding on something deeply private.

"Come on." She turned and clapped her hands on Haru's shoulders, giving the two girls their privacy. "Let's see if we can get some food around here."

The last thing Kurara noticed as she wheeled Haru away was Sayo's fingers gently hooked around Tomoe's hand.

FIFTEEN

$S\Lambda IL I N G$ with the *Kuroi Kame* was just as uncomfortable as Kurara feared. Sure the nights were warm and the stars bright, but Captain Morita was unpleasant, the sailors hated them and the food was slop. She slept poorly, constantly jolted out of her sleep by the rocking waves and the sailors drunkenly singing into the night. Knowing that there was nowhere to run if they were attacked did not help either.

She and the others kept to the back of the ship, sitting inside the lifeboats or on top of Banri's back while the *Kuroi Kame* sailed ahead at full speed. When Kurara did sleep, her dreams were fraught and full of terrors. They were always the same: filled with the sound of paper wings and a shikigami screaming at her in fury.

This time when Kurara fell asleep, she was standing inside a large impact crater. The ground was shaped like a bowl; the walls of rock surrounding her curved upward toward the sky. Emerald grass carpeted the ground and trees grew sparsely across the land. A series of small, turquoise lakes shimmered beneath the sun as something landed in the center with a monstrous splash.

"Aki! Akiiii!"

A furious shikigami loomed over her, its marble-white eyes gleaming, its snaking neck jerking from side to side as if trying to pin her down in its glare. Kurara could just about make out the creature's paper wings and sharp eyes, yet her mind could only focus on those fractured parts of the shikigami. When she tried to look at the beast as a whole, its form slipped from her mind like smoke between her fingers.

The creature bristled with rage. *"Aki! What have you done to me? What have you done to us all? We should never have let you join us! We should never have given you the Star Seed!"*

Just like in her other visions of Haru and Aki, Kurara felt the strange floating feeling of being a spectator in her own head.

"Be quiet!" She—or rather Aki—summoned up enough courage to shout back at the bird. There was a note of steel in her voice. The promise of violence yet to be realized. "The Seed is all that is left! It is my duty to keep it safe! I will never—"

"We should never have let you come here! We should never have given you the Star Seed!" The shikigami interrupted her with a harsh shriek, its wings fanning outward as if to curtain the entire world with its feathers.

A second later, it lunged toward her, ready to swallow her whole.

Kurara jolted awake like a swimmer desperately coming up for air. She gasped and squeezed her eyes shut, unable to deal with the sudden sight of the ship's deck.

"Are you OK?" someone asked.

She blinked until she could finally see Sayo's face. The girl was leaning against the lifeboats, looking at her with a cautious expression. Kurara could hear the slow creak of the ship, taste the salt in the air and feel the unrelenting summer heat pulsate against her skin as the sun rose. Banri was behind her, looking down at her with concern. She had been leaning against the bear's side when she had fallen asleep.

"I'm fine. I just had a bad dream, that's all." Kurara rubbed her eyes.

"Akiii! Aki! We should never have let you join us! We should never have given you the Star Seed!" The paper beast had screamed at her with eyes so full of hatred. Why had it been so angry with her? What had she done?

It had called her Aki. That could not have been a normal dream. It had felt far too real.

Sayo snorted. "You didn't dream of choking to death on the disgusting swill these sailors insist on calling food, did you? Because that's what I've been dreaming about."

Kurara shook her head. She had perfectly normal nightmares about death and failure and murderous shikigami, thank-you-very-much.

"A dying star fell from the heavens and from that star grew a tree," Banri sang to soothe her.

Something about the old song struck her. She had heard it plenty of times before. From Akane. From her own memories. But she had never really paid attention to the words until now.

"Where does that song come from?"

"It is an old lullaby all shikigami are taught," said Banri. *"About the Star Tree."*

"A Star Tree?" Sayo scoffed. "I've never heard of such a thing."

"That is because they are no more. By the time I was born, there were no Star Trees left. All that remains is the song. My master was a Grave-keeper—it was an important job looking after the dead and he knew many important songs and legends from the old times. He used to tell me all about them. He said that a Star Tree could grow five hundred feet tall. He said that the very first of the trees grew from falling stars. Its sap was a deep crimson and its leaves were dark blue and purple like the night's sky. Its branches were as golden as the stars."

Kurara tried to imagine a tree like that: leaves as dark as the night, golden branches that glowed like stars, and blood-red sap running down the bark.

Blood red . . .

"The blood of stars!"

Like a missing puzzle piece, everything clicked together. Haru had mentioned that the symbols on their cores were painted with the blood of the stars, and sap was sometimes known as tree blood. If this tree grew from a star then perhaps its sap was what people had meant when they said "the blood of the stars."

That was it! That had to be the answer! The sap must be special; it must be what made Haru and her different from other shikigami.

Just as her hopes began to soar, they quickly crashed to the ground. Banri had said that there were no more Star Trees. Was that why Haru had told her that he did not know how to grant the shikigami their freedom? Because there were no more trees left to harvest their sap?

Kurara felt as though someone had punched her in the gut. She had found a way to save the shikigami only to be kicked back to square one.

A loud shout stole Kurara's attention. The sailors of the *Kuroi Kame* were gambling and drinking again, as was their habit. Even as the midday sun beat relentlessly over the deck and burned into the backs of their necks, they shouted and roared and threw down their cards with drunken glee.

Except this time no one seemed particularly happy.

"You cheated!" A large, balding man stood over a circle of sailors; his face was flushed red with too much drink as he roared, "You! You bloody sky rat, you cheated!"

In the middle of the circle sat Tomoe and Haru, trying to swindle some travel funds from the sailors. At least, that's what Tomoe had claimed. Truthfully, Kurara reckoned she just wanted to thrash a few arrogant sailors at a game of cards.

"I did nothing of the sort!" Tomoe crowed in triumph. "Now pay up!"

In the corner of her eye, Kurara noticed Sayo tense.

The sailor's mouth narrowed in fury. He was not the only angry sailor among the group of foul-mouthed, drunken men, but he was the only one who seemed spoiling for a fight.

"You definitely cheated! I saw you that time!"

"Sit down, Joro, you're just drunk." Haru tugged at the man's sleeve.

Joro would not sit down. His face went from red to purple. Veins bulged at the side of his head. Without warning, he brandished the long, curved sword tied to his waist. His blade gleamed in the sunlight as he raised it above his head and brought it swinging down toward Tomoe.

In a flash, Sayo was by Tomoe's side, shoving Joro away with a snarl.

"*Stop!*"

In a single bound, Banri landed in the middle of the chaos. The sailors scattered in fright as the bear slammed its paws between them all, shaking the deck.

Most of the men had the good sense to give up when a giant, angry shikigami was yelling at them, but Joro, fueled by liquid courage, roared with rage and charged at the bear.

Haru was the closest to Banri when the sailor lifted his sword and brought it whistling down toward the bear's chest. Before the blow could hit, Haru stepped in the path of the swing. The tip of the blade pierced his arm, eliciting a sharp cry of pain.

Banri's eyes flashed with anger. "*You—!*"

"Everyone, stop!" shouted Kurara.

The men froze. It took a moment for Kurara to realize that they were afraid of her, of what she, the big bad Crafter with the sinister control over paper, might do to them.

Her ofuda circled around the sailors in slow, threatening circles. Kurara fought the giddy thrill of power as she looked from one pale face to the next.

"*L–little one?*" Banri's voice was a small, startled thing, as if it were afraid of disturbing the air with the sound of its voice. *"Did I do something wrong? I thought I was helping by jumping in, but did I make things worse?"*

"No, you didn't do anything wrong, Banri. Thank you for trying to help," said Kurara, though if she were honest the shikigami had probably stirred up more panic than necessary.

"That's right, everyone! Cool yer heads! All this drama over a little card game? You buncha girls!" One of the sailors took charge as the rest of the men dragged a furious Joro away.

"Oh gods, why did I do that? It hurts like the seventh circle of hell! Oh gods, Tomoe, don't touch it, I'm dying, woman!" Haru wailed. Kurara turned to see a smear of blood over the cut in Haru's arm.

"Oh, don't squawk like a baby chick! It's such a shallow wound!" Tomoe scolded him, but when she turned away Kurara noticed Tomoe quickly hide her bleeding palm.

"Rara, Rara, I think I'm dying!" Haru's face was the picture of misery.

A sailor turned to him. "You're bleeding. Let me—"

"*I'll* take care of him." Kurara stepped between them. Grabbing Haru by the wrist she yanked him below deck.

The corridors of the *Kuroi Kame* were like a wooden maze, the hallways narrow and creaking. Lamps hung on metal hooks that barely offered enough light to see. Kurara was not sure where she was going, but she was too frazzled to care. She could not forget the flash of fear that had coursed through her body when she saw the blade stab through Haru's arm.

"Phew, that was close! I'll have to thank Tomoe for

bleeding on me. Is that a weird thing to thank someone for? She sliced her own palm with her tanto and slapped her blood on my wound so it would look like I can bleed. It was so cool! She didn't even wince!" Haru babbled as Kurara yanked him along.

"Y–you!" she hissed. "What were you thinking?"

"I was thinking that maybe Banri might freak out if it had a sword sticking out of it. You know how much of a crybaby that shikigami is." Haru sounded petulant, more like a boy caught playing in the mud than the victim of a stabbing. "Besides, you'd be upset if Banri got hurt."

"So you got yourself hurt instead?"

Haru grinned. "Aww, Rara, were you worried? Does that mean you'll nurse me back to health?"

Kurara stopped to glower at him. When she said "You're insufferable," what she meant was: *I'll never forgive whoever hurts you.*

"If it was for you, Rara," said Haru, "then I'd gladly let myself get stabbed a thousand times."

SIXTEEN

THE very first door Kurara came across led into a large, dimly lit storeroom. Like everything below the *Kuroi Kame*'s deck, the dull wooden walls and floorboards were old and creaking. The room itself was lit by a small oil lamp hanging down from the middle of the ceiling. The porthole window was closed, covered by a thick sheet of canvas that kept out the daylight. Cold, metal shelves lined every wall, each packed with labeled boxes of food and other supplies.

It was not an infirmary, but Kurara preferred it that way. An infirmary would have a healer—someone that she, or rather Haru, would have to talk into giving them some bandages without them looking too deeply at the injury, and she would rather not deal with anyone right now. The first box she cracked open contained nothing but tins of sardines. It took some rummaging before she uncovered the medical supplies, and longer still to locate the bandages.

"Will it heal on its own?" Kurara steadily unwrapped a roll of gauze.

Haru shook his head. "No, not for a wound this large. You'll have to use your ofuda to fix it."

"Hold still," she instructed. Hovering a hand over Haru's wound, she focused her mind on the edges of the injury and pulled the paper fibers of his arm back together, leaving behind a slim white scar that ran over the curve of his forearm. Kurara frowned. No one would know it was paper unless they looked really closely; but still, the very sight of it made her feel as though she had failed somehow.

"Don't make that face, Rara. Scars just make a man look rugged!" Haru took the roll of gauze from her and began wrapping his wound. Though the injury was closed, he still needed to play the part of a normal boy and pretend that he was healing. Spots of Tomoe's blood seeped through the gauze, staining it a convincing red. Kurara would have to thank her later.

"Thanks for protecting Banri." It should have been her. She should have defended Banri herself. She was the one who could still use ofuda, the one who had been trained like a Crafter.

"Like I said, I didn't do it for Banri, I did it for you. Because I knew you would be upset if the bear got hurt." Haru finished tying his bandage in place.

"Oh!" She suddenly remembered. "I left Banri on the deck with those awful sailors!" Even with Sayo and Tomoe, Banri was delicate. The shikigami hated noise and strangers, and the sailors were the noisiest, crudest bunch Kurara had ever met. If they said something mean to Banri, she would turn her paper arm into a tentacle and throttle them.

Something of her thoughts must have shown on her face, because Haru wrinkled his nose and said, "Aren't you a little too attached to that shikigami? I mean, we're going to split up eventually. Even if we go all the way to Kazami, it's not coming with us to the Grand Stream."

"I know that, but I still want to help it in any way I can. I know what the blood of the stars means now! It's the sap from a special kind of tree called a Star Tree."

Haru's smile disappeared. "Did Banri tell you that?"

"Well, sort of." Everything on deck had happened so quickly, she had not had the chance to share her discovery. Banri had only known what the Star Tree had looked like. She had been the one to figure out that its sap was the blood of the stars.

"Then did Banri also tell you that there are no more Star Trees left?"

"So you *do* know about the Star Trees?" said Kurara. "But you said you didn't know what the blood of the stars really was!"

"No, you asked me how to *find* the blood of the stars and I told you the truth: that I don't know."

Something in Haru's tone frustrated her; he sounded as though he did not understand what he had done wrong. But even if Haru hadn't lied, he had not told her something that would have been useful for her to know. What else would he keep from her?

"You could have told me about the Star Trees as well! You deliberately held that information from me!" she said, angrily.

"I didn't want to give you a reason to be upset! What's

134

the point of talking about Star Trees when they were all cut down so long ago?"

"Cut down? By who?"

"By Crafters, of course," said Haru.

"Why? Why would they cut them down?"

"Why do you *think*, Rara? So that shikigami would not have the freedom to betray them. Who wants a tool that might disobey orders?"

Kurara almost dropped the box of bandages. Crafters had cut down the trees to keep shikigami shackled to them? So that shikigami could never disobey their masters?

"Bu–but that's . . ." She could hardly finish her sentence. It was awful. Barbaric. How could anyone do something so terrible?

"Originally, shikigami were meant to be like you and me: as close to a living human as possible. But shikigami like us are not as useful as the ones like Banri. Not for fighting, anyway. We eat their food, we get tired, we argue with Crafters and, worse, we can betray them. That's why they made shikigami like Banri. Shikigami with bodies that never tire and never need food. Shikigami that cannot disobey."

"So . . . that's why you told me you didn't know how to free them." Kurara fiddled with the box of bandages simply to have something to do with her hands.

Haru was right: knowing about the Star Trees did upset her, but Kurara would rather know the truth and be upset than be kept in the dark.

"Like I told you, Rara, there's nothing to be done. I know it's a hard truth to swallow, but there's no way to grant shikigami their freedom. Not anymore."

But the shikigami in her dream had screamed something at her, something about a Star Seed.

"We should never have let you join us! We should never have given you the Star Seed!"

"Even if the trees were cut down, there must be some way to revive them. Or to grow another one. They can't all be gone! What about their seeds? There must be some seeds left that we could plant . . ."

Haru sighed. He had never lost his patience with her before, but Kurara could hear it in his tone: his eagerness to be done with this conversation. "The Star Trees were special. As far as I know, they didn't produce seeds or fruit. You might as well go looking for a flying pig or a jewel that grants eternal life! Chasing after fairy tales will only hurt you, Rara." His expression softened. "And I don't want to see you hurt."

"No, there *is* still a Star Seed! I . . . I saw it!"

"Saw it? What are you talking about, Rara?"

Kurara clamped her mouth shut. Should she tell Haru about her dream? Doubt crept into her mind like a thief. There was more to Haru than who he had been when they lived together on the *Midori*. He kept his secrets close and his memories locked away inside himself. Away from her. If she told him about her dream, she could not be sure that he would help her.

The realization that she didn't trust Haru any more brought a strange kind of grief. She used to tell everything, used to share all her dreams and desires without a second thought. Back then, the mere thought of doubting Haru would never have occurred to her. He had always been a guest in her mind, welcome to peruse her thoughts and feelings at his leisure.

Kurara opened her mouth. She did not want anything to be different between them, but her desire to grant the shikigami their freedom was more important than anything else.

"Nothing," she said. "It's nothing."

SEVENTEEN

"A crater?" Sayo looked at Kurara as if she were a cat who had just dropped a dead bird at her feet. "Why do you want to know?"

Kurara shrugged. She was not sure how to say "I saw one in what was probably a dream-memory of a previous life and I think it might be my best clue to finding a way to free the shikigami".

Seagulls flocked overhead, their sharp calls piercing her ears as the waves heaved and rocked the ship. While the sun beat against the deck, a soft breeze ruffled the sails. Sayo leaned back as she considered Kurara's question.

"I don't know of any crater in Mikoshima."

"But you're a navigator! I thought you knew everything when it comes to geography!" cried Kurara.

Sayo glared at her. "I do know everything when it comes to *current* geography. Land changes over time. Perhaps this place no longer exists. Have you tried asking your friend?"

"I asked, but Banri didn't know either."

"I meant Haru."

Kurara snapped her mouth shut.

Sometimes, she remembered the day Himura walked away from her as she called out to him for help. The memory brought back a familiar, smoldering anger that she had nursed over time into a constant, low-burning flame. She had trusted Himura and he had betrayed her. She did not want to trust Haru only to be hurt again. She did not want to end up a fool, pleading with someone who had already turned their back on her.

"You're thinking about unnecessary things," Sayo snorted. "Our only priority is to reach the Grand Stream and join the *Orihime*. Don't forget that."

Kurara's nails dug into the palms of her hands. Unnecessary things. That was right. To everyone else, to the whole world, the plight of the shikigami was not something worth worrying about. Shikigami were tools at worst, pets at best. The military treated them like useful weapons and Crafters ordered them about with no regard for a shikigami's own desires.

But I'm a shikigami too, and I'm a person. Sometimes, she felt as if Tomoe and Sayo forgot that—they forgot that she was made of paper, that she had a core instead of a heart—as if they could not square the idea of her being a shikigami with the idea that she was an individual with thoughts and feelings of her own.

No, that wasn't fair. Kurara knew she was just being bitter because she was tired and feeling hopeless.

"We should never have given you the Star Seed!"

At the very least, her dreams had taught her one thing: at some point, there had been a Star Seed. What happened to it afterward was what Kurara needed to find out. If it still existed, then there was still hope for the shikigami. There was still a chance they could be given their freedom.

———◦———

As each day aboard the *Kuroi Kame* blurred into the next, Kurara felt as if the sun was trying to roast them alive. Tomoe and Sayo sat on top of the lifeboats, leaning back so that the wind and surf trailed through their hair. Occasionally, one of them would say something, to which the other would reply before lapsing into silence, rendered useless by the heat. Haru had disappeared into the cool dampness below deck to listen to the sailors' stories, returning only on occasion to relay an interesting bit of trivia or a weird account he had heard from the men.

It was a shame the sailors were all such miserable louts because their tales were actually quite interesting—stories of sea monsters and sky whales and tsunamis that would cover the deck in a carpet of fish. Kurara would have liked to hear more. Or perhaps what she missed was hearing the excitement in Haru's voice, watching his eyes light up with boyish wonder and seeing his infectious grin overtake his face.

At some point Tomoe put her head on Sayo's lap, but when Kurara glanced at them again, Sayo's fingers were balled up in fists at her side, very deliberately not touching anything. Her gaze lingered on the small red line on Tomoe's palm where the girl had cut herself for Haru. The wound had mostly healed by now, leaving only a thin scar that seemed to annoy and upset Sayo in equal measure.

Though it looked as though they were back to being friends again, there was at times an oddly strained tension between them that Kurara hadn't noticed before. She opened her mouth, then thought better of it. It was better not to get involved in their . . . whatever this was.

Kurara's ofuda fluttered around her, swirling like a vortex of paper butterflies that circled her body. With a single thought, the pieces of paper crashed into one another, merging and stretching to form a large peacock with a fanned tail, a prowling mountain lion, a stag with antlers that pierced the sky. The sailors might not like being reminded of her power, but she was not going to let a bunch of burly men keep her from doing something she enjoyed. From a dagger to a sword, she ran through a gamut of paper weapons, concentrating so that each was as sharp and strong as the next.

Banri watched with a wide-eyed wonder that reminded her of her days on the *Midori* when Haru used to giggle at the origami animals that would leap over their beds.

"Master was also very good at shape-changing," said Banri. *"When he was not tending to the graveyard, he would teach Oda how to make large landscapes of paper."*

Kurara looked up from her ofuda. "You said that before— that he was a Grave-keeper. So he looked after the dead?"

"When a Crafter dies, they are cremated. A Grave-keeper's duty is to tend to their ashes. It is an important and honored role. Grave-keepers are elders who know all sorts of things."

Cremation. The act of burning a body to ashes. Kurara reckoned there was some profound meaning in submitting a body to the flames, allowing the flesh to be burned just like paper, but thinking of it made her a little queasy. Perhaps she had simply been around Sorabito for too long; in the sky cities, it was tradition to allow the birds to pick apart their dead.

"I've heard about Grave-keepers before," Sayo interjected. "About ten years ago, the Emperor began rounding up as many Crafters as he could for his army. They had lots of books and stuff that they were hoarding. Books that went straight into Princess Tsukimi's library. What if this Crafter that Banri's looking for was also taken away? They might not be at Kazami anymore."

"*N—no, that cannot be.*" Banri shrank away from her.

"Stop it, Sayo, you're frightening it," said Tomoe.

Sayo sniffed airily. "I'm just saying it's a possibility. It's not my fault this huge lug is such a crybaby."

Banri lowered its head in shame. "*A crybaby . . . Master said that too. Shikigami are not meant to be cowards. We are supposed to be strong and brave and fearsome. We were built for war after all. We were built to—to—*"

"You're not a coward. And you're not just built for war. You're just you, Banri, and I like that. I like who you are now." Kurara patted the bear's side. Her ofuda swayed around her in gentle waves, forming soothing patterns in the air above the shikigami's head.

"*Little star, you are very kind, but I fear you are simply saying things.*"

"No, I mean it! Remember that huge tiger shikigami at Nessai? It attacked you and yet you still leapt onto the boat!"

"*I suppose.*" Banri did not look convinced.

"You suppose? A big lump like you shouldn't be scared of anything," said Sayo.

Kurara shot her a displeased look.

"Ugh, OK. *Fine!*" The girl rolled her eyes. Taking a deep breath, she turned so that her body was level with Banri's head and said in a stiff voice, "Even though there were so many people about, you charged into the city as soon as you saw Kurara's signal. That was very brave too. And even though you were hurt and in pain, you endured it well."

The bear's ears pricked up. "*Truly?*"

Sayo looked like she was choking on a lemon. "Truly."

A pleased rumble shook Banri's chest, but just then the sound of heavy footsteps interrupted their conversation.

"I've got good news and I've got bad news! Which of 'em do you want first?" Captain Morita strolled toward them with an excited gleam in his eye.

Banri backed away as the man approached. Despite being more than three times her size, the shikigami still attempted to hide behind Kurara as she stepped forward.

"What's the good news?"

Captain Morita did not answer until Tomoe echoed the question.

"Our destination's close now. We'll reach Zeka within a day," said Morita. "You'll be in good company. Our comrades have contacted me. Sohma has been doing good work in the city! Even better, Kazeno Rei is in Zeka too."

A flicker of something crossed Tomoe's face—anger, or perhaps irritation—but she controlled her expression well.

"And what's the bad news?" she asked.

"The bad news is there might be a shikigami traveling around these waters. The lookouts spotted some great gawping bird in the distance."

A bird? Kurara felt the tight bundle of nerves in her chest loosen. That could not be Fujiwa. A wild shikigami was easier to deal with than an imperial Crafter. Perhaps she could even reason with it.

"Do you think it will attack?" asked Sayo.

"Well, we're not hunters, but we've dealt with shikigami before. If it attacks, we'll lure it into the sea. The saltwater will mess its body up good," Captain Morita replied, with the sickening glee of someone who enjoyed destroying something beautiful. When the crew of the *Orihime* hunted, there was no pleasure in destruction, only in a job well done.

As the clouds shifted, Kurara spied something moving through the clouds. At first, she thought that the light was playing tricks on her, but the more she squinted the more she could make out the curve of a head and the sharpness of tail feathers. It was coming closer.

"Um, when you say there's a shikigami in the area, do you mean *that*?"

The others turned around as Kurara pointed to the giant bird heading straight toward them.

EIGHTEEN

"THAT'S not a shikigami," said Tomoe.
Morita's brow furrowed. "It's not?"

"You fool, can't you tell the difference?" Sayo was on her feet now, craning her head back to take in the sight of the giant, paper-white buzzard making its way toward the ship.

Tomoe was right; even from a distance Kurara could tell that there was no intelligence in its eyes.

"That's not a shikigami, it's just ofuda!"

That meant someone was controlling it. Someone like—

"Fujiwa!"

Haru burst onto the deck like a man possessed, his mop of ink-black curls looking even messier than usual. "Rara, Master Fujiwa is here!"

As the buzzard drew closer, the prickle of electricity dancing across Kurara's skin confirmed it. There was a person clinging to the bird's back, dressed in a military uniform and accompanied by an unmistakable white tiger.

"That's impossible—how did he catch up so fast?" Captain Morita gawped as he and the sailors scrambled to the edges of the deck, drawing their weapons. Pride kept them from fleeing, but from the ashen looks on the men's faces and the shaky way they held their guns, they did not want to get in the way of a battle between Crafters.

"Tell your men to get us out of here! Full speed ahead!" Tomoe grabbed Haru and pulled him into an arm lock so that he could not fight against them when Fujiwa appeared. A handful of men peeled away to do her bidding, but Kurara knew that it would do no good. They would not shake Fujiwa so easily this time.

"Someone, toss me a pistol!" she heard Sayo shout, but she was not sure if anyone else did. Gritting her teeth, Kurara watched as the paper buzzard crumbled in midair. A stream of paper trailed after Fujiwa and his shikigami as they crashed onto the deck like vengeful gods descending from the heavens.

Fujiwa sized her up as one would a wild animal. His ofuda moved around him at a slow, cautious pace.

With a flick of her fingers, Kurara sent a handful of paper whizzing toward him, each white square as sharp as a blade. They shot past Fujiwa's face, drawing a thin line of blood from his cheek. It was a warning shot.

"Stop that, Rara!"

"Sayo, help me hold him down! We'll drag him onto a lifeboat and toss him out to sea!" cried Tomoe as she struggled against Haru's thrashing limbs.

"Haru!" Fujiwa shouted without taking his eyes off Kurara for one second. "Come here!"

Haru strained to obey even as Tomoe and Sayo held him back. Kurara's ofuda formed a long, white chain. With a crack, she lashed out at Fujiwa—only for Banri's hulking body to block the blow as it lunged straight for her.

"Banri! What are you doing?" she cried as the bear swiped its paw at her head and forced her to retreat to the edge of the deck.

"*Master, please don't leave me, please!*" the bear roared.

Kurara's jaw clenched. Not again! This was the worst time for Banri's sanity to start slipping.

Banri shook its head as if trying to fight off the memories haunting its mind. No matter what Kurara did or how many times she called its name, the bear did not hear her.

"*Forgive me! Forgive me, Master!*" it cried.

While she was distracted, Fujiwa took his chance to attack, but he too was blocked by Banri as the shikigami suddenly lunged for him.

This was a nightmare. Kurara could not fight Fujiwa while keeping Banri at bay and making sure that Haru and the others were safe. She needed to put some distance between them. She needed to separate Fujiwa from everyone else.

Before she could attack again, Ruki crashed into her, sending her flying across the deck. Pain blossomed along her side as she hit the mast and slammed into the ground. Her ears were ringing from the blow, but she could just about make out the sounds of panicked voices and hurried footsteps.

"Rara!"

"Kurara, are you OK?"

"Oi, girl, do something about your shikigami!"

Voices yelled as the world lurched into sickening focus. Kurara looked up, too stunned to fully process what had just happened. By the time her mind finally caught up, Ruki was standing over her, one paw in the air, ready to squash her like a bug.

"Stop it!" Banri's scream tore through her head. A second later, the bear hurled itself into Ruki's side. Both shikigami rolled across the deck, growling and snapping at one another like ancient forest gods locked in battle.

Kurara scrambled to her feet. Her ofuda swirled around her, folding together to form a staff in her one good hand. Pushing all her might into the swing, she brought the tip of the staff crashing into the side of Ruki's head.

It was a direct hit. The force of the blow sent the tiger staggering away from Banri.

"How dare you!" Fujiwa's fluttering ofuda formed a paper katana that flew toward her.

Kurara readied herself to block the blow, but before the sword reached her, Banri stepped in front of her once more. The katana pierced the bear's side.

"Banri, get out of the way!" she cried. She did not know if the bear was back to being itself again or still fighting against the erosion of its mind, but she was more than capable of protecting herself.

"No, I am brave! I will protect you and your friends!" the shikigami shouted through the pain.

Kurara clenched her teeth in frustration. When she trained with Himura, it was always one on one, and that was how she liked her fights. She could handle a single Crafter and their shikigami. But when there were so many people about, even if they were on her side, the battlefield became too crowded for her to control. She needed to clear the deck.

"Everyone, get to the boats! Banri, you too!" she shouted as Ruki rolled back onto its feet.

"*I will not leave you!*" Banri stubbornly swung a paw at Fujiwa. The Crafter dodged and struck the bear's flank with a hail of paper bullets that sent the bear stumbling to one side.

With a roar, Kurara lunged at the imperial Crafter. She grabbed a handful of paper from the air, merging them together into a long, white sledgehammer. She pulled her arms back and slammed it into the deck.

The floorboards in front of their feet cracked. Upon the second blow, they shattered, sending both Fujiwa and Kurara tumbling through the deck and into the ship below. Landing on a bed of dust and broken wood, Kurara rolled to her feet.

Shouts of alarm echoed above her, but she paid them no mind. Now that they were both below deck, she knew Fujiwa would follow her. After all, he already had control of Haru, and he did not care for the others; *she* was the wild card, she was the untamed shikigami that he was supposed to drag back to the princess's side. Down here, Kurara could bait him away from the others.

Down here, she could deal with Fujiwa alone.

NINETEEN

THE ship was dark and damp, its hallways like narrow warrens. Kurara knew Fujiwa was behind her as she ran through the dimly lit corridors of the *Kuroi Kame*. Muffled voices of alarm echoed through the walls, but it was impossible to tell how far away they were. The floors creaked so loudly that Kurara wondered if the ship was ripping in two.

As she turned the corner, a paper shuriken embedded itself in the wall in front of her face. She ducked, still refusing to turn around even as the throwing star pulled itself free and sped after her.

"Halt!" Fujiwa's booming voice echoed down the tight passageway.

Kurara bolted through the ship as his ofuda snapped at her heels, running until she found the storeroom where she had patched up Haru a few days before. Slamming the door shut behind her, she stacked everything she could get her hands on against the door: crates of tinned seafood, sacks of rice and heavy rolls of cloth. Kurara prised open another wooden box and unearthed a pair of expensive sake bottles nestled against the silk.

The door burst open behind her, wood splintering. She had known that her makeshift barricade would not keep a Crafter at bay, but she had hoped that it would have bought her more time. Kurara drew back, pressing herself into the far wall. More boxes crashed to the ground around her, each one filled with books and old star charts and smoking pipes with wooden matchboxes.

"Stop!" She held the sake bottle like a weapon. "Don't come any closer!"

"Enough." Fujiwa was not deterred. "You have defied the princess for too long. And even though she could give you a good life, even though she has been generous, you continue to defy her."

"A good life!" Kurara scoffed. "You mean as her pet shikigami!"

She threw the bottle at Fujiwa. As it soared through the air, Kurara shot a bolt of paper right through it, shattering the glass and spilling alcohol over Fujiwa's head.

"You—!" The Crafter swore as Kurara snatched up a pack of matches and struck one against the side of the box.

"Come any closer and I'll set you on fire!"

How ironic would it be if Fujiwa burned just like a shikigami? The fire might not kill him, but drenched in sake as he was, it would do some serious damage.

The man's face twisted into a look of anger. "You're just

a shikigami! A mad, wild one if your behaviour is anything to go by! Once you have a master and a bond, you'll settle down. You'll come to your senses."

Kurara snarled at him like the beast he thought she was. "Your princess is the mad one! She's so obsessed with shikigami that she's willing to make you attack a ship full of innocent people!"

Before Fujiwa could reply, a loud creaking sound ripped through the ship. A second later, something crashed through the ceiling in front of her, sending splintered wood flying everywhere. The match slipped from Kurara's hand, landing in the corner of the room where it began to burn through the rolls of fabric.

Kurara gawked at the bear that had suddenly plummeted into the room with them. "Banri! Why haven't you escaped on the lifeboats?"

The storeroom was barely big enough to contain Banri. The shikigami moved with difficulty.

"*I shall not leave without you!*" it roared as it swung its paw at Fujiwa.

The Crafter jumped back, using his ofuda to block the bear's claws. Banri stepped on the bottles of sake scattered over the floor, shattering them and spilling their contents. Smoke curled through the air.

"Stop, Banri!" cried Kurara, but it was too late. The small fire from the matchstick had grown, gorging itself on the fallen bits of cloth and paper tossed about the room. A moment later, it found a puddle of alcohol and roared to life.

The flames took hold of the room. Kurara panicked.

In her head she was inside the forest again, watching Haru burn. She could not watch another shikigami she loved go up in flames.

"You damned shikigami!" roared Fujiwa.

"Fire! Fire!" screamed Banri in alarm as the flames latched onto its paws and began to crawl up its body.

Despite the chaos, Kurara had enough sense to break the porthole window. Smoke billowed out from between the broken glass and rose upward like a signal flare. She grabbed the edge and heaved herself up, ignoring how the jagged edges of the glass cut her hand.

"Banri! This way! Jump!"

She had forgotten that Banri was too large to fit through a tiny window. Instead, the bear barreled through the wall, taking Kurara with it in a burst of broken wood. The last thing she saw was Fujiwa with his sleeve pressed over his nose and mouth. His eyes shone with frustration as he retreated from the room.

As Kurara hit the water, the breath was knocked out of her paper lungs. The sea heaved, pushing her farther away from the boat as she floundered to stay afloat. She squeezed her eyes shut and tried to fight against the waves, but with each desperate kick she only sank farther. Panic made it worse. She blindly pushed through the water, hoping that she was heading in the right direction.

She forced her eyes open at the sound of Banri crashing into the ocean. When she looked, she could just about make out a massive ball of white sinking into the depths. Rushing forward, she managed to grab a handful of paper fur. She tried to swim to the surface, but Banri's body was a sodden weight pulling her down. Her grip on the shikigami slipped. When she tried to shout, water invaded her mouth, stinging the back of her throat.

Was she going to die? No, as a shikigami, this would not kill her, but perhaps that was worse. To be lost at the bottom of the ocean for the rest of eternity was far more frightening than the thought of drowning.

Dark spots danced across the inside of her eyelids. Her chest burned. The last thing she saw before the waves carried her away was Banri's body drifting farther and farther down into the depths of the ocean.

TWENTY

WHEN Himura had left the *Orihime* with Kazeno Rei in tow, he knew things would not be easy. Taking the leader of a terrorist group like Sohma anywhere was not going to be a walk in the park; he had been prepared for all sorts of things to go wrong.

He had not been prepared for this.

Never in his wildest dreams had he anticipated meeting a shikigami in the middle of a city. Wild shikigami that had lost their minds would sometimes attack villages and towns, and bonded shikigami would follow their masters anywhere they went; but given the choice, and in their right minds, a shikigami would never willingly spend time near large groups of people.

He glanced around for the creature's master. Shikigami stuck close to those they bonded with, not just because Crafters tended not to let their shikigami stray too far, but because distance had ill effects on a shikigami's mind. Even though they would not go completely mad, they would become depressed if they were away from their masters for too long.

This shikigami appeared to be alone.

"I have been looking for a Crafter such as yourself," it repeated, coyly. *"I have an interesting proposal for you."*

He stared at the snake. He could not believe it. To find a shikigami now, after he had lost Akane . . . was it a sign from the gods?

Shikigami were made to serve us, his parents had whispered to him when he was a child. They were valuable but replaceable. If he bound this shikigami to him with his blood, he could have another Akane. A second chance.

His bracelet crumbled away into a dozen pieces of paper.

Sensing his intention, the snake darted across the alleyway like an eel through water. In a flash of white, it coiled up Himura's leg and wrapped itself around his ankles, bringing him crashing to the ground. Its head hovered menacingly, just inches away from his face, forked tongue flicking.

"Child, you dare to attack me when I have so graciously blessed you with my presence? What arrogance! Cut your head off in apology! Cut off your head and present it to me on your knees. Perhaps, then, I may just forgive you!"

Himura froze. The shikigami's scales were brittle as they slithered over his skin. The weight of its body was like a cannonball resting against his chest.

He opened his mouth to reply, but the words jammed in his throat.

I've upset it. Kurara aside, the only shikigami he had ever met were either completely mad or completely in awe of their master. Something like this—all fire without the insanity, eloquence without the fawning adoration—was completely new to him. Himura thought of Akane and the fox's sunny smiles. He wondered if Akane would have loved him quite as much if it had not been forced to.

"If I cut off my head, I won't be able to get on one knee and give it to you," he wheezed. The weight on his chest was cutting off the air to his lungs. He was starting to feel faint.

The snake considered this for a moment. *"Very well then. I wish for you to stab yourself with your own ofuda instead."*

Himura stared at the shikigami. Though it was not mad, there was something very wrong with its personality. Who in their right mind would create a shikigami with such an attitude?

The snake slithered off Himura's chest. *"I see Crafters rarely, and when I finally find one, you try to attack me! I am here, alone in this stinking city, because my master bids me to bring all Crafters that I encounter to her. Yet you look at me with such foul eyes! You are hardly worth bringing to meet the Grave-keeper."*

"Grave-keeper?" Himura echoed.

Even the backwater village where he had grown up had heard of the Emperor's attempts to force more Crafters into the military. He knew that the princess had seized the books that had once belonged to the Grave-keepers. That was why Himura had wanted to see her library—he knew the princess's sources were reliable. After all, she had stolen everything she owned from his people.

"There are still Grave-keepers left?"

"First you want to attack me and then you expect me to answer you!" The way the snake flicked its tongue seemed very much in lieu of a rude gesture.

"I . . . apologize for that," said Himura. Distantly, he was aware of the absurdity of apologizing to a shikigami. It was like apologizing to a hammer; they could not really be offended. "Please don't go yet. I—I beg you."

"Well," the snake preened, the offence quickly forgotten. *"If you're willing to beg . . . But first, tell me your name."*

"My name is Himura."

In the distance, the crowd's roars began to fade. They were moving on, taking their anger and discontent with them.

"I am Mana," said the shikigami. *"My name is spelled with the words for truth and summer. My master is the great Grave-keeper, so do not bother thinking you can bond with me. Try anything again and I will crush your throat."*

Though the shikigami seemed fairly sound of mind, there was something in the fiery confidence with which it spoke that intrigued Himura. Surely, the snake was not lying.

"And why are you so far away from your master?"

"Master is getting old. She will die soon. She needs a student to take over her duties. I came here in search of someone who might wish to study beneath her. There were a lot of Crafters passing through earlier. Military Crafters with their shikigami trundling by their side and a bunch of soldiers staring at them like they were wild animals, but I had no chance to speak to them. They all got on an airship and took off to the sky cities. Ever since then, this city has been in turmoil. Things keep blowing up and people keep getting angrier."

Himura mulled over the shikigami's words. The military only deployed Crafters in dire situations; most were overseas fighting in the Emperor's wars. If they were being sent to the sky cities, then the situation in the clouds was worse than Himura had imagined.

He was glad Rei had slunk off somewhere. Imagining the man's triumph was about as much as he could stand.

"And where is your master?"

"The Grave-keeper lives far to the south in Kazami village. It will take two weeks to get there," the snake replied.

Two weeks! Himura did not have time for that. He needed to meet the *Orihime* at the Grand Stream. He wanted to tell Sakurai and the crew about the situation in Zeka, to warn them that the relationship between the Sorabito and the groundlings was dangerously tense.

But . . . he was heading south anyway. What was the harm of visiting this Kazami place? The book he had stolen from Tsukimi's library sat heavily at the bottom of his travel pack. He had done worse things in his pursuit of knowledge than take a slight detour.

"If I go with you, I'm not committing myself to anything. I would like to see this master of yours, but I'm not promising that I'll stay and become your master's apprentice," he said.

"Of course," said Mana, smoothly. *"And I make no promise that my master will want you anyway. But I have my orders to bring Crafters to her, and I cannot disobey."*

Himura nodded. Maybe all he would find when he followed Mana was a hermit who had gone mad from years of seclusion. Or perhaps Mana's master was a sham of a Crafter who knew nothing more than how to make paper cranes, but he would never find out unless he accompanied the snake.

If Mana's master really was a Grave-keeper, it would be worth the visit. A real Grave-keeper would be well versed in Crafter history and tradition—they would know about the great war, about shikigami, about the Crafters that had once ruled this land. Either way, it was in the same direction as he needed to go.

He had already sacrificed so much. After everything else, what did it matter if he was a little delayed in returning to the *Orihime*?

"Lead the way."

Interlude

Oh, to be a cloud
To be a fish or a frog
A bird with blue wings
To be anything except
Small and painfully human

—from *On Life in Our Empire*
(banned by the Patriots Office)

Princess Tsukimi did not think of herself as a rash person. She had endured plenty of insults—from her father, her brother, the imperial court, and the masses who whispered malicious rumors about her.

She knew restraint. She knew how to not stab the very annoying military official standing in front of her right now.

"I'm afraid you just missed him, Your Imperial Highness."

Princess Tsukimi stared out of the window from the top floor of the Patriots Office. The moment the *Jurojin* had landed in Nessai Harbor, she and her imperial Crafters had

been met by a very worried military officer who ushered her up a dozen flights of rickety staircases, along the curve of Nessai's broken dome, and into the red-brick Patriots Office and the antechamber where she now sat.

Apparently, an imperial princess turning up out of the blue, when she was supposed to be in Sola-Il, was considered "alarming".

Tsukimi tapped her fingers against her knee. The crystal chandelier above her head cast a constellation of too-bright lights across the carpeted floor that irritated her. Tapestries of famous battles hung on ice-white walls trimmed with gold. Goro, Tamada, and their shikigami stood to attention at the door, pretending to be invisible.

Someone had placed a cup of green tea and a selection of mochi on the table closest to her, though she could not remember any maids entering the room. Both the tea and the officer were ignored as she turned to sweep aside the curtains covering the antechamber windows. People milled across the land below, as tiny and insignificant as ants.

"F—Fujiwa left a few days ago and hasn't been back since. There was some commotion by the harbor. A shikigami showed up," the officer stammered, his eyes flitting from the princess's bored expression to the untouched plate, as though his promotion depended on exactly how many pieces of mochi she ate.

"A shikigami?" Tsukimi finally turned her attention to the man.

"A large bear. Apparently, it had a master, so there was not much damage. Fujiwa disappeared shortly after, but he

left you a note." The man pushed a piece of paper across the table to Tsukimi.

The oaf should have started with that! She could have left by now instead of enduring his tedious fawning and inferior-looking tea.

Tsukimi snatched up the note. It was written in code, but Fujiwa's handwriting was neat and precise.

Following ship Kuroi Kame. *Heading to Zeka,* it said. *Shikigami children spotted.*

At last, some good news. She crumpled Fujiwa's message into a ball and tossed it into the air. It did not spin around her or transform into an origami lion. Catching it with a hand, she cast aside her irritation and got to her feet, ready to leave, when the door burst open.

"Sister!"

Tsukimi's mood plummeted.

"The men outside told me you were here. Honored sister, it is a pleasure to see you again!"

Ugetsu, she wanted to snarl. What in the seven hells was he doing here? She thought he was a thousand miles away, fighting the northern savages for scraps of land to add to the empire. No one had told her that he was on his way back to the country. She needed better spies.

Prince Ugetsu was an excellent soldier, though one would never guess it from the way he looked. He was tall and thin, with arms like soba noodles. Yet he wore his uniform as though he had been born for military service. His hair was neatly cropped beneath the broad-rimmed cap he wore, and his mustache was finely oiled. A katana lay strapped to his

waist, though he rarely drew it from its sheath. Sometimes, the appearance of power was all one needed.

Her brother strolled into the antechamber as though he were the guest of honor at a party. He was flanked by his own imperial Crafters—two young men who could almost be mistaken for twins, dressed in red and black uniforms.

"P–Prince Ugetsu! W–what an honor! We have heard much of your deeds in Estia. Is it true that you single-handedly defeated the Demon General of the North?" The officer was quick to pour her brother a glass of brandy from the decanter on the table.

Princess Tsukimi frowned. No one had offered *her* brandy, but of course, Prince Ugetsu was the golden child, the darling of the nation, the loyal soldier who was going to bring glory to the empire. In contrast, she was the "selfish oddball" who spent all her time studying Crafters and shikigami. It was no wonder the common rabble preferred Ugetsu.

"Leave us," she interrupted the stammering officer. "All of you."

Both her brother's and her own bodyguards exited the room. The officer trailed behind them, clearly unhappy to be lumped in with the Crafters.

As soon as they were gone, Tsukimi held her breath and counted to ten. Just long enough for the silence to become uncomfortable. She bet her brother thought he had her trapped by appearing out of the blue like this, but wild animals were at their most vicious when they were cornered.

"Ugetsu, I thought that you were abroad. If father doesn't have another colony to add to his empire by the end of the

year, he really will have words with you." Personally, she had hoped Ugetsu would die overseas, but so far he had shown the hardiness of a cockroach.

Her brother took a seat on one of the armchairs, propping his feet up on the impressive mahogany table in front of him.

"Oh, he'll have his colony soon enough. But what about you, dear sister? I was worried about you when I heard what happened in Sola-Il. There are rumors, you know. I have allies among the Sorabito who tell me what goes on in the sky cities. People say that the shikigami that almost destroyed Sola-Il was one of your escaped experiments."

Ha, that was rich! She was sure Ugetsu was involved in at least three attempts on her life, though she did not hold it against him. It was never personal, even when they tried to kill one another; this was simply how they had been raised. The world was a battleground, and every encounter was an intricate dance to dominate the other. There were no such things as allies, only enemies and servants. Why should she hold it against Ugetsu?

"So did you rush back to defend my good name, honored brother?"

"But of course. I couldn't let the rabble speak ill of my beloved sister."

Tsukimi snorted. Though he was an uncultured oaf that she would someday slaughter, her brother did amuse her sometimes.

"I also came for your opinion on something. Have you heard the news?" Her brother wore that smug smile that said he knew something she did not. Tsukimi did her best not to bristle.

 165

"I hear many things," she replied coolly.

"Then you know about this." Ugetsu strode forward and placed a tatty paper ball on the table next to her.

Princess Tsukimi was about to wrinkle her nose at its disgusting appearance when she realized just what it was: a shikigami core. The blood markings were faded and covered in dirt, but still visible over the discolored paper, which was broken and flaky like a wasps' nest torn in two.

What could have done this? Shikigami cores were not easy things to break open; despite being made of paper, they were hard as bone and encased deep within a shikigami's chest or head. Moreover, they were valuable. Tearing one apart was no better than ripping money in two.

"During one of the battles in Estia, a shikigami was killed in a rather . . . unusual way. The men who were there at the time report that a monster emerged from inside the core and killed all the nearby soldiers. Everyone except the shikigami who were also present on the battlefield that day." Ugetsu spoke slowly and deliberately, trying to gauge her reaction to every word. He need not have bothered. Tsukimi had far too much practice keeping her emotions from her face.

"What nonsense is this?" she snorted, even as her interest piqued and her pulse quickened. A monster emerging from a shikigami core . . . how fascinating!

"The shikigami that were affected all claim the same thing: that they saw a vision when the monster touched them. They say that they saw a man in a white cocoon. And someone who repeated the same thing over and over: 'All that lives shall die. All that lives shall die, and be reborn'."

Tsukimi stood up and walked to the window. "Does father know about this?"

"Not yet. I wanted you to be the first to know, dear sister."

Her eyes narrowed. "And why is that?"

Ugetsu smiled at her. His teeth were boneyard white. The golden decorations on his military cap gleamed.

"You are the expert in shikigami, are you not? I thought perhaps you might have an idea of what this is all about."

"You flatter me, but I'm not nearly as good as you think. I'm afraid I have no clue what all this is. A bunch of nonsense perhaps."

"Tsukimi," said Ugetsu. "How long will you allow father to play us off against one another? You must know by now that he has no plans to give the throne to either of us."

"That doesn't matter. He will die one day." She flipped a strand of hair over her shoulder.

"And when will that be? When we are both old and gray as well, and he even older and grayer, feebly clinging on to what little life he has?"

"Why are you so interested in this?" she asked.

Ugetsu came to stand beside her, his hands carefully folded behind his back. "That monster killed an entire battalion. It would be a useful weapon, don't you agree? A weapon we could both profit from."

Tsukimi's smile curved like the edge of a katana. If Ugetsu was mentioning it, that meant he already had plans to use this discovery in some way. Her spies would need to keep a closer eye on him.

"I'm afraid I'm after more interesting things than your little shadows, Ugetsu. If that's all . . . ?"

"More interesting things?" Ugetsu smiled pleasantly. "You mean like those shikigami children you're chasing? You're not the only one with spies, dear sister," he said when Tsukimi's demeanor soured.

The trick to power was to never appear flustered. Even when someone had their hand around your throat, you had to act as if you wanted it there. Anything that could not be used to gain the upper hand over your opponent was worthless; emotions were no different. Smoothing out her expression, Tsukimi inclined her head and smiled as if Ugetsu had done her a favor by reminding her why she had come to Nessai.

"Well, if you must know, then yes. Those children interest me far more than any strange shadow monsters you have stumbled upon." She did not rage at him for admitting to spying on her, did not demand that he tell her who had betrayed her trust; if she had, he would have only laughed at her for being so childish.

Ugetsu turned away from the window. "I see. That's a shame, sister. I thought we could finally work together toward a common goal."

Tsukimi snorted.

"Have fun with your shadows, honored brother."

In the end, Ugetsu was nothing more than a boy playing at war. He was no threat to her. One day the empire—and everything in it—would be hers.

TWENTY-ONE

KURARA spluttered as the tide tossed her onto solid ground. The world spun around her as she rolled onto her hands and knees and hacked up what felt like a small pond's worth of seawater.

Clutching her chest, she squeezed her eyes shut against the pain. Her core felt as though it were on fire. She breathed through her nostrils, fighting back the waves of nausea. Why did living feel so much like dying?

Slowly, her vision swam into focus. She was no longer drowning. The ground beneath her was sandy. Harsh sunlight beat down upon the back of her neck and waves crashed against the shoreline. A beach. Kurara had never seen one before, but she recognized it from the songs the entertainers on the *Midori* would sing.

The dirt was yellow and grainy, and the air smelled of saltwater.

Her gaze darted from one end of the empty beach to the other. Pieces of wood washed ashore with the tide. Then she remembered. The ship. The attack. Fujiwa. Falling into water and being swept away.

"Haru?"

Where was everyone? Haru? Tomoe? Sayo? In fact, where was *she*? The tide had pushed her to some unknown shore and Zeka was nowhere in sight.

"Banri?"

"Here, little star." A giant, sodden thing waded out of the water. Rivers poured from its flank as it emerged onto the beach with slow, lumbering steps.

Water was not as damaging to shikigami as fire, but being soaked in the sea was not ideal either. Some of Banri's paper fur was peeling off. Its ears drooped and its legs moved as stiff as trunks. Misery lay clearly etched upon its face.

"Oh, Banri, are you all right?" Kurara leapt up and hugged the bear's front. Her clothes made an uncomfortable squelching sound.

The bear gave an embarrassed nod. *"I . . . I hurt you,"* it whimpered.

Kurara shook her head. She reckoned she would forgive Banri almost anything.

At the point where the beach ended, the sand turned to soil, leading to a line of dense trees. The trunks pressed so closely together that Kurara could not see what lay past the jagged edge of greenery. Nothing stirred from within the forest's ominous darkness. There was no sign of Sayo warily peering out from behind the cedars, no Tomoe scrambling onto the shore like an awkward foal, or Haru waving brightly from the edge of the coast. Surely they could not have drowned? Maybe they were still out at sea, clinging to pieces of driftwood. Or perhaps they had ended up somewhere farther down the water's edge, past the point where the beach curved out of view.

Banri made a choking sound as if trying to hack up a lungful of seawater.

Kurara's anxiety was a tangled thing. It knotted inside her chest, snarling up her throat. What if the water had really damaged Banri's body? What if the others had drowned? What if Banri was about to lose its mind once more? What if she never saw any of her friends ever again?

"I'm fine. Don't worry about me, little one. Or your friends. I am sure they're fine." Banri's rumbling voice echoed inside her skull. It was almost as though it could read her thoughts.

Kurara took a deep breath. Banri was right. Worrying would get her nowhere.

"I'm afraid you won't be able to ride me until I dry out. My body feels rather fragile at the moment."

As if to prove a point, the shikigami shook itself, unleashing a torrent of water and loose bits of paper. It was not Kurara's imagination: Banri's body was far thinner than before.

"Don't worry about it. In this heat, you'll dry out in no time." She reached a hand up to pat Banri's flank when something flashed in the corner of her eye.

She jumped back just as a white harpoon landed in the sand, inches from her feet. Before she could grab the weapon, it crumbled into a dozen pieces of paper and swirled out of her reach.

A roar echoed through the air.

Kurara's heart sank. Turning to face the edge of the shore, her gaze fell on Fujiwa and Ruki.

"Don't move, shikigami!" Fujiwa's stern voice carried across the windswept shore as he jumped from the tiger's back and landed on the sand.

The sight of him set Kurara's teeth on edge. The fact that they were perfectly dry when Kurara could feel sand in her underwear and an uncomfortable dampness at the back of her neck filled her with irritation. She was sick and tired of Crafters. Sick of being chased. Sick of running.

Her ofuda was wet but still usable. Holding out her paper arm, her fingers twined together to form a blade at the end of her hand.

If Fujiwa wanted a fight, she would give it to him.

"*Little . . . star, something is . . . wrong*," Banri gasped. "*My core . . .*"

Before Kurara could attend to the shikigami, Fujiwa formed a spear out of his ofuda and hurled it at her. It whistled past her face as she dodged, then crumbled, reformed in midair, and shot toward her once more. Banri surged to its feet, pushing Kurara out of the way as the spear struck its body. The tip of the blade pierced its skin and fur, slicing through paper muscles and penetrating the cavity of its chest.

Banri's eyes widened. Its mouth opened in a soundless cry of pain.

Kurara swore she heard mountains crack. Her breath caught in her throat. Even Fujiwa seemed surprised. He quickly withdrew the spear from Banri's chest, and his ofuda returned to flutter around him like startled butterflies.

Banri's body folded inward like a house of cards, limbs

buckling, fur crumbling. Kurara jumped back with a look of horror as the paper that had made up Banri's origami body caved in and swept across the sand in a tidal wave of white.

Its core rolled free of the paper mound. There, in the middle of the core, was a hole where Fujiwa's spear had struck it. A coarse, gray powder spilled onto the sand.

Kurara was glad she had no heart or else it would have broken under the weight of her grief. The pain was swift and overwhelming. It was like drowning all over again.

This could not be happening. Shikigami cores were stronger than steel. The crew of the *Orihime* hunted shikigami all the time without ever breaking the bone-like paper sphere at their center. Kurara had carried Haru's core with her for weeks, and it had shown no sign of wear or tear. They were not easy things to break.

Perhaps the saltwater coupled with the force of Fujiwa's attack had been enough to crack open the normally ironclad sphere. Maybe it was just a matter of bad luck. Kurara did not know. The only thing she felt was the horror and fury swelling inside of her.

She would kill Fujiwa.

Struggling to her feet, Kurara readied her ofuda, but before she could strike, a thin wisp of smoke emerged from Banri's broken core. It coiled as it rose into the air, forming an almost human figure.

Slowly, the smoke began to solidify into one writhing, shadowy mass. A tumble of broken limbs and darkness. It turned its head—or rather, what passed for a head—to stare at Kurara.

Then it lifted a finger and pointed straight at her chest.

TWENTY-TWO

SHE didn't dare move, though every instinct inside was shouting at her to run. Whatever that thing was, it was dangerous.

But it had come from Banri.

Banri was . . . Banri could not be . . . Kurara wanted to cry, to scream, as the paper that had once been part of the bear's body fluttered around her feet.

The smoke thickened and formed farther into a mangled version of a human figure; its limbs swung, long and boneless, by its side. As it stepped forward, its hands dragged through the dirt. There was something primal and malicious about it, as though it were a being composed of pure darkness.

The shadowy monster moved with unnatural speed. Its arms flailed like empty sleeves caught in the wind. Its head dangled past its neck, swaying like a pendulum on a string.

Toothless mouths covered its torso, soundlessly flapping open and shut as the thing moved.

Kurara took a step back.

It was heading straight for her.

At last, her legs agreed to move. Kicking up the sand as she ran, she raced across the shore toward the line of trees at the crown of the beach. Though she was distantly aware of Fujiwa and Ruki fleeing in the opposite direction, she did not have time to pay them any mind.

The thing gave chase. While Kurara battled against the sand which sank beneath her feet and worked against her legs, the shadowy monster appeared to glide across the shore like an insect skating over water. Kurara clenched her teeth, squeezed her eyes shut, and put all her energy into running. She could feel it. The thing was closing in. Her knees ached. Her legs screamed at her. It was close. Too close.

She glanced over her shoulder.

It was right behind her. Kurara stumbled on the sand. As she did, the thing phased through her.

Then came the pain. Excruciating. Intense. It was worse than when Princess Tsukimi had cut her open, worse than the sensation of drowning. Waves of nausea rolled over her. She was on fire. Her core felt like it was being ripped apart from the inside out. She fell to her knees and writhed in the sand, clawing at her face and throat as she struggled to speak.

"Rara!" someone shouted. It sounded like Haru, but Kurara could not tell whether he was really there or if it was just her mind desperately searching for comfort. When that thing had passed through her body, it must have left something corrosive behind. How else could she explain the burning pain wracking her body right now?

The sky spun. Her vision kept flickering in and out. Somewhere above her, she could hear the sound of ringing bells.

"*A dying star fell from the heavens, and from that star grew a tree . . .*" someone sang as the pain grew into a blinding heat that consumed her body.

TWENTY-THREE

THE agony faded into a dull ache. When Kurara looked around her, the shore had disappeared. She was no longer on the beach but in the middle of a small clearing encompassed on all sides by tall cliffs.

How did I get here? She could have sworn that a moment ago she had been running across the sand.

She glanced at her new surroundings. The curving walls created a cage around her, too high to climb. A thin waterfall flowed down one side of the cliff, pooling into a small pond by her feet. Lotus flowers poked their pink heads above the water, swaying in time with the sound of ringing bells echoing from somewhere. Their movements were so hypnotic, it took Kurara all her effort to tear her eyes away from them.

"H–Haru?" Kurara called, but her friend was nowhere to be seen. Both the shadowy monster and the beach had disappeared as well.

That thing touched me. It passed right through me and then—

Before the panic could fully seize her thoughts, Kurara heard what sounded like soft chanting. Startled, she spun around only to find the previously empty clearing was filled with people. A line of men and women stood close to the rocky walls, forming a circle around a large bonfire that had not been there before.

She wanted to ask what was happening, where she was. But the people standing around the clearing did not even glance at her. Perhaps they could not see her at all.

Something on the ground caught Kurara's eye. When she stepped back, she noticed a circle etched into the ground. Inside the circle, someone had carved the symbol of an eight-pointed star.

Kurara's stomach knotted with unease. The bonfire in the middle of the clearing created flickering shadows that danced across the rocks like prancing yōkai. Coils of smoke curled upward, escaping into the sky. She wished she could flee that way too.

"All that lives shall die. As cicadas at the end of summer, as mayflies before the autumn moon, all that lives shall die," a deep, sonorous voice rang across the clearing.

Kurara jumped at the sudden appearance of a monk standing right next to her. His crimson robes were the same color as the flames; he looked as though he were burning as he stepped into the engraving on the ground and swung his shakujo. The six iron rings that looped around the top of the staff made a ringing sound that echoed through Kurara's body.

178

"Hey!" She finally found her voice. "Where am I? What's going on?"

The monk did not answer. His eyes were as dark as ink, like the sea on a moonless night. His expression was pensive, his face downcast as he continued to chant. Kurara stepped forward to place a hand on his shoulder when the people standing around the walls suddenly chanted in a single, monotonous drone: "All that lives shall die. With your life, you shall be a sword in times of war, a shield in times of misfortune, a companion in times of solitude. All that lives shall die, and be reborn."

The flames of the bonfire flickered, splitting shadows across the rock wall. The monk lifted his staff and struck it against the ground. Without warning, the circle of men and women around the cliffs unleashed a torrent of ofuda. Paper swirled around the monk's body, merging together to form a human-sized cocoon that enveloped him from head to foot. A small gasp escaped the man's lips as he dropped his staff, but he did not struggle. Soon, he was completely wrapped in paper. As ofuda whirled, faster and faster with each rotation, they merged together, stretching and transforming into a dozen paper spears.

"Wait!" cried Kurara, but it was too late. The spears pierced the cocoon from every angle. Blood seeped through it, slowly pooling onto the ground.

Hands clapped over her mouth, Kurara could only watch as someone stepped away from the circle, dipped a torch into the bonfire and set the bloody cocoon alight.

The smell of smoke and blood rose into the air. The engraving on the ground—the eight-pointed star within a circle—began to glow. A voice, magnified by the walls, echoed through Kurara's skull as they addressed the roaring flames.

"From this day forth, you shall be known as Banri. Though you wander ten thousand leagues, you shall always find your way home."

Like grass bending in the wind, the circle of Crafters moved in one fluid motion. They prostrated themselves, their palms pressed flat to the ground, foreheads touching stone as they whispered.

"May you be worthy of your name."

The thing that surprised Kurara the most was waking up. She could not remember what had happened to her, but she remembered the pain. No one should be able to survive anything that hurt that much.

Then again, she was not just "someone." She was a shikigami, and among all the other inconvenient things her body did, dying from pain did not seem to be one of them.

The world spun around her as she sat up. Someone had dressed her in a simple gray kimono. She lifted up her sleeves to stare at her new clothes. When she put her hand against the ground to steady herself, her fingers brushed against something soft.

What on earth . . . She stared at the cotton bedding beneath her fingers with startled alarm. It was not the futon that confused her, but what she was doing lying on top of one, inside what appeared to be a simple bedroom, when the last thing she remembered was the ocean and a beach and . . .

Pain blossomed through her body. She doubled over, clutching her hands to her chest. Her eyelids fluttered as her vision blinked back into focus. She remembered the attack on the *Kuroi Kame*, washing up ashore, Fujiwa and Ruki's sudden appearance, and Banri . . .

She had been dreaming. No, that had not been a dream but a memory. Banri's memory.

Kurara slapped a hand over her mouth as pain rolled through her stomach. Banri was gone. The bear's core had split open like an egg, spilling gray powder onto the sand, and inside was . . . Inside was something horrific.

"Ah, awake at last! I was beginning to worry!" Someone shoved the sliding doors open with such force they slammed against the frame.

A short woman strolled into the room. A dark red cloak, ragged and full of holes, fluttered around her ankles like a tail of fire. Cloth bracers reached up to her elbows. A chipped red oni mask—golden-horned, with thick red eyebrows—hid the top half of her face from view, but Kurara could clearly see her smile.

Both the mask and the woman's cloak were made of paper—Kurara could feel its presence teasing at the edges of her mind. Electricity prickled at her nerves, sending a lance of white-hot lightning crashing down her spine when the woman was close: the telltale signs that she was in the presence of a Crafter.

"Who are you?" She scrambled to her feet.

The woman tipped her head in greeting. "Oda Suzue, at your service."

Oda. That name sounded familiar, but Kurara could not quite remember where she had heard it before.

"Don't worry. I haven't cracked your chest open and put my blood on your core like some Crafters would. Besides, your friend Haru would kill me if I tried," said the woman.

Kurara looked at her sharply. So Oda knew that she was a shikigami. Apart from Tomoe and Sayo, everyone she met who knew the truth had thought of her as a tool—or as a strange curiosity to be pinned down and studied. She wondered which camp this woman would fall into.

"Haru's here?" So that had not been a hallucination. But then where was he now? In fact, where was *she*? Who was this odd woman? And where were Tomoe and Sayo?

There was a knock at the door and a small paper deer poked its head around the corner. It was a nervous thing, bug-eyed, with stick-like legs and tiny nubs for horns, though Kurara supposed the bug eyes were on account of how it was staring at her.

"Ah, Yaji!" Oda grinned. "My dear Yaji was the one who found you and brought you back."

"I thought she was a Crafter," the deer squeaked. *"B–but Haru said she's a shikigami like me! Is it true that you eat the hearts of Crafters that try to bond with you?"*

"Yes," Kurara lied. "And I grind their bones to dust and drink sake from their skulls."

The deer squeaked.

"Yaji, don't you have a job to be getting back to?" The woman ushered her shikigami away.

The deer seemed only too pleased to leave. With a quick

bow to its master, it darted around the corner of the door and disappeared.

Kurara hated to admit it, but she was glad that it had gone. The deer reminded her too much of Banri—young and nervous and driven by the need to please others.

"Where am I?" she asked.

Oda's expression lit up. "This is Kazami village. And I believe that you were looking for me."

TWENTY-FOUR

KURARA stared at the woman. *This* was the person Banri had wanted to see? The person the shikigami wanted to form a bond with? Kurara was not sure what she had expected, but it certainly was not this: a short, old woman playing about in an oni mask.

"*You?* You're the Crafter Banri wanted to meet?"

Oda's smile slipped for just a moment. "You don't remember, do you? Haru told me that you wouldn't."

"No, I remember," said Kurara, though it hurt to do so. "I remember what happened to Banri."

"Yes, I heard about that. What a shame. Several years ago, Banri and my master left to look for more Crafters. When they did not return, I assumed both were dead, so I took up the mantle of Grave-keeper in his place."

Kurara shook her head. Oda spoke about Banri's death,

but she had not seen exactly what had happened. She did not know of the horror that Kurara had witnessed.

"Banri's core broke, and then this—this *thing* came out!"

How did one describe something as awful as the shadowy creature she had seen? No words could do it justice. Kurara could only stare at Oda with wide, frightened eyes and hope that the woman understood.

"Calm down," said Oda, as if being attacked by primordial shadow monsters was something one could simply shrug off. "I'm afraid there's nothing you can do now. Fire destroys shikigami. Some would say it purifies them. But if the core is broken open, then it's too late."

"Too late for what? Do you know something about that shadowy monster? Could I have saved Banri?" Kurara's voice trembled.

The woman sighed. "You've only just woken up. You should not strain yourself. Tell me your name."

Kurara opened her mouth to protest, then reconsidered. Pelting the woman with questions would not get her anywhere.

"Kurara. My name is Kurara."

Oda was silent, as if she had not expected that. Though it was difficult to read the woman's emotions through that annoying mask strapped to her head.

"Kurara." She smiled suddenly, testing the taste of it on her tongue. "What a curious name. You know, names are important for shikigami . . . Kurara. How do you spell that?"

"With the words for 'sorrow' and 'joy'."

The memory of Banri's naming cut through her like a knife. Had she been named in the same way? With blood and paper? No, but she would have been Aki back then. Then who had given her the name Kurara? She could not remember. As far as she knew, she had always been Kurara.

As if on cue, her stomach growled. Now that she thought about it, she had not eaten anything since the *Kuroi Kame* sank.

Laughing, the Grave-keeper turned on her heel. "You must be hungry. Come on, follow me."

The way Oda walked through the house reminded Kurara of how the entertainers on the *Midori* would seem to float across the floors, as if even the ground was not worthy to touch their feet. The paper doors that lined the hallway were all dark, but Kurara could sense a faint glow of blue light coming from the other side. She had no idea what time of day it was—perhaps night, judging from the fact that the lamps inside Oda's home were all lit. Polished wooden floorboards reflected back the candles hanging from burners attached to the ceiling.

A narrow hallway led to a single room with a cooking pit in the middle. The fire was out, but steam still rose from a large, cast-iron pot hanging over the pit. The smell of ginger and soy wafted into the air.

"I have a lot of questions," said Kurara.

"I imagine you do, but can it wait? You should eat, and then we should go and tell your friend that you're all right. That poor boy was beside himself when you wouldn't wake up." Oda gave her a knowing smile and settled by the fire pit. Kurara glanced around the otherwise empty room. Where *was* Haru?

Oda lifted the lid to the iron pot and sniffed its contents.

186

After giving it a quick stir, she scooped the food into two clay bowls and handed a serving to Kurara.

It was all so very mundane, Kurara could not help but wonder if this was the person Banri had really wanted to meet. She did not know what she had expected, but certainly she had thought that a Grave-keeper would be more impressive. Someone who would wear her sacred duty about her like a cloak, who would *feel* as ancient as the rocks themselves and as immovable as the cosmos. Someone who spoke with the weight of all that history and ceremony behind her words.

Instead she was sitting here, eating watery rice porridge topped with thin strips of ginger and chives. Kurara tossed her head back, tipping the contents down her throat without waiting for it to cool. There were more important things on her mind than eating.

"I've wanted us to talk ever since Banri mentioned you. I am looking for the Star Trees. Anything you might know would be helpful."

Oda laughed. "If you want to see a Star Tree, I suggest you invent a time machine. They were all cut down a long time ago."

The okayu would have been tastier if Kurara was not also biting back her annoyance. Oda was definitely not treating this with the gravity it deserved. This was not a game. The fate of the shikigami—their freedom, their very lives—all depended upon Kurara.

Setting aside her bowl, she looked Oda in the eye. "But couldn't there be a Seed left? A Star Seed?"

Oda poured herself a cup of tea. "Star Trees were not

ordinary trees. They grew from the remains of a fallen star. They did not produce fruit or seeds."

That was what Haru had said, but everything in Kurara's dream contradicted that. There had been a Star Seed. Someone had given it to her once and then . . .

Then what had happened to it? She needed to find someone who knew. She needed to figure out the location of the crater, and talk to that furious shikigami. But could she trust Oda enough to tell her about her dreams? The woman was a stranger after all, and a Crafter to boot. What if Oda tried to stop her from finding the Star Seed? What if she tried to destroy it?

"How can you be so sure?"

"How do you know that the inside of a volcano is full of molten fire if you've never seen one before? How can you be sure that the moon revolves around the earth if you have never tracked its course? Because those you trust have documented it for future generations to learn. There is no such thing as a Star Seed," said Oda, with infuriating serenity.

"But a lot of the knowledge about Crafters and shikigami has been lost to time. You could be wrong!"

"Then when you prove things to be otherwise, I will graciously accept my mistake."

Kurara gritted her teeth together and said nothing.

At length, the woman sighed.

"You *really* don't remember." Oda had said that before. At the time Kurara had thought that she was talking about what had happened to Banri, but now she was not so sure.

"Remember what?"

Oda took a sip of steaming tea and looked at Kurara.

When she smiled—all teeth and a gaze that could cut through your soul—her eyes shone through the holes in the mask like a kitsune's. She stood up and walked to the set of paper doors behind her.

"Here, let me show you."

The doors slid open to a view of a cave. Kurara's breath caught in her throat.

She was underground.

Kurara had to crane her head back to stare at the vaulted ceiling arching far above her head. The cavern was large enough to fit a dragon. Luminous mushrooms provided a faint blue light, around which bright green moss gathered. Long curtains of flowstone split the cavern into sections, draping down from the ceiling like cobwebs of rock. Stalagmites, large stone fangs, grew from the earth to make loose pathways through the cave.

The entertainers on the *Midori* used to tell tales of hapless humans who got lost in dream-worlds while sleeping, or wandered into the domains of powerful yōkai without realizing it, but there was something about this place that was achingly familiar.

Sloping paths carved into the walls led up to a myriad of tunnels, each one a dark doorway leading off to who knew where. There were buildings too: small stone huts that seemed to grow out of the rock walls themselves, and squat, wooden storehouses clustered together like the clumps of mushrooms Haru had shown her back in the forest.

In the center of the cavern, water had collected into a wide but shallow pool. Despite the lack of sunlight, a large tree stump stood in the middle of the water just a few inches above the surface, like the world's largest lily pad. An odd smell emanated from the gnarled roots, not unlike the scent of the air after a storm.

Kurara's eyes fluttered shut for a moment, and she imagined what the tree had looked like in its prime; its leaves like the midnight sky, its branches as golden as the sun, its trunk oozing a blood-red sap.

Now a stump was all that remained. Broken. Dead.

It would save no one.

Oda came to join Kurara by the edge of the water. "This, like all the other Star Trees, was cut down during the Great War. It will never produce sap again." As she pulled off her mask, it crumbled into a hundred pieces of bright gold paper that swirled around her in a colorful storm. Her eyes were a pale, sickly blue. The color of corpses left to rot in the open air.

"Awful, isn't it? This is how Crafters are, Kurara. Greedy. And selfish. All they wanted were slaves that could not disobey them."

Yes! Yes, exactly! Kurara wanted to shout. At last, there was a Crafter who understood! Then again, Oda had shikigami of her own. Who knew whether Oda's disdain for other Crafters was righteous indignation or hypocrisy?

"You said this was Kazami village." She changed the subject instead.

"It is," said Oda. "The village is underground. It was built during the Great War. There are tunnels that run for miles in all directions, all the way to what is now known as the Grand Stream—a confusing maze meant to baffle any intruders."

"And where are all the people?"

"It's just me and my shikigami, I'm afraid. Kazami village was built to prevent intruders from finding them, but no place is impenetrable. There was a battle here. Well, not here *exactly*, but somewhere in these tunnels. I believe it was quite a glorious final stand for the people of Kazami, but they were all killed and this place was abandoned, forgotten for years until I arrived. I rather like it down here, I must say. It's quiet and no one bothers me."

No, that's not what happened, something inside Kurara whispered, but when she thought about the people of the village, all she felt was a sharp pang in the back of her head.

Shaking it off, she stepped closer to the Star Tree. Something was carved into the stump. A circle and an eight-pointed star. It looked familiar: Kurara had seen the same symbol in Banri's memory.

When her gaze traveled to the foot of the pool, she noticed something beneath the surface, something round and tied with rotting ribbons that floated just below the water.

Kurara swallowed around the lump in her throat. It was a clay urn. No, several urns—at least a dozen arranged at the bottom of the pool in a semicircle. Judging from the tarnished red prayer beads wrapped around their sealed lids, they were the type that stored the ashes of the dead.

This was a graveyard.

TWENTY-FIVE

TRAVELING with Mana was quite literally a pain. Even when they rode upon Himura's paper falcon, the snake clung to his shoulders and would only let go at night and during meals. Its weight made his back ache, but whenever he complained or tried to shake the shikigami off, Mana would chuckle and cling a little tighter—never enough to hurt, but enough that Himura felt his breath catch.

"You're a stingy child! Don't you know that young folk should care for their elders?"

The snake talked like a nattering grandmother, enjoyed flicking its tongue against the curve of his ear, slapping his shoulders with its tail, and complaining of how the rain made its ancient body ache whenever the weather turned foul.

Mana's coils squeezed against his ribs. *"You're nothing but skin and bones, aren't you boy? Are you eating properly?*

Are you consuming enough greens? You won't get any taller if you don't."

Himura wondered if humoring the snake was worth it. What was he doing abandoning everything like this? If Rei were around to see him submit to the whims of a shikigami, he would no doubt have something scathing to say. He tried not to think about Rei. Or what he was doing now that he was free to wreak havoc in the world.

There were many things he tried not to think about.

The longer he and Mana traveled together, the more Himura could not help but compare the snake to Akane. They were so different in personality that sometimes he had to remind himself that they were both shikigami.

If only Akane were here. He wondered if he had any right to think such things.

Before the guilt could chip away at his thoughts, Himura's stomach rumbled. After his food packs had run out, he had spent more time on the ground, hunting and foraging as they journeyed south, but the things he found were hardly enough to satisfy his hunger. The shoots were bitter, the mushrooms tasted like mud and, worst of all, every time he scrunched his face up in a grimace, Mana would look at him with such an insufferably smug expression that he was tempted to stuff a few mushrooms down the snake's throat too.

"*Can't you control your belly?*" Mana complained as Himura's stomach gave another embarrassingly loud rumble.

"You were *just* asking me if I was eating enough!" he snapped in reply. "I'm sure it must be awfully convenient to not need to eat."

With a sigh, Mana slipped off his shoulders and slithered

through the grass. *"Very well,"* it said. *"This forest is full of boar. Because I am kind and generous, I will catch you your dinner."*

The snake darted away before Himura could stop it. That was another thing he was having trouble getting used to: a shikigami making its own decisions.

Following Mana, Himura pushed through the bushes. The forest was alive with the roar of cicadas. The sound seemed to swallow him. As he stepped over a small, dried-up stream, he heard a loud rustle just ahead.

A second later a large, brown blur suddenly burst out of the foliage right in front of him. Himura only just had time to leap back to avoid being hit by the boar. The beast was easily as tall as his knee and likely half his weight—a fully grown male with wild, black eyes and tusks that gored its predators.

Not a moment later, a flash of white darted through the grass.

"Catch it! Catch it!"

Himura drew a long string of ofuda from his bracelet. The paper hardened as he pulled it out, transforming into a sharp, white spear. He took a step back, then hurled his weapon at the fleeing boar.

His aim was off and he had not put enough strength into the throw, but that did not matter. As soon as the spear left his hand, it honed in on its target and struck the boar's flank. The animal gave a loud squeal as it stumbled into the dirt, where it moved no more.

"Well, that was exciting! I'm glad you weren't 'boared' to death!" Mana sniggered at its own joke.

Himura fought the urge to say something sarcastic in return —then he noticed a long gash along the side of Mana's body where the boar's tusks had slashed through its paper scales.

"You're hurt!"

"'Tis nothing but a flesh wound. A paper cut," Mana scoffed. *"You can close it for me."*

We don't have a bond, Himura wanted to say. *Why did you get hurt on my behalf? Why did you even care enough to think about finding a proper meal?*

Mana gave a loud cough.

Jolted from his thoughts, Himura pulled the paper spear out of the boar's side. He discarded the pieces stained with blood and laid the rest carefully over Mana's wound. With jerky hands, he melded the ofuda into the snake's side. Paper fused into Mana's scales until it was impossible to tell there had been a gash there at all.

"I could have killed that boar myself. There was no need for you to get injured," he muttered. If Mana noticed the slight tremble in Himura's voice, it did not say so.

"I'm sure you could have, but it does me good to keep my instincts sharp."

They made camp by a small stream overshadowed by ginkgo trees, and Himura settled down to skin and spit the meat. Working on the boar's carcass kept his hands busy and his mind occupied. He did not want to interrogate Mana on why it had decided to find food for him, or think about why his heart had jumped with worry when he saw its injury.

He ate his first good meal in days while Mana spoke animatedly about how it had tracked down the boar, using its tail to illustrate how it had flushed the creature out of the bushes. When it was time to settle down for the night, Himura did not dream of flames. For once, there was no Akane diving into the fire. No Kurara staring at him with her hardened gaze. Instead, he heard singing. It was a familiar song, one Akane would sing sometimes when he had trouble sleeping. When Himura awoke—peeling one bleary eye open—it was still dark. A soft, haunting voice by his side crooned.

"A dying star fell from the heavens. And from that star grew a tree."

"Akane?" Himura sat up, rubbing the sleep from his eyes.

"Who is Akane? I am afraid it is just me." In the soft firelight, Mana's gaze was almost kind.

He stiffened. For a moment, he wondered if the snake would look at him the same way if it knew what he had done to Akane.

The thought of Mana's hatred, of its sharp fangs and even sharper eyes filled with seething anger, was enough to keep his mouth shut. He turned away from the firelight, trying not to wonder why he cared what a shikigami thought of him in the first place.

His parents had told him that shikigami were tools made to serve a Crafter. If they had been wrong, then everything he had known, everything he had been taught to believe all those years ago, was wrong too.

"We are almost at Kazami," said Mana.

"I haven't seen any sign of a village at all."

Mana flicked its tongue with glee. *"Oh, Kazami is special. You cannot find it unless you know exactly where to look. You shall see what I mean soon enough."*

Its delight made something squirm inside Himura's chest. He stood up with a jerk. The flames in the campfire burned low, but there was another pyre raging inside his

196

body. He paced around the camp as if to escape the burning feeling inside of him.

"You have a blood bond with the Grave-keeper, right? Tell me . . ."

"If you wish to know anything about shikigami or how they are made, you will have to ask my master directly."

"I was going to ask you if you love your master." He was not sure what expression he was wearing when he asked, but Mana gazed at him with a pitying look.

"When it comes to bonds between Crafters and shikigami, it is best not to talk about love."

"Why not?"

"Because I do love my master. She infuriates me and yet I love her still." Mana's voice was wistful, colored with a fondness that Himura had never heard in its tone before.

"When Master is kind, I feel a surge of affection toward her and wonder if I only feel that way because of the bond. And when she forces me to do something I do not want to, I wonder if I would hate her if not for the bond.

"Sometimes, I wish she would keep me closer. I would not be questioning these things if I were always by her side. When I am not with her, my doubt grows and I feel the madness creep at the corners of my mind. But then I go back to her and everything is all right. What was I so worried about in the first place? Of course I love my master. How could I not?"

"You leave your master often, then?" That was unusual. Most Crafters kept their shikigami close.

"For . . . errands, yes." Mana sounded reluctant to talk about it. *"Master is a bit of a hermit after all. Sometimes, I think I like that about her. Sometimes, I think I hate it.*

197

"Whether it is love or hate or something else, I am always wondering if these feelings are my own."

"Then why bother thinking about it? Shikigami were made to serve Crafters and that's that," said Himura. His parents would lull him to sleep with stories of a time when his people had ruled the land with their strength and skill and mastery over shikigami. His parents had always told him how clever and brilliant ancient Crafters were. His ancestors had been so much better than the Crafters of today. So much more, his parents had whispered. So much more.

Mana snorted, though surprisingly it did not seem offended by his words. "Poor little boy. People don't worship Crafters as they once did, and that hurts, doesn't it? I know why you want to see my master. You wish to find something there— something that will make you feel special. Something to show once and for all that your kind is superior to everyone else, but I shall tell you one thing,"—the snake's tone softened—"you won't find what you seek in the past."

Himura felt as though the snake had wrapped its scaly tail around his body and thrown him sideways. He felt undone. No, Mana was wrong. What did a shikigami that he had just met know about him or his wants, anyway?

There was no reason to feel guilty. Not about Akane. Not about Kurara. He wasn't guilty.

"Goodnight, Mana," he said, sharper than he intended.

The snake's eyes flashed with hurt. "I'm only trying to—" it began, before something in its expression hardened and it coiled into a ball with a barely audible, "Goodnight."

Interlude

Sow the fields with ash
The dead will have their banquet
Upon the pyre

—Written by a Crafter of Unknown Origin
(from the personal library
of the Imperial Princess)

Princess Tsukimi mulled over everything her brother had said as her airship cut through the sky. His story about the broken core did pique her curiosity, but her focus now could not stray from the search for the shikigami children. She put it on her list of things to investigate later, right after dealing with her father's anger—Ugetsu was sure to blab about her whereabouts, the little snitch.

Fujiwa's note about heading to Zeka was the only lead she had on the children. As the airship approached its destination, Tsukimi could see the large stairs and floating gardens that decorated the city slowly come into view. She

gripped the armrest of her chair, her impatience growing. On the table in front of her, pieces of folded and crushed origami lay scattered about.

The ship's engines rumbled just as the doors slid open and one of her imperial Crafters stepped into the lounge.

"What is it?" Tsukimi glanced up at the bald man who had just entered. If it was another game of cards, she was not interested.

Goro saluted. He was twice her size and three times as wide, yet he seemed like a child next to her.

"Your Imperial Highness, we've managed to contact Fujiwa."

"And he doesn't have the children with him! What a failure!" the crow shikigami on the man's shoulder squawked.

"He says that we should avoid landing in Zeka. The city has been attacked by Sohma rebels; it might not be safe. The Patriots Office was burned to the ground." Goro wiped his sleeve against the side of his shaved head.

Tsukimi snorted. She was not interested in the petty squabbles between Sorabito and the groundlings. Whether they lived in the clouds or on the ground, ants were still ants.

Still, she would rather avoid unnecessary headaches. If she landed in the city, someone from the military might ask her to help them contain their Sohma problem. Or worse, they would tell her father where she was and he would order someone to keep her in Zeka. No, better to avoid the city if possible.

"Very well." She slowly rose to her feet. With a wave of her hand, she gestured for Tamada to hurry to the navigation

room. "Tell the men to bring us down farther south. We'll meet Fujiwa there—he can follow the ship."

The female Crafter and her wolf shikigami bowed and quickly left. A moment later, the airship veered right, away from the city.

The ship landed in the sea a few miles south, where the shoreline curved like a sickle. Farther inland, the sand turned to soil, and then to a forest made up of heavy pines and beech trees. Goro created a paper bridge across the water that connected the bottom of the airship to the shore, and Tsukimi made her way across the water to where Fujiwa and Ruki were already waiting for her.

The first thing she noted as her feet touched the golden sand was Fujiwa's disheveled state. His clothes were a mess, his black hair sprinkled with golden sand so that it seemed to glitter in the light. Even Ruki looked rather tattered. A line of trees stretched finger-like shadows over the tiger's displeased face.

"What happened?"

Flustered, Fujiwa relayed everything that had occurred while they were separated: from spotting the shikigami children in Nessai to tracking the girl down when she had washed up on shore.

A dark shadow haunted his expression as he described his fight with the girl. "And then the bear's core cracked open and—and—!"

"And a monster came out?"

Fujiwa gave her a startled look. "H–how did you know that, Your Highness?"

"Is there anything in this world that I don't know?" Tsukimi pressed her lips together in a thin line. A cracked shikigami core. A strange shadowy monster. It was exactly as Ugetsu had reported. If the shadowy thing had touched Fujiwa, would he have died? Would Ruki have reported seeing a hallucination of a man in a white cocoon?

All that lives shall die, and be reborn. What did that mean?

"I would never doubt your genius, Your Imperial Highness!" cried Fujiwa. "In any case, when that monster emerged, I lost the girl."

"You mean you ran away?" said Tsukimi.

Fujiwa looked aghast. "No! Your Imperial Highness, I would never abandon my duty to you!"

Ruki brushed its tail against its master's cheek to comfort him. Tsukimi frowned. She never enjoyed these moments of tenderness between master and shikigami. She generally did not like things that did not involve her.

"And where is the girl now?"

Before Fujiwa could answer, there was a loud boom in the distance. A squawking flock of birds took off in fright as a handful of trees came crashing down, followed by a loud roar that echoed through her head.

Tsukimi's heart skipped a beat. That was the sound of a shikigami.

She doubted it was the children—that roar sounded more like something wild and furious—but she could never pass up the opportunity to see a shikigami, especially not when one was so close.

She bid Tamada and her wolf remain by the airship with

her soldiers while she took her other two Crafters and their shikigami with her into the forest. With eager steps, she hurried beneath the gnarled branches.

As they got closer, Tsukimi felt the ground shake. The next thing she knew, a large white monkey—a macaque, to be precise—emerged from behind the remaining trees. It beat the surrounding clearing with its fists, digging large trenches out of the earth with its fingertips and throwing clouds of dirt into the air.

The shikigami was at least six feet tall, with arms as long as tree branches and deep, hollow gouges beneath its eyes that made it appear exhausted. Its paper fur was disheveled and covered in dirt that got stuck in the creases and folds of its body, attracting insects that crawled over its skin and moss that grew over the ridge of its back. Despite its tattered state, there was an intelligent glint in its eye that said it was still in possession of its mind.

Not a wild shikigami then. Or if it was, it had only very recently lost its master.

When the macaque spotted Tsukimi and her men approaching, it suddenly stopped and faced them with a grin so wide that it split its face in two.

"Crafters!" The shikigami ambled forward on its hands and feet. Though it looked happy to see them, it could not quite hide the look of spite in its eyes or the look of vicious glee that reminded Tsukimi of little boys sprinkling salt over slugs.

Her eyes darted around the clearing as the shikigami made its way toward her. Something else—someone else—was

watching them; she could feel the cold weight of their eyes from somewhere beyond the trees. When she moved closer, a figure quietly darted to a remote thicket.

Tsukimi stopped. She swore that she saw the flash of a skirt, the whisk of red hair.

"Who are you? Where is your master?" Fujiwa's ofuda swirled around him like a small whirlwind as he continued to glower at the shikigami.

"Wait," Tsukimi ordered. Everyone stood silent and to attention. She pointed to the thickets where she had seen a flash of clothing. "There's someone over there. Grab them."

The moment she spoke, the bushes rustled in alarm. Despite Fujiwa's surprise, he did not hesitate to obey. His ofuda darted into the undergrowth. A moment later, Tsukimi was rewarded with the sound of a frightened yelp followed by angry cursing.

From beneath the bushes, Fujiwa's ofuda dragged out two dirty children, kicking and shouting. The girls were quite different from one another—one with short black hair that curled around her ears, the other with a messy red braid that was turning brown at the roots—but they both wore similar clothing and had the same willowy appearance.

"Sorabito." Tsukimi smiled down at the girls. "You two wouldn't have anything to do with the riot in Zeka, would you?"

"There's a riot in Zeka?" one of them squeaked.

"I recognize these two. They were with the shikigami

children. I believe they're comrades." Fujiwa stared at the girls bound in paper chains as if he could not quite believe that they were really there.

"We're friends!" the girl with red hair spat.

Tsukimi's face lit up with a smile. "The girl—Kurara, was it?—where is she now?"

"Even if I knew, I wouldn't tell you!" The girl scowled and thrashed uselessly against her restraints.

"Is that so?"

With a nod to Fujiwa, Tsukimi had the two girls hauled to their feet. They were filthy little things, covered in mud and dirt with bits of leaves stuck in their hair. They smelled like they hadn't had a good wash in two weeks. Tsukimi wrinkled her nose and grabbed hold of the redhead's braid. She yanked it like a rope, twisting it harshly until the girl shrieked.

"Tomoe!" Her companion lunged at Tsukimi, but Fujiwa's ofuda yanked her back.

"I–I don't know where she or Haru are," the girl—Tomoe —panted.

The redhead seemed to be telling the truth. With a disappointed sigh, Tsukimi released her grip on the girl's hair.

"I know where she went."

Everyone turned to the monkey shikigami.

The macaque bared its teeth in an all-too-human grin, eyes twinkling with malevolence as it scraped its knuckles against the ground. *"I know where that girl went. I saw it. One of my comrades picked her up and took her to the village."*

"Wait, Kurara was here?" The Sorabito girl gasped, though no one paid her any mind.

"I was minding my own business when these little creatures attacked me then tried to run away."

"You attacked us first!" the short-haired girl protested. "We were minding *our* own business, trying to get our bearings, when you suddenly came out of nowhere!"

"And where is this village you speak of?" asked Fujiwa.

The monkey grinned again.

Goro cracked his knuckles against the palm of his other hand. The paper rings on each of his fingers clicked as well. "He asked you a question. Speak, you beast!"

With a hooting laugh, the shikigami stooped down so that its face was inches from Fujiwa. It leaned in closer, until it could easily bite Fujiwa's head off. In a low voice, it said, *"It is my master's village, Kazami. Would you like to see it? Would you like to see the Grave-keeper? Shall I show you the way?"*

In the corner of her eye, Tsukimi noticed the two Sorabito girls exchange knowing glances.

"Well, looks like I know where Kurara went now." She sauntered closer to the girls. "But have no fear, I'll find some other use for the two of you, I'm sure. Perhaps as bait. Has anyone told you that you have a lovely scream?"

"Has anyone told you that's a really creepy thing to say to someone?" the redhead shot back.

Tsukimi laughed. She liked them fiery. The short-haired girl did not seem to appreciate her laughter, though. The moment Tsukimi got too close to her friend, the girl lunged at her, growling like a wild animal.

"Sayo!" her friend snapped.

The princess shook her head. It seemed she and the red-haired girl understood something this Sayo did not: to show others what you cared about was to show them exactly where they could stick the knife. It made you weak, made you an easy target, and now Tsukimi was confident that she could make the Sorabito girls do as she wished.

"Very well." She turned back to the monkey shikigami. "Show us the way to this village of yours."

The macaque turned to her as if it had only just realized she was there.

"Who are you? You are not a Crafter."

Princess Tsukimi lifted one finely plucked eyebrow. Her expression remained placid, but the beast's words roared through her ears. *You are not a Crafter.* You are inadequate. Unworthy.

She smiled, all teeth and hunger.

"I am Princess Tsukimi. The soon-to-be Empress of this country. And who are you?"

"My name is Zagi." The creature spoke not to Tsukimi but to her Crafters, swaying from left to right as it did. *"That is the name I was given. That is the name by which I live. For I am righteousness. For I shall judge all souls that come to me."*

"Fine, Zagi, will you take us to this village, or are you just going to sit around like a child and taunt us?"

The shikigami said nothing, but it suddenly turned around and ambled away as if it had forgotten all about Tsukimi and the Sorabito girls. Or perhaps it did not care, as long as the Crafters followed it.

Turning back to the Sorabito, Tsukimi smiled. "Come on, girls."

Fujiwa yanked them along. They made for an odd picture: a princess, two Crafters, their shikigami, and two Sorabito all following behind a giant paper monkey.

"This feels like a trap," murmured Fujiwa as they made their way deeper into the forest.

Tsukimi smiled. "I hope it is."

TWENTY-SIX

I am a lotus. Kurara tried to calm herself down. *I rise above the muddy waters. My fears are below me.*

Of course, Kurara thought. She should have known there would be a graveyard here. What was a Grave-keeper without a graveyard to look after?

"These are . . . dead Crafters?"

"That's correct." Oda waded into the water without a care for the bottom of her drenched clothes. She bent down and scooped an urn out of the water, snapped the rotten seal on the lid and turned the urn upside down.

"What are you doing?" Kurara flinched as the woman dumped the contents of the urn onto dry ground, but what came out was not ash but a tumble of cores.

Shikigami cores.

There had to be at least a dozen: some with blood markings on their cores, some without. "What *is* this? Why are there shikigami cores in the funeral urns?"

"You already know the answer to that, Kurara."

"No, I don't. I have no idea what you're talking about," she said, stubbornly.

"You do, you just haven't put it together yet. Haru told me what happened to Banri. You saw the thing that came out of its core, didn't you?"

Whenever Kurara thought about the *thing* that had emerged from Banri's core, she felt a shiver run down her spine. If she closed her eyes, she could still see its dark, smoky shape, its broken limbs and many mouths.

"You know what it was," Oda insisted.

"I don't!" cried Kurara. How could she possibly know anything about a monstrosity like that? Banri had been so gentle and sweet, so scared of strangers and noise and the dark, and yet so brave in the face of danger. That thing that had come out of the core was nothing like Banri.

"Rara!"

Kurara turned to see Haru emerging from one of the cavern's tunnels.

"Thank goodness you're up!" He grinned at her with a brightness that rivaled the sun.

Relief and irritation warred in Kurara's chest. She was glad to see Haru and thankful that he was safe, but she was also annoyed that he had let her wake up alone and then left her in Oda's care.

"Where are Tomoe and Sayo?" She glanced around Haru in the vain hope that maybe they were hiding behind the rocks to surprise her.

Haru shook his head sadly.

"I'm trying to teach your friend here about an important aspect of shikigami cores. However, our dear *Kurara* seems unwilling to learn," said Oda—though the way she pronounced Kurara's name made it sound as though it were a joke only she found funny. She turned and pointed to the tree stump. "See here. You recognize it, don't you? You know what it means."

Kurara turned to give it a proper look. She stared at the symbol engraved into the rings of wood and thought back to the vision she had seen after that shadowy thing had touched her. There had been a man surrounded by Crafters. And a ritual of some sort. The other Crafters had wrapped the man in a paper cocoon, killed him, and burned his body.

"From this day forth, you shall be known as Banri. Though you wander ten thousand leagues, you shall always find your way home."

That man who had died. Had he really been Banri? Or rather, had he become Banri?

Kurara shook her head to clear her thoughts. If that man had truly gone through some kind of ritual to become Banri, then that meant . . .

"Shikigami were once humans."

That was the only explanation Kurara could come up with. That was why shikigami were not merely paper puppets, but living beings with thoughts and desires of their own. They had been people once. When they became shikigami, their personalities carried over into their new forms.

Oda nodded, her gaze steady and her eyes bright.

"It's a soul," said Kurara. "Inside their core is a human soul. I'm right, aren't I? Crafters were sacrificed and turned into shikigami and their souls were contained inside their

211

core. It's the soul that gives a shikigami life. It's what makes them different from just conjuring up an animal using plain old ofuda."

She could make a paper fox like Akane right now, but it would be nothing more than a large piece of origami that she could control. It would not be a shikigami. It would not be *alive*.

She needed a soul for that. She needed a life.

"There's a ritual," said Haru. "Crafters who are sacrificed during the ritual become shikigami. The way they move, their personalities, their intelligence, the reason shikigami seem so human—it's because they *are* human. Or rather, they were *once* human."

Then Banri had once been a person. Akane and Ruki too. When the *Orihime* hunted shikigami, they were not just hunting wild beasts but creatures that had once been people.

I am a lotus. Kurara tried to calm herself down under the weight of everything she had learned. *I rise above the muddy waters. My fears are below me.*

It was not working. The more she thought about it, the more it felt like everything she knew was buckling and crumbling beneath her feet. She stared at the urns below the lake. This was not just a cemetery for the dead, it was a storehouse. A birthing ground. She was standing over a hundred lives that were yet to be born. A hundred lives that had been cut short. Could those dead Crafters sense anything while they were sealed in those urns? Were they staring back at her from beneath those murky waters?

If shikigami were made from Crafters and she was a shikigami, then . . .

No, she didn't want to think about it. She squeezed her eyes shut for a moment and thought of lotus flowers. She was Kurara. Not Aki. Not some other woman. She was Kurara.

"That's why shikigami need blood bonds," Haru continued. "The dead do not belong in this world. They can't exist in the here and now without an anchor. If they don't have one, their souls are slowly corrupted. They turn violent and they lose their minds."

A corrupted soul. Like the thing that had come out of Banri's core. Kurara felt a stab of horror at the thought. How could such an ugly, horrendous thing come from such a gentle and kind shikigami? Banri had done nothing to deserve its fate; why were shikigami always getting the short end of everything?

"This is why, to really kill a shikigami, you must use fire," said Oda. "When their cores burn, the fire purifies them. It is difficult to crack open a core, but if you do, you unleash something that was never meant to exist on this mortal plane. Something that turns putrid and corrupt."

Putrid. Corrupt. No matter how true that was, it was not a shikigami's fault. They were created, used, then discarded like broken toys. The unfairness of it gnawed at Kurara's core. She could feel it coming up her throat like bile.

"Why didn't you tell me that shikigami were once Crafters?" Kurara shouted at Haru. She thought she was used to him keeping things from her. She had been wrong. His secrecy stung like an open wound.

"What difference does it make? You always thought of shikigami as people."

"But don't you see? That means that I was right! If people knew—if Crafters knew—what shikigami really are then maybe they would understand that they can't treat their shikigami like mindless tools!"

"Is that what you think?" Haru looked at her oddly, as if she were the strange one for believing that this discovery made a difference to anything.

"What do you mean?"

Haru's expression was carefully blank, his shoulders stiff. He only looked like that when he was annoyed with her, though why he would be annoyed she did not know. From the very beginning of this conversation, Kurara had felt out of her depth, like she was wandering through the dark with no end in sight.

"During the war, Crafters cut down the Star Trees so that shikigami could only obey them. They knew the truth and yet they still cut down the trees! They still treated our kind like weapons. And when they went to war, whenever they won a battle against another clan, they would capture the enemy and turn them into shikigami too. Even knowing that they might end up sacrificed themselves didn't stop them from using shikigami as tools. Doesn't that disgust you? Do you think knowing the truth now will make a difference when it didn't all those years ago? Knowing what they used to be, do you really think shikigami deserve freedom? Isn't this just karma for what they did as humans? Isn't this divine punishment?"

Divine punishment. Those words echoed through her very being.

A sudden wave of dizziness washed over her. Kurara rubbed her temples as her vision flickered. Divine punishment. She shook her head, trying to rid herself of the strange buzzing sound in the back of her brain.

"You can't honestly believe that, Haru!"

Haru's bottom lip jutted out at a stubborn angle. "Why not?"

"Because—because it's wrong! Besides, even if there were bad Crafters, I'm sure there were good ones too. Ones that don't deserve this. No, even if every Crafter was a terrible person, that doesn't matter. A Crafter is a Crafter and a shikigami is a shikigami. They're not the same person anymore and they don't deserve to be punished for something that happened in another life!"

This was not like Haru. Sure, he used to play pranks on the other servants and the entertainers of the *Midori*. He would cause trouble and then charmingly smile his way out of the consequences, but he had never been mean-spirited. He had never held any grudges.

Then again, what did she really know about Haru? She only remembered their time together on the *Midori*. In terms of their lives, that was nothing more than the tip of a giant iceberg.

"You say that you don't care about who shikigami used to be, but you didn't always think that way. You used to agree with me." Haru sounded hurt, as if she was the one betraying him.

Kurara wanted to scream in frustration. "I don't care what I—what *Aki*—thought or what she did. Shikigami are human, and they don't deserve to be treated like . . . like *things*!"

"Is that true?"

Kurara felt a thunderstorm strike her spine.

She spun around.

Himura was the last person she expected to see standing before her, and yet there he was, looking rather worn and tired since the last time she had seen him. Gone was his careful poise, his stern manner. Between the dirt clinging to his skin and the disheveled state of his clothes, he looked like he had just wrestled a bear.

"Shikigami are human. Is that really true?"

TWENTY-SEVEN

LOOKING back, Himura should have known something was wrong. He had awoken that morning from another dream of fire, and Mana had been acting strangely since the moment he opened his eyes.

"Are you sure you want to see the Grave-keeper? I think you'll be disappointed."

The hesitation in Mana's voice had, in turn, made Himura pause. During their travels, Himura had wavered between believing that the snake really was leading him to someone who had all the answers about shikigami, and the certainty that he would find a mad fool prancing about in a cape. Was Mana hesitating because it knew its master was a fraud?

"Why do you think I'll be disappointed?" he'd asked.

"I told you," said Mana. *"You won't find what you seek in the past."*

At the time, Himura had not wanted to consider Mana's words. His parents had died longing for the glories of the past, seeking the truth that lay there. He would not be the same.

"I need to see them. I want to know . . . I want to know everything."

Yet the moment Himura had stepped into the eerily lit cavern, he'd known things would not go as planned.

The underground tunnels snaked around each other in a maze of dead ends and looping passages that he could not keep track of. When he emerged into the cavern, instead of being welcomed by an old Crafter who would show him all the secrets of the Grave-keepers, he found the last person on earth he wanted to see.

"What are *you* doing here?" Kurara stared at him as if she had just seen a ghost, but her horror quickly turned to anger. Mana coiled around his ankle, its presence an anchor against the storm of Kurara's ire.

"What do you *mean* shikigami were once human?"

That could not be right. His parents had said that shikigami were made to serve them. Every Crafter Himura had met said much the same. In fact, he used to sneer at those Crafters who tried to pretend otherwise, the ones who would treat their shikigami like a friend or a loveable pet. It was stupid to act as though a shikigami was anything but a tool made for a Crafter's benefit.

Shikigami were not human. There was no way the Crafters of the past—the wise, brilliant Crafters, the Crafters who were so much more than he was—would ever do such a thing. Why would they? Treating shikigami badly was foolish when there was the risk of one day becoming the very same thing that was abused and mistreated. Himura could not wrap his head around it. It had to be a lie. No one in their right mind would consider a shikigami human.

Except . . . Kurara had.

Kurara had always thought of shikigami as, if not people, then something damn close. She stared at him now, a mixture of shock and outrage warring across her expression. Himura stepped back, searching for Mana for support, but the snake had darted away and was heading toward a strange, short woman in a paper cape.

"Master, I have done my duty, but this time, please can we just send him back?" said the snake.

Himura flinched. Did even Mana not want to be around him anymore?

The woman said something to the snake that obviously upset it, but her words were too quiet for Himura to hear. He could hardly concentrate anyway. Between Kurara's sudden appearance and the discovery of how shikigami were made, he did not have much room in his head for anything else.

His gaze trailed up from the bottom of Kurara's clothes to her paper arm and across to where her hair brushed against her shoulders. Her collarbones peeked from beneath the collar of her kimono, the skin bare. She no longer wore the daruma pendant he had given her.

It hit him like a blow to the gut. It was such a small thing and yet it took aim and pierced through everything soft and tender about him.

This was his fault, he knew that, but knowing did not lessen the sting.

Kurara pressed her lips into a thin line.

"Where's Akane? Did you leave Akane on the *Orihime*?"

Himura took a deep breath.

"Akane . . . is dead."

It was difficult to gauge Kurara's reaction. He was too lost in his own thoughts. This was the first time he had ever said it aloud, and speaking it made it feel all the more real. He was wholly unprepared for the shame that hit him like a physical blow. No matter how many times he repeated that he had no reason to feel guilty, his words echoed hollow in his skull, useless even to him.

"While the library was burning, I asked Akane to fetch me the book I was reading. I thought that it would be able to make it back to me in time, or that I could at least save the core, but . . . I miscalculated. It was my fault."

Those eyes. Himura had seen those eyes in his dreams. Whenever the flames consumed Akane and transformed into Kurara, she always looked at him with those same eyes full of disgust.

"I know how much you liked Akane," he said, as if the more he talked the more he could smooth away the sharp edges of what he had done. "I never meant to do it. It was an accident. I regret it of course. If I could rewind time, I would take it all back, but I cannot."

Kurara took a deep breath. When she spoke, her voice was as soft and deadly as a viper.

"You . . . You're *sorry* that you led Akane to its death? You regret it? What good does regretting it do? Akane is dead, but it's OK because you regret it! Akane is dead, but it's fine because you're *really sorry* about it?"

The next thing Himura knew, pain blossomed across his chest. He was flying backward, hitting the ground with a crash.

"Stand up!" Kurara glared down at him, her voice tight with anger as her ofuda flew around her. "Stand up! I'm going to kill you."

TWENTY-EIGHT

OF all the people Kurara did not want to see, Himura was at the top of the list. Logically, she knew that they would have to see each other again at some point, if she returned to the *Orihime*, but she had imagined that would not be until she reached the Grand Stream—when she was less emotionally drained than she was now. When the sting of his betrayal no longer hurt as much.

Seeing Himura here and now felt like a chasm opening beneath her feet. Her stomach plummeted and her breath caught in her throat. She was angry. If she kept being angry, she did not have to be hurt. Beneath that rage, she knew that despair was waiting like a wolf, ready to pounce the moment she let her guard down.

Banri's core had broken. She had helped to destroy the eagle that had attacked the *Orihime* outside Sola-Il and cut off the head of the paper dragon that had rampaged through the sky city. Every shikigami she had ever encountered was either dead or their body had been destroyed. And now Akane too.

At least Akane's core burned. At least it didn't break open. At least Akane's soul hasn't been left to wander across the land, like Banri's. The thought made her sick. She never wanted to be glad that a shikigami had burned to death. Her fury howled through her. Himura eyed her, his body tense and ready to spring away, but he did not remove his bracelet just yet.

Kurara's ofuda struck him in the gut, sending him flying backward into the dirt.

She would be lying if she said that didn't feel good.

Her next hit caught him in the chest, sending Himura tumbling across the ground again.

Kurara hit him a third time.

"What are you even *doing* here?" She stalked over to where Himura lay, wheezing. "What more could you possibly want from me?"

"I . . . I came to see the Grave-keeper." As he picked himself up, he did not quite meet her gaze.

"So, you abandoned the *Orihime* to chase after rumors?"

"I didn't abandon them. The Grand Stream is not too far from here. I planned to join the ship again after a brief detour."

Kurara glowered at him. Why was she disappointed? If Himura would sell her off for a chance to read some books, of course he would not think twice about abandoning his duties.

"Well, you've learned a lot now, haven't you? How does it feel?"

Himura did not say anything. Common sense, or perhaps just self-preservation, kept his mouth firmly shut. Kurara had never seen him so uncertain. The Himura she knew never hesitated. Whether it was about shikigami or her training, he was always so sure that he knew what was best.

Now that he knew the truth, Himura looked . . . smaller, somehow. As if uncertainty had diminished him. Was knowing that shikigami were once human, that they had souls, really that important? Even if Oda had told her that shikigami were made from mushrooms, she would have thought of them as thinking, feeling individuals, and not tools to be used and thrown away.

Himura stood up slowly, cautiously, as if he thought Kurara might knock him down again if he startled her.

"I can take you back to the *Orihime* with me."

"And why would I go with you?" Kurara looked at him as if he had suggested she eat rat droppings. "You were desperate to sell me off only weeks ago, and now you want me back on your—?"

"Rara!" Haru's sharp cry warned her of something coming her way, but she did not have time to move as a pair of paper vines suddenly shot toward her.

She braced herself for the blow, but to her surprise they flew past her, just an inch away from her leg and toward Himura.

They would have pierced his chest had he not stepped to the side just in time. Instead, the tips of the vines stabbed deep into his shoulder, drawing blood that soaked into the paper and dripped to the ground.

With a click of Oda's fingers, the vines yanked themselves out of Himura's shoulder with such ferocity that they brought him to his knees.

"What are you doing?" cried Kurara.

Oda smiled. "Oh, Kurara, why do you think my shikigami

224

brought you here? Why do you think Mana brought this man here?"

Kurara racked her memory as she tried to recall what Oda's other shikigami had said to her when she had first woken.

"That deer thought that I was a Crafter," she said.

Oda nodded. "Fortunately for you, you're not. No, you're something much more magnificent. This man, however"—Oda gestured to Himura—"is nothing more than an ordinary Crafter. And all Crafters who come to my graveyard are to be sacrificed. That is why I send out my shikigami. To lure Crafters back here to die. That's all there is to it."

The paper vines plunged into the ground and disappeared beneath the earth. A beat later, they erupted from beneath Himura's feet, stabbing upward like a spike-trap. Himura jumped aside just in time to avoid being impaled on their wickedly sharp tips. Pulling his bracelet off, the paper crumbled into a long spear that he gripped in one hand while he continued to dodge Oda's ofuda.

The twin vines—one made of the red paper from her cloak, the other from the golden paper that had been her mask—swerved through the cave like flowing water. It seemed Oda was not able to control more than two vines at once, but they were more than enough to keep Himura on his toes. The tip of each vine was as sharp as an arrowhead, piercing the ground with such force they left holes in their wake.

A flash of white swerved around the stalagmites and lunged for Himura's leg, missing by only an inch.

"You—!" Himura cursed as the snake shikigami leapt for him.

"I'm sorry. But I must do as I am ordered. This is how it is

225

with shikigami." The snake sounded none too pleased with itself even as it continued to attack.

Kurara watched in numb shock as the two continued to battle it out. How quickly everything had dissolved into pure chaos. Her anger and grief over Akane were lost in the anarchy of battle.

Himura was red in the face, though Kurara could not tell whether that was out of anger or from dodging Oda's vines. "So, this is your game? You lure Crafters here, drawn by rumors—and then you sacrifice them?"

"Consider it karma. Now you can get a taste of what it's like to be a shikigami!"

"Then why don't you turn yourself into one?" Himura retorted.

Oda's vines darted around the curtains of flowstone, through the gaps between the hanging stalactites and around fangs of jagged rock. They were going to kill one another. Yes, Kurara was angry—furious—at Himura. Yes, she wanted to punch him until he could no longer stand, but did she actually want him dead?

There was no time to examine her feelings. In the next second, Kurara thrust herself between the two Crafters, flinging her arms out to block them both.

Oda's eyes widened. Her vines froze just inches from Kurara's face.

Kurara stared, almost cross-eyed, at the blade-like paper tips right in front of her. Her chest heaved, but the danger of what she had just done had no time to hit her.

"No one is killing anyone," she said.

At least, not without her permission first.

TWENTY-NINE

SILENCE resounded through the cave. No one spoke. No one moved.

"Put away your ofuda." Kurara's tone left no room for argument. She watched Himura and Oda's paper return to their usual forms even as her mind bubbled with doubt. Himura had let Akane die. He had betrayed her. Why not let Oda kill him? Didn't she care about shikigami? Didn't she want revenge too?

She shook herself free of such thoughts. A life on board the *Midori*, where everything had been structured and orderly, had taught her only how to deal with things on a timetable. Her doubts would have to wait their turn.

"You're too soft!" Oda scoffed. "After everything that Crafters have done, you want me to suddenly forgive them all? I have spent my life luring Crafters here to be sacrificed, and if you were still yourself, you would agree with my ways!"

"If I were still myself?" echoed Kurara.

"If you were *Aki*! Don't forget that I know what you and Haru are. What you once were! If you were still Aki you would agree that Crafters deserve to be punished for what they've done to their shikigami!"

"But Crafters *are* shikigami!" Kurara's head was starting to throb. It was like a snake eating its own tail—a vicious circle of blame. "Besides, how would you know what I would or would not have thought?"

No, that did not matter.

The important thing was how she felt *now*.

"And this one?" Oda spat venomously. "Didn't he kill his own shikigami? Can you honestly tell me that Crafters are not selfish and greedy?"

"Himura is Himura. He doesn't represent every Crafter in the country."

"Oda," said Haru. "Please. Could you drop it?"

Perhaps because he was a shikigami, or perhaps because people tended to do as Haru asked, Oda clamped her mouth shut. She looked distinctly unhappy about it, though.

Kurara fought the oncoming ache that was building up behind her eyes. When she had first met Banri, she had been full of excitement and hope for what she might find in Kazami. Now, Banri was dead, Tomoe and Sayo were missing, the Star Trees were all gone, and she had discovered the horrific truth behind how shikigami were made.

Her only hope lay in a dream of a crater and the screams of a shikigami who had looked at her with murderous eyes. And that might only have been a dream.

"Oda." Kurara turned to the Grave-keeper, lowering her voice. "Can we speak somewhere else? Somewhere private?"

If Oda hated Crafters so much that she was willing to use her shikigami to lure them in and kill them, Kurara was reasonably sure that she could trust her with information about the Star Seed.

Oda hesitated before nodding. "Come with me; we can speak inside my home. As for you . . ." She pointed at Himura.

"I'll watch over him," said Haru.

Kurara wanted to separate the two Crafters before they decided to attack each other again, but she trusted Himura about as far as she could throw him. Leaving him alone with Haru was a recipe for disaster. She opened her mouth to protest, but Haru simply rolled his eyes.

"I'll be *fine*, Rara! He knows that if he does anything funny you really will kill him."

"If my word counts for anything—" said Himura.

"It doesn't." She scowled.

"—I promise I won't do anything to hurt you or your friend."

"Good to know you'll only betray us once," Kurara scoffed, then turned back to Haru. "If he tries anything . . ."

"I'll shriek like a baby chick and wait for you to rescue me." Haru gave her hand a comforting squeeze.

With one last glower at Himura, Kurara followed Oda back to her home. The paper doors threw themselves open at her approach. Flicking her fingers in the air, Kurara snapped them shut behind her.

"What do you wish to speak to me about?" asked Oda. "If you want to lecture me about the importance of life and the evils of murder, save your breath. What my shikigami and I do is none of your business. You may be one of the first shikigami, but as you are now, you are just a child. Besides, I have already sent Yaji away to look for more Crafters. And I have no plans to stop."

"Don't you think it's a bit hypocritical that you hate other Crafters for using shikigami as tools when that's what you're doing too?" snapped Kurara.

Oda's eyes flashed with anger. "*My* shikigami agree with me! They also want revenge."

Kurara was not so sure about that. Thinking back to Mana's reluctance to attack Himura, she did not think Oda knew her shikigami nearly as well as the woman thought she did. Was it self-loathing or self-righteousness that made her so vicious? Did Oda even realize that she was just as bad as the Crafters she hated?

She could not force Oda to change though, and she did not think anything she said would make a difference.

"I'm looking for a crater," she said instead.

Oda looked at her in surprise. "A crater?"

"I've been having dreams." Kurara told the woman about the things she had seen; how her past memories were starting to leak through into her sleep; how she had dreamed of a furious shikigami yelling at her about the Star Seed.

"And you think that these dreams mean something?" said Oda, skeptically.

"They're no ordinary dreams." At least, Kurara hoped not. "They're memories. Aki's memories."

"Aki?" Oda perked up. As far as Kurara could tell, Oda respected the original shikigami. Perhaps it was because she was a Grave-keeper, but she had obeyed Haru the moment he had asked her to be quiet.

"If I can find this crater, if I can speak to the shikigami in my dreams, perhaps I'll remember something important."

"Something that will make you more yourself," said Oda.

Kurara wanted to disagree. She wanted to say that she was perfectly happy being who she was now. But if Oda thought that helping her might bring the old her back, then she could bite her tongue.

"You said that the Star Trees don't produce seeds, but they must exist. If you know anything, please tell me!"

"I stand by what I said before. There is no such thing as a Star Seed. However . . ." Oda was silent for a moment. The unnatural stillness of the air made the quiet feel almost eerie. "There is a crater very close to here. In fact, it's in the heart of the Grand Stream. The shikigami you saw in your dreams—I think that may be Suzaku."

Kurara sucked in a deep breath. "That can't be right! Suzaku is . . . I mean, that's just impossible!" she spluttered. It was one thing for a shikigami to hate her, it was quite another for that shikigami to be Suzaku—to be that towering bird whose wings created the winds of the Grand Stream. A shikigami so huge and monstrous that no one dared go near it. A shikigami that could crush her like a bug.

I am a lotus, Kurara told herself. Lotus flowers did not fear anything. They did not worry about giant shikigami pecking off their heads or getting ripped apart by the wind. If she went to the Grand Stream, perhaps she would find Tomoe and Sayo there. Maybe she would find out what had happened to the Star Seed.

And maybe in the process she would learn why Suzaku was so furious with her.

"Come with me, Aki. I'll give you something that will show you the way."

Oda walked past the kitchen and through the polished hallways to the end of the corridor. There, she crouched down and moved aside a loose floorboard to reveal a hole that led farther underground. The paper from her mask drifted down to form a flight of steps leading into the darkness.

"When I began living here, I thoroughly inspected the tunnels and caverns. The few things that I could salvage from the ruins, I kept down here," Oda explained as she led Kurara into the basement. She lit a single oil lantern hanging by an iron hook in the middle of the room. The resulting light illuminated a cramped and dusty storeroom filled with junk.

Among the wood carvings and half-broken statues, the various pots, jars and reed baskets, Oda pulled out a thin, yellowing piece of parchment upon which someone had inked a map of Kazami village. It looked like a child's drawing: a squiggly mess of lines and circles that split off and curved back into each other.

"As I was exploring, I made a map for myself to keep track of my progress. The tunnels lead all the way to the heart of the Grand Stream. The eye of any storm is the least destructive part; the winds are the weakest in the center of the hurricane where you will emerge."

Kurara took the map from Oda and folded it carefully into quarters.

"Do you really think the Star Seed is a fairy tale?" she asked.

Oda sighed. "I have already told you what I think about this Seed of yours, but if you won't believe me then speak to Suzaku. I'm sure your conversation will be . . . illuminating."

Sure, Kurara planned to talk to Suzaku. *If* the shikigami was not already mad. If it would deign to talk to her at all. If it still remembered her and was not so angry that it pecked her eyes out first.

If the *Orihime* had not already destroyed it.

"Thank you." What Oda did to Crafters—what she made her shikigami do—was horrendous, but if the map helped her reach the Grand Stream, she could at least be grateful. Perhaps one day, if—no, *when*—she had found the Star Seed, she could return here to free Oda's shikigami.

"Aki."

Something in Oda's voice made Kurara pause.

"Kazami is a place of misery and death. We Crafters killed each other. And when that wasn't good enough, we took our dead and put their souls into paper creatures so that they could keep on fighting and killing. Everything that Crafters touch becomes tainted. One day, you'll understand that."

THIRTY

HIMURA'S thoughts were racing. Shikigami. Kurara. Akane. The Grave-keeper. In a single moment, his entire world had been turned upside down.

He wished that he had never come here, that he had never left the *Orihime*. Despite the luminous fungi scattered across the walls, glowing softly blue, the cavern was oppressively dark. A cold draft from the tunnels bit through his clothes and made his injured shoulder sting, as if even the underground village itself did not want him here.

Something flickered in the corner of his vision. A flash of white. Himura looked down to see Mana slither across the ground toward him.

"I have no wish to talk to you. You knew what you were doing when you brought me here. You lied to me," he said.

The snake paused. Hurt glimmered in its eyes. *"I asked you before if you were sure you wanted to see the Grave-keeper."*

Himura glanced at Haru, who was standing only a few feet away, doing his best to pretend that he could not hear anything they were saying.

"You knew that I wouldn't say no."

Mana coiled itself into a tight ball. *"I cannot disobey my master's orders. You know that well. To tell the truth, even if I had the will to choose, I do not think I would have disobeyed. Not at the start. Again and again I have seen Crafters treating their shikigami as something that they can throw away when it suits them. Yet watching my master grow increasingly obsessed with luring in other Crafters, I have come to understand that there is nothing to be found in the past but bitterness. If I were free, I would like to simply move on with my life. As I traveled with you, as I saw how you too were obsessed with the past . . . I felt sympathy. I have led dozens of your kind to their deaths. You are such a fool. Just like my master."*

"Who are you calling a fool?" snapped Himura. He was nothing like that insane woman.

Was it his fault that he had treated Akane badly? He had only done as his parents had taught him. He had never imagined they could be wrong about anything.

Deflated, the snake slunk away, disappearing in the direction its master and Kurara had headed. Himura tamped down on the sting of guilt in his chest as he watched the shikigami go. Perhaps this was karma.

Wincing against the pain, Himura pulled down one side of his kimono and wiped away the dried blood around the puncture wound in his shoulder. After binding the injury in paper bandages, he gingerly straightened his clothes and looked up to find Haru staring at him.

"You didn't have to be so harsh, Mr. Himura. I know you were betrayed, but it was not as if Mana had a choice; we shikigami must obey our masters."

The boy wore a wan smile, but his eyes were cutting: as if he could read Himura's mind a little too perfectly.

"If you want to be forgiven, you have to learn how to forgive others."

The breezy way Haru spoke felt like he was trying to make some kind of joke. Himura was not in the mood for whatever this was. His throat felt tight and hot. His shoulder throbbed with pain. A stew of anger and guilt bubbled just beneath his skin.

Turning his attention to the shallow pool of water, he stared at the dark clay urns submerged below, and the rotting ribbons and prayer beads wrapped around them. These urns had all been people once. People who had been murdered, perhaps. People sacrificed to make shikigami. His gaze traveled to the stump of a giant tree that peeked just above the surface of the water. There was something familiar about it. Himura recalled his parents once telling him a fairy tale about a giant tree.

"Do you know what that is?" Haru, noticing the object of Himura's attention, pointed to the symbol carved onto the tree trunk—an eight-pointed star within a circle.

"I've seen it before. In here." Careful not to move his shoulder too much, Himura pulled a small, red leather-bound book from his knapsack. The parchment was singed and the binding was coming apart. There was no title on the spine. Or perhaps the title had been burned away in the fire that stole Akane's life.

"Where did you get that?"

"From Princess Tsukimi's library."

Haru whistled, impressed. "You stole something from the Imperial Princess?"

Himura grimaced. Nothing about how he got the book made him feel proud.

"It's about the markings on shikigami cores. About what they mean; which marks control memory and which marks affect a shikigami's strength and thoughts," he said.

"So, you know almost everything about making shikigami. There's just one thing you're missing. One thing even Princess Tsukimi doesn't know," said Haru.

"You mean about the soul?"

"Yes and no. I've heard that Princess Tsukimi was experimenting on humans before, so she was on the right track regarding needing a life to create a shikigami. She probably knows that souls are a necessary ingredient, but she thinks that regular humans will do just fine." Haru placed his hands on his hips. "I'll teach you the real way to make a shikigami."

Alarm and shock were not emotions Himura thought he'd ever feel in response to those words. Before he had come to Kazami, he would have done anything to learn what had been lost to his people for so long, to learn the things he believed he deserved to know. What a fool he had been.

"Why would you do that?" asked Himura, but Haru had already launched into an explanation.

"First, you need to draw this pattern." Haru used

his finger to trace the image of an eight-pointed star and a circle on the ground. "The next important step is to have a sacrifice—a Crafter—we'll use this stone as our pretend sacrifice." Haru placed a large white stone in the middle of the symbol. "Then you wrap the subject up in a cocoon of paper. To tell the truth, the cocoon isn't actually necessary. It's just useful to keep the subject from running away, but let's go with it."

He looked at Himura expectantly. Holding back a sigh, Himura reluctantly wrapped the chunk of stone in a few pieces of ofuda.

"After that, you set the cocoon on fire and burn the whole body," Haru continued. "Once everything's burned, you collect the ashes into a paper ball."

"I assume the next step is to write my blood on the ball to turn it into a core?"

"You're a fast learner, Mr. Himura! Yes, exactly right. Your blood creates the bond, but the patterns and sigils that you draw on our core will dictate our appearance."

"And that's it?"

"Well, you have to name the shikigami. Names are important. They represent your hopes and dreams for us." Haru clapped his hands together as if in prayer. *"May you be worthy of your name."*

Himura gave a bitter laugh. His hopes and dreams for a shikigami? He doubted Crafters thought enough about their shikigami for that. What had been the creator's hopes and dreams for Akane when they had given it that name?

He stared at the dozens of urns around the cave. For years he had longed to understand how one made shikigami, to recover the knowledge his kind had lost, to come one step closer to that "something more" his parents had often spoken of. Now, he wondered if he might have been better off never knowing.

"If you want to try it out, I won't stop you," said Haru. "There are plenty of cores here. You can take your pick."

It was like being punched in the gut. Did Haru really know what he was saying? Was this some kind of trap? Himura eyed the boy with suspicion. If he tried to make a shikigami here and now, both Oda and Kurara would probably barrel out of the nearby building and slit his throat.

As if reading his mind, Haru offered him an infuriatingly gentle smile. "Don't worry, Mr. Himura. Even if Rara objects to it, I'll protect you."

"I don't *want* a shikigami." Himura bristled and was surprised to find that it was true. Any shikigami he created would obey him, not because it had chosen to, but because the bond compelled them to do so. He did not want a shikigami that had no choice but to love him, a shikigami that would stay with him only because he was its master. What he wanted was something *real*. Something . . .

Something like he thought he had with Mana. Before everything had gone so horribly wrong.

"You can take a core for other purposes too. Did you know they can be very useful weapons if you break one open?"

Himura glowered at him. Was Haru trying to get him killed? Besides, cores were valuable. Who in their right mind would break one open? And what would happen to the soul inside the core if he did? Wouldn't it be unleashed too?

"Why are you telling me this? Why are you teaching

239

me how to make shikigami?" asked Himura. He doubted the boy was telling him out of the goodness of his heart. If Oda knew that he now possessed the knowledge and understanding of how to create a shikigami, she would definitely try to kill him. Again.

"It's a gift, Mr. Himura! There's nothing more valuable than the gift of knowledge!" said Haru, brightly.

"All right, but *why*?"

The boy smiled.

"Because I need you to do something for me."

THIRTY-ONE

THE moment Kurara stepped out of the basement with the map in hand, she sighed. By the skies, she was exhausted. Her ofuda fluttered around her in a slow parade of confetti.

After a moment, Kurara forced herself to leave Oda's house. She flicked her hand, and the paper doors slammed open with more force than necessary. To her relief, Himura and Haru were still standing by the pool near the old tree stump where she had left them.

"We're heading to the Grand Stream." Kurara clutched the map even tighter as she made her way to him.

Haru looked concerned. "What? Now?"

"Yes, there's no time to waste."

"I can help you travel," said Himura.

Kurara could barely look at him. "Oh, I'm sorry, were you under the impression that you were invited?"

Himura lowered his eyes, but that only annoyed her even more.

"We can't leave him here, Rara. Oda will kill him," said Haru. As if he thought he was being reasonable for not wanting a murderer to be killed by another murderer.

But I did defend him from Oda as well, an unhelpful voice in Kurara's head reminded her. If she really wanted Himura dead, she should have just let Oda do as she wished.

"He can leave on his own then."

"Rara . . ."

"I'm leaving, Haru. I need to reach the Grand Stream." Kurara turned and headed toward the rear of the cavern. She ignored Haru's calls and his hurried footsteps chasing after her.

Statues of shikigami stood by the entrances to the many tunnels that lined the rock wall. Kurara poked her head around the exit to the furthest right. There was no light coming from the other end of the tunnel—just a passage of darkness that seemed to stretch all the way into some unknown abyss—but even though she could not see what lay at the other end, she could sense something in the walls.

Paper. There were tiny scrolls of rolled-up paper embedded in the rock, allowing her to sense the way forward even in complete darkness.

Without a moment's hesitation, Kurara stepped forward. The tunnel was narrow, only just wide enough to walk down in single-file. As she made her way through it, the soft glow from Oda's cavern grew dimmer and dimmer until it disappeared completely, leaving her in the dark. She could not see her own hands in front of her face, or even her feet, as they took one shuffling step after another; if she did not know better, she would question if her eyes were even open. Only the paper in the walls gave her any indication of where she was going. She could sense them close to her—two thin unbroken lines of paper like guide rails keeping her on track.

"Rara, c'mon Rara, wait! I don't know where you are!" Haru's voice echoed against the walls as he chased after her.

Kurara stopped. Haru could not sense the paper in the walls like she could. If he got lost, who knew if he would ever find his way out again?

"I'm here." She stopped to let him catch up.

"Don't run off without a plan!" Haru's breath brushed against the back of her neck. "Do you even know where you're going? We should stock up on food and supplies. And you should get another night's rest!"

"I can't!" Her footsteps grew more harried as she resumed walking. She wanted to tear her hair out in frustration. Why couldn't Haru understand how important this was?

"Of course you can, Rara. Why are you in such a rush?"

"Because!" she cried.

Because when I reach the Grand Stream, Suzaku will tell me everything. About why it's so angry at me. About whether there's a Star Seed out there and where I can find it, she told herself.

Akane was dead. Banri was dead. She could not wait another day to reach the Grand Stream. Another day meant another shikigami dying somewhere. Another day was another shikigami she could not save.

"Rara," said Haru, gently. "What aren't you telling me?"

In the darkness, it felt like a surprise blow. Like an assassin's knife beneath the ribs. She couldn't see Haru's

243

face, but she could feel him; how close he was to her, the warmth of his breath against her skin.

Did she trust him? If she told him about the Star Seed, would he help or try to hinder her?

Things used to always be simple with Haru. Easy. She loved him without thinking; as if love were something engraved deep within her core. Whenever they fought, it was like she was fighting with another half of herself. She did not know what she would do if Haru wasn't on her side.

A gentle glow caught her attention. There was a soft light at the end of the tunnel. As she hurried forward, the passage brought her to a small cavern.

There were no statues, no buildings, no luminous mushrooms or large stalactites dripping down from the ceiling like blades of stone; just rocks and moss growing bright green in the sunlight that crept through the cracks in the ceiling.

"Oh," said Haru. "So this is where the people of Kazami got their sunlight."

Kurara craned her head back to peer at the long fissures running along the top of the walls and the whorls of flowstone that had formed from the moisture collecting there like crystalline flowers. In another life she might have enjoyed the sight, but now worry gnawed at her. Had she taken a wrong turn somewhere? This wasn't the way to the Grand Stream.

While she pored over the map, muttering to herself and wishing that Sayo were with them, Haru shuffled his feet against the mossy rocks.

"Listen, Rara," he said. "If you don't want to tell me anything that's fine. I suppose it's only fair, but ever since

244

we fell from Sola-Il, it feels like you and I have been drifting further apart. I know it's my fault. I know that it's because I've kept things from you, because I'm still keeping things from you, but there's been a lot going on in my head too. On the *Midori*, I was content to just stay there and pretend that we were nothing more than war orphans living day to day. Even though we always talked about leaving and going on an adventure, I never thought we would actually leave—I thought it was all just a nice fantasy and that we'd stay there forever."

He moved away from the sunbeams, as if the thought of confessing in the light of day was too much for him.

"When the *Midori* went down, I thought maybe we'd have fun running around the country, but then—well, then my core was burned to pieces and when I finally came back . . . you were different. You could use ofuda better than you ever could. You *knew* things, but you weren't Aki.

"It's weird for me to think of you and Aki as two different people, but I think I need to accept that. I need to understand that. I know you've been frustrated at me for all the things I don't tell you, but the truth is, even if I hadn't made that promise to Aki, I wouldn't say anything. *I* don't want to talk about those memories. If I tell you about your past, I have to tell you about mine too, and I . . . I don't want to. I can't. I can't relive some of that stuff."

It took a moment for Kurara to take it all in. Ever since coming to Kazami, she had suspected that whatever had happened in her past had not been pretty. *War* was never pretty and she—Aki, rather—had lived through it. Perhaps she had done awful things. Perhaps one of those awful things was why Suzaku was so angry with her. She had been so preoccupied with her own mysteries, she had never stopped to consider that Haru had lived through it all too.

"So you keep your secrets and I'll keep mine," said Haru. "But whatever we do, let's not hate each other, all right? Even if you can't understand it, my priority has always been your happiness."

Kurara stared at him. Before she knew it, she had reached out for his hand, hooking her last two fingers around his.

"Thank you," she whispered.

The relief on Haru's face was like the sun finally breaking through the clouds after days of gray skies.

This was how things should be between them: gentle and soft and without regret. Despite the secrets, despite her lack of memories, Haru had always been there for her, cheering her up whenever she felt down, looking out for her whenever one of the servants tried to make trouble, and pulling her along into his own adventures. She could not imagine a world without him.

"I'll tell you what I know, Haru," she said. "I'll tell you everything."

The look on Haru's face was inscrutable as he searched her expression for some sign that she was lying. As much as it hurt, Kurara understood why he was looking at her that way. Outwardly, they had acted as though nothing was different, but they had both felt the small cracks form in their relationship, causing them to drift away from each other ever so slightly.

He swallowed and then, as if trying to drag stones up from the bottom of a well, he said, "Then I'll tell you everything too."

THIRTY-TWO

"*YOU* and I were some of the first shikigami ever created. We were made before the war, that's why we're different from all the others. The shikigami you see nowadays were made for war, but we were made to live."

Haru sat her down on the edge of a moss-stained rock as he spoke, his voice soft and gentle as if he were afraid that he would scare her with the things he said. Kurara closed her eyes in the hope that Haru's explanation would jog something in her memory, but came back with nothing. Perhaps those memories would eventually leak back to her in the form of dreams, but for now she felt only a hollow emptiness where they should have been.

"To become a shikigami used to be an honor granted to only the most respected of Crafters. It was not something done often. We were special. We were given eternity," said Haru. "And then the war happened—and everything changed. Suddenly making shikigami was not about granting people a chance to live forever, it was about making weapons. Making *tools*. Crafters wanted servants that would obey them unquestioningly."

"And so they came up with the ritual to bind a shikigami to them. They began cutting down the Star Trees," said Kurara.

"Not all Crafters wanted to destroy them. You and I worked with others to protect the Star Trees. You came to Kazami to help the people here defend their tree."

"And I failed." It was not a question. Kurara had seen the stump of the Star Tree peeking above the water in Oda's cavern.

"It wasn't your fault. In case you haven't noticed, all the Star Trees are gone. We both failed!" Haru's hands curled into fists.

Kurara could only guess what it must have been like to travel from place to place, each time hoping that things would be different, only to meet with the same end, the same bitter taste of failure.

"Over and over, we went to protect the trees and failed. We fought, we did things neither of us are proud of, and yet we still failed. The guilt ate at you until it was too much."

"Was that why I wanted you to erase my memories?" asked Kurara. To make her forget her failure? Had it really been that bad? She could no longer recall the horrors of living through a war.

"But there's still a Seed left. There's still a chance we can bring back the Star Trees," she insisted.

She had watched Haru's expression carefully as she told

him everything she knew: about the crater, about Suzaku's fury, and about the Star Seed that Suzaku kept yelling at her about in her dreams.

"So you think the Star Seed really exists? And that Suzaku might know where it is?" he said. He gave her a hopeless look. "Even if the Seed is real, Suzaku is mad and dangerous. You won't get any answers out of it."

"But I have to at least try."

For a moment, Haru seemed lost in thought. When he looked at her again, a weight seemed to have lifted from his shoulders.

"Well then, what are we waiting for? Let's go! Rara and Haru: two plucky young adventurers off on a search for justice and freedom. It'll be the quest of a lifetime!"

"Haru." Kurara stopped him before he could run off to another tunnel. "Thanks," she said.

Haru gave her a weak smile. "I broke my promise to Aki. I don't know whether I should be relieved about that, but I am."

"If it means anything coming from me, I doubt she could hold it against you," she assured him. If Aki had been anything like her, if she had cherished Haru even a tenth as much as Kurara did, there was no way she could hate him.

Despite Haru's initial enthusiasm, the more they walked, the more Kurara understood how the layout of tunnels and caves were designed to confuse an invader. Even with a map, navigation was difficult. More often than not, they had to walk in complete darkness, with only the paper in the walls outlining the passages and guiding Kurara's steps. There were only so many different paths to take, and they looped around and split into forks so many times that she could barely keep track.

Some of the tunnels had collapsed in on themselves, blocking the way, while others led to dead ends. There were traps too. Lots of them. One minute she had been walking with one hand against the rock wall, the next she heard a clicking sound and a large rock catapulted out of nowhere and hit the ceiling. It was so dark that Kurara had not realized there was a colony of bats roosting above their heads until they were suddenly screeching in fury and flying straight toward her.

"This way!" She pulled Haru into another tunnel and stretched her ofuda across the entrance, hardening the paper like a rock.

There were several thumps as the bats hit her ofuda wall, but no matter how hard they tried, they could not break it. Shadows flitted against the paper in a rush of tiny, furred bodies. Kurara stood her ground and concentrated on keeping the wall up as the sound of flapping wings eventually faded into silence.

"That was close!" She breathed a sigh of relief.

"Where are we now?" Haru squinted at the map, but even if there was enough light to make out the mass of squiggly lines, they had got so hopelessly turned around while running from the bats that neither of them could guess where they were.

Kurara closed her eyes and concentrated. It was distant,

but she could just about sense a roll of ofuda up ahead. Curious, she gave it a little tug with her mind but, wherever it was, it was deeply embedded in the wall.

"There's something that way." Kurara pointed in the direction of the paper. The longer she remained underground, the more she learned that the people of Kazami only ever marked places of importance with paper.

Haru did not look quite as convinced, but he followed without complaint. Eventually the passage opened up into a wide cavern.

Kurara's mouth fell open. The cave was so large she had to crane her head back to look at the ceiling. Houses grew on large spires of rock, and stone bridges arched over deep chasms in the ground. Stairs carved out of the walls zigzagged upward to large bell towers that shone in the slanted light seeping through the ceiling.

The buildings were almost as white as paper. At first, Kurara thought that they *were* paper, but upon closer inspection she realized they were made out of some kind of thin, layered stone with cracks that looked like the folds in origami. Some were covered in blackened scorch marks that slashed across the stones like tar over snow. Icy mineral deposits along the walls and ceiling spiraled outward in tusks of hardened crystal that looked like horns in some places and flowers in others.

Kurara gawked at the shikigami statues covered in white, woolly fungi.

Haru frowned. "This place feels strange, doesn't it?"

She nodded. The closer she looked, the more evidence she found that a great fire had once raged through the ruins.

Charred wooden beams poked out of crumbling stone windows, next to broken statues that had been cracked, chipped and scorched by fire. There was something eerie about the wreckage of civilization—a reminder of how easy it was to wipe out everything others had worked so hard to build. People had lived here once. Families. Human beings with dreams. Now where were they? Just dust to the ashes of time.

"*Kazami is a place of misery and death,*" Oda had said. Was this what the woman had meant? Kurara did not like how still and silent it was. It all felt so familiar. These houses and bell towers, the curving stone bridges and torii gates felt like things she had seen before—like an old painting with its color faded.

A loud growl echoed across the walls.

Haru looked embarrassed as he held his hand against his stomach. "I told you we should have gone back to Oda's place to prepare," he grumbled.

"We won't die if we don't eat," said Kurara.

Haru gave her a horrified look. "Not eat? Have you tried not eating, Rara? After a while it feels like your stomach is gnawing at itself, then it feels like there's a hole in you. Then every part of your body feels hot then cold and your vision starts to blur! We might not die, but it's a miserable experience. Let's take a break. These mushrooms are edible." He pointed to the white, furry mushrooms that resembled cotton balls.

Kurara groaned. Not more mushrooms!

"Fine!" She squared her shoulders back and resigned herself to her fate.

Gathering as much as they could between the two of them, Kurara and Haru settled down to cook their depressing meal of fungus, fungus and more fungus. Haru rubbed two rocks together until he had made a small fire.

While the mushrooms slowly roasted, Kurara pulled a piece of paper from her arm and let it spin on the tip of her finger. Haru's gaze flitted from the fire to Kurara and then back to the fire in that restless manner that meant he was gearing up to ask her something she was probably not going to like.

"Hey, Rara, don't take this the wrong way or anything, but why are you so obsessed with the Star Tree? With shikigami freedom. Is this really what you want to spend your life doing?" he said at last.

Her ofuda stopped spinning. "Are you saying I should give up?" she snapped.

Haru gave her an indecipherable look. "I'm saying that what happens to the shikigami isn't your responsibility anymore. It's not a burden you have to bear."

"If it's not ours, then whose?" Each time a shikigami was hurt, each time their bodies were destroyed, was like a knife to her chest. Though she had promised herself not to, she thought of Akane, of Banri, of the dragon shikigami she had defeated at Sola-Il. She had wanted them all to live much happier lives than fate had dealt them. It was unfair. So unfair. Kurara felt like she was hitting her head against a wall, begging for a kinder world.

If the world would not grant the shikigami their freedom, then Kurara would snatch it for them.

Haru smiled at her as if he had just thought of something hilarious.

"What?" she asked.

His smile widened. "When you think about it, we're kind of heroes, aren't we? Defenders of freedom and justice like in those plays the entertainers would perform. Do you think anyone will write a story about us?"

Kurara gave Haru a playful shove. "If they did, you'd be the annoying sidekick rather than the hero. Or maybe the fair maiden in need of rescue."

"Ooh, the fair maiden, definitely! I'd get a better costume that way. Or maybe I could be the wise mentor."

"That would require you to be wise," said Kurara. "And to mentor someone."

Haru clutched the front of his kimono with a theatrical gasp. "I taught you how to tell different mushrooms apart, didn't I? And that's not all I can teach you! Come, let Great Teacher Haru give you an important lesson in the nature of ofuda!"

"I'm not calling you that!"

"You might be familiar with shape-changing," Haru continued, undeterred. "But did you know that before my core was injured, I could transform my whole body into whatever I wanted?"

That sounded . . . extreme. Changing her arm was one thing, but changing her entire body was quite another. What if she got stuck and could not turn back? What if she turned her entire body white?

Noticing her hesitation, Haru gestured to his clothes. "If that's too much, there's another trick I used to do. You can wear ofuda. You know, like Oda's mask? Only it doesn't have to be a mask; it can be claws or wings or the body of an entire animal. Think of your body like that of a hermit crab and the ofuda 'clothes' that you put on as your shell." He gave Kurara an encouraging grin. "Go on, try it! Maybe try wearing a bird's wing on your arm to start and then go from there."

Taking a deep breath, Kurara wrapped more paper around her arm so that it encased the entire length of the limb from hand to shoulder like a long glove. She had missed this: the joy of creation, the thrill of making paper dance, the pleasure of listening to it rustle as it moved. Her ofuda stretched downward and molded into feathers. It encased her head like a helmet, stretching down to form a beak. The detail of the feathers, the way the pinions held together in order to catch the wind, was tiring. It was heavy too, like she was holding a thick curtain over one arm; the weight of the wing made her tilt to one side, but she held onto the form and looked at Haru expectantly.

"What's that supposed to be?"

"A sparrow! I'm clearly a sparrow!" The tail! The wings! There was even a small beak in front of her mouth, muffling her words. It was obvious what she was meant to be!

Haru shook his head, grinning from ear to ear. "Nice try, Rara. Maybe you should start with something simpler. Something like a snail, maybe?"

Kurara scowled. She would show him.

Lying down on her stomach, she wrapped her ofuda around her body, locking her arms and legs together. The paper on her back ballooned into a shell while the ofuda covering her head stretched into two antennae. She kicked her legs, which were bound together inside the tight paper wrapping. If she tried, she could just about crawl.

"Like this?"

Haru stared at her in stunned silence. Then, suddenly, he burst out laughing.

"You . . . you look ridiculous, Rara!" Haru dropped to his knees, clutching his sides as his entire body shook.

"You're the one who told me to be a snail!" she cried, indignant.

Haru was not listening. He was too busy trying to breathe. Kurara looked at herself. At her ridiculous antennae and the hard shell on her back. She tried to hold it in, but it was no good. The snail's body crumbled around her and she rolled onto her side, clutching her stomach with laughter.

THIRTY-THREE

THEY slept on the ground by the stone bridge, huddled together for warmth. When Kurara closed her eyes, her dreams were haunted by the familiar beating of wings and the sound of a shikigami screaming at her in anger.

"Aki! What have you done to me? What have you done to us all? We should never have let you in! We should never have given you the Star Seed!" The paper bird she now recognized as Suzaku pinned her with its wild gaze.

When Kurara awoke, Haru was still asleep and snoring lightly. Her back screamed at her for spending the night on the hard ground. By the skies, she missed her futon on the *Orihime*. She would even take the *Midori*'s lumpy beds or the forest floor outside Sola-Il over the floor of the cave.

Carefully, so as not to wake Haru, Kurara stood up and looked around the silent, abandoned city. The eerie stillness of the cavern remained, hanging ominously in the air, like an ancient crypt. Her feet moved on their own, leading her down narrow, fire-scorched stone paths that curled between empty houses, up crumbling staircases carved into the rock walls, and beneath giant torii gates that had been chipped and blackened by flames. Bits of chipped stone and burnt charcoal lay scattered across the ground, clattering whenever her feet accidentally kicked them out of the way.

Kurara knew this place. With the same kind of innate knowledge that taught sparrows how to fly and salmon how to swim back to the place of their birth, when she closed her eyes she could see Kazami as it had been in its prime: filled with Crafters and shikigami and the sounds of life. As she plunged deeper into the ruins, something cracked beneath her foot.

Kurara glanced at the heel of her shoe.

Human bones lay scattered across the ground: small, cracked fragments covered in burn marks.

She clapped a hand over her mouth to hold back a scream. A wave of dizziness washed over her, but when she leaned against the nearest wall to steady herself she was suddenly assaulted by a sharp, throbbing pain in her skull.

"This is the only way to keep the Star Seed safe!"

"Are you insane? I didn't agree to this! None of us agreed to it!"

"Please, Lady Aki, you promised us an honorable death!"

Ghostly voices echoed through her head. Kurara hissed in pain and pressed the base of her palm to her temple as if she could beat them out of her skull. The voices grew louder inside her head. She swore she could smell the choking stench of fire and burning flesh.

"Rara? What's wrong?" Kurara jumped. Blinking, she turned to find Haru hurrying through the ruins toward her.

The voices faded to a whisper before disappearing, and the stench of smoke grew fainter, leaving Kurara frightened and dizzy.

"I've been here before. In this cavern," she muttered, clutching her head.

Haru frowned. "You have? How do you know?"

Because this all feels too familiar. The voices she had heard, the smell of smoke, teased the edges of her memory. She did not know how to explain it in a way that would not sound silly, how the very curve of the walls and the towering ruins felt like a dream she had had a thousand times before. There was no doubt Aki had stepped into this very cave before.

A strange, prickling feeling skittered over her skin. She turned to glance at the walls of the cavern. "Do you feel that?"

"Feel what?"

Paper. Not just in the walls but in the ground, too. It was faint, but if she concentrated she could feel the presence of paper buried below the layer of bones.

"Here!" As if seized by a sudden madness, Kurara grabbed a piece of blackened wood and followed the line of paper she could sense beneath her feet. "Here too. And here. And all across here."

When she was done, Kurara had drawn an eight-pointed star on the floor of the cavern and traced a circle on its walls.

It was the same symbol Kurara had seen in Banri's memory. The one during the ritual that had turned Banri into a shikigami.

"Why would there be a shikigami symbol here?" Kurara

259

thought of the human bones she had found in the center of the ruins, the evidence of fire that swept across the buildings . . .

"Why else? To create shikigami," said Haru.

"Yes, but here?" Kurara felt sick. This was obviously a place where people had lived and gone about their daily lives. For there to be a shikigami symbol here, to have burned and sacrificed a Crafter in this place . . . something was very wrong.

Kazami is a place of misery and death.

"I was here before because I . . . I came to Kazami to defend it," she said, as if trying to memorize the words to a poem she had forgotten long ago.

Yes, Haru had said as much before, but now it was truly starting to sink in. She had come to Kazami to help, and she had failed. Even if the dead stump of a Star Tree in Oda's cavern was not enough evidence, the destruction here told her everything she needed to know. There had been some kind of battle here—perhaps part of the war she had heard about that pitted Crafter against Crafter in a bid for power and territory. She had not been able to protect the Star Tree. She had not been able to save the people of Kazami.

It was horrid. No wonder she could not take it, no wonder she had asked Haru to make her forget. Kurara could not help but think about the people here who had been dragged out of their homes and turned into shikigami against their will, how the echo of their screams sank deep within the stone, the fire leaving permanent marks upon the ruins.

She shook her head to rid herself of those thoughts. No matter how much she regretted it, she could not change the past. She could not let herself be distracted now; she needed to reach the Grand Stream. That was all that mattered. Perhaps if she found this Star Seed, she could do the people of Kazami some justice by bringing back the Star Trees.

"I think I know where we are," said Haru behind her, checking the map that he had slipped from her pocket.

He gestured toward a huge stone door that blocked the way out of the cavern. Beyond lay another long series of tunnels and then, hopefully, the Grand Stream.

As Kurara reached the stone doors, a tingle of electricity pricked at her skin. Before she could react, the doors opened with a loud rumble that shook the earth. A moment later, something large and white burst through the opening and into the cavern.

Ruki.

A woman dressed in a splendid kimono and a rich blue hakama jumped down from the tiger's back. Kurara froze. No matter how long she lived, she would never be able to forget that icy presence, that feeling that you were standing on the brink of a chasm, about to be swallowed whole.

Kurara stared at the woman in horror.

Princess Tsukimi smiled back.

Interlude

Rustle of paper
The sound of eternity
Fills my hungry soul

—Written by a Crafter of Unknown Origin
(from the personal library
of the Imperial Princess)

Following Zagi's directions, Tsukimi and her men had found the entrance to Kazami. The journey had been long and made more tedious than it needed to be by the monkey's childishness and the captive Sorabito's constant attempts to escape. The redhead in particular had a mouth on her that seemed incapable of saying anything without sarcasm, and the short-haired girl kept glowering at Tsukimi as if she wanted to set her alight.

The princess was thinking of torturing one of the girls to make the journey go faster when Zagi finally announced that they had arrived. Her heart skipped as she followed

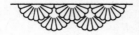

the monkey below ground. This was just like the adventure games she would play as a child, when she used to pretend that she was a conqueror, discovering new lands and new peoples to rule over.

The Sorabito girls followed behind, bound in ofuda ropes. Tsukimi pretended not to hear them whispering to one another; it was most amusing how they still thought they could escape, even after Tsukimi had thwarted all of their other attempts.

"I can distract them for you!" the short-haired girl, Sayo, whispered. Tsukimi had to hold back her snicker. The girl thought that she could distract an imperial Crafter long enough to give the redhead a chance to escape? How cute. "This is more important than me and you, more important than any of us! Something is happening in Zeka, something between the groundlings and the Sorabito. Things are getting dangerous, I can tell. Your father is there, causing trouble! Someone has to stop him!"

"I'm not running away without you, stop being so stupid!" the redhead hissed as she was pulled along like a dog on a leash.

Neither of the girls seemed willing to back down and so they settled for lapsing into tense silence.

The tunnels of Kazami ran in a circuit purposefully built to ensure one lost their way. If not for Zagi, she doubted they would ever find the exit or the entrance again. Using what little light peeked through the holes in the bedrock, Tsukimi strode forward as the tunnel opened up into a giant cavern, resplendent with buildings made of white stone

and wide, arched bridges. Goro and Fujiwa gawped up at the stone architecture, at the houses carved out of the very rockface, decorated with intricate engravings of shikigami, but Tsukimi had eyes for one thing and one thing only.

The shikigami girl.

Behind her, Sayo swore beneath her breath. Tsukimi grinned. Of course Kurara was here. The world was made to bend to her will, after all.

Her heart raced as her gaze fell upon the girl standing in the soft glow of luminous mushrooms. In her mind's eye, she was seven years old again, standing in the imperial courtyard and staring into the eyes of the very first shikigami that had set her blood aflame.

Kurara's response was immediate and intense. Tsukimi delighted in watching as ofuda swept toward her like the angry tide, morphing together into a vicious dragon with snarling jaws and scales as sharp as knives.

The princess did not move. As the dragon made its way toward her, Fujiwa ordered Ruki to take the brunt of the blow. As the shikigami and Kurara's paper creation clashed, the impact sent the tiger tumbling across the ground, its fur tearing on the stalagmites dotting the cavern.

Kurara winced as Ruki screamed in pain. Regret danced in her expression.

You're too soft, Tsukimi wanted to scoff. Once the girl was under her control, Tsukimi would teach her how to be merciless.

"Haru, grab the girl and bring her to the princess!" Fujiwa tossed the boy a katana made of sharpened paper.

"Of course, Master!" Haru chirped and cheerily swung Fujiwa's katana at Kurara.

Kurara's paper dragon crumbled into dozens of tiny squares and merged together into a sword, which she snatched out of the air.

"Haru! Haru, stop!" she shouted, blocking his blade with her paper arm.

"Stop fighting and come with me, Rara!" Haru grinned as if they were merely playing.

The shikigami children continued to exchange blows. Princess Tsukimi watched in delight as the two danced around one another. Haru swung the blade—all power and no finesse.

"I would stop fighting if I were you, girl!" she cried. "Or do you not care what happens to your friends?"

With a wave of her hand, Goro dragged the two Sorabito girls to the front. They struggled and cursed, but they could not break the ofuda ropes around their arms and legs.

Kurara's eyes widened in shock. "Tomoe? Sayo? What are you doing here?"

"Forget it! Don't worry about us, Kurara, just beat 'em up!" shouted Tomoe.

Tsukimi chuckled. "By all means, try to 'beat us up.' If you don't care about what happens to—"

Before the princess could finish her sentence, the monkey shikigami slammed its fists into the ground. The ground shook from the force.

"No fighting! I have brought you here to see my master. Come, we are not there yet." It scowled like a child who did not want to play.

Tsukimi glared at it. Gods, she could not wait to burn it to ash. "To Yomi with your master! I'm here for the girl."

"*You* will *see my master!*" With an outraged howl, the shikigami slammed its fist into the ground again and again until dust rose up and stalactites wobbled from the ceiling and crashed to the ground.

"Goro, Fujiwa, stop that beast!" cried Tsukimi. If it did not cease this foolish behaviour, the thing would cause the cavern to collapse on top of their heads.

The macaque swung its arms at her men as they tried to approach. In the corner of her eye, Princess Tsukimi noticed a shadow moving. She turned just in time to see that Kurara had managed to slip away from Haru. The shikigami girl lunged at her instead, but before they could come to blows, Ruki snagged the back of Tsukimi's kimono and yanked her out of harm's way.

The princess laughed with glee as her feet swung through the air. Now *this* was exhilarating. She could not remember the last time she had felt so alive!

"Good work, Ruki. Stay close to Her Highness and protect her!" ordered Fujiwa. "Haru, don't let the girl escape!"

"Yes, Master!" The boy continued to cheerfully swing his sword at Kurara, though he need not have bothered. In its rage, the monkey shikigami charged at them all. One moment it was swinging its arms through the stone ruins, the next it had grabbed Kurara by the leg and hauled her into the air.

That was quite enough. As much as Tsukimi enjoyed the chaos, she did not want anyone to break her toys, especially not before she got a chance to play with them.

As Ruki set her back down on the ground, she ordered her Crafters to destroy the macaque.

Without a moment's hesitation, both Goro and Fujiwa sent chains of paper snaking through the air, wrapping around the monkey's wrists and ankles. The shikigami screamed and dropped Kurara in order to claw at the restraints, and the girl went rolling across the ground into the corner of the cave. The beast wriggled its fingers underneath the paper bonds and tried desperately to yank itself free.

With practiced ease, Tsukimi pulled out the hand cannon holstered to her hips. The barrel was larger than her usual pistol, and when she lit the chamber and fired, the bullet erupted from the muzzle and hit the shikigami in a burst of flames that rapidly licked up its paper body.

With a scream that echoed throughout the cavern, the shikigami crashed into one of the stone bridges and plunged into the water, but it was too late. The fire had taken most of its body, and as it reached its feeble limbs toward the broken bridge to haul itself out, Tsukimi drew her katana and stuck the blade through the monkey's chest. After she had drawn her weapon back, she reached into the hollow of its chest.

The sensation of wrapping her fingers around the shikigami's core gave her a giddy thrill. To hold a creature's life in her hands was the kind of power Tsukimi lived for.

Her heart thundered just as it had that day her father had set fire to a god. Squeezing her fingers around the core, Tsukimi held tight and yanked it out with all her might.

"Curse you! Your end . . . will come . . . soon enough . . ." Zagi's body crumbled like a statue, collapsing inward into

a white heap that quickly soaked into the water and swept over the ground.

Tsukimi dropped the core on top of the sodden mound where it rolled down into the shallows of the lake. It was moments like this, when all eyes were on her, that Tsukimi enjoyed the most. Nobody moved, everyone too frozen in shock at what she had done.

Quick as lightning, Haru grabbed Kurara by the arm and twisted it behind her. She cried out in surprise as he threw her to the ground. Before she could push him off, Haru's knee pressed into the small of her back, pinning her in place.

"I've caught her, Master! She can't escape!" He sounded so proud of himself, so full of adoration.

"Now everyone calm down." Tsukimi held her hands up for silence, as though she were overseeing a classroom full of boisterous children.

She had all the cards in her hand; with the shikigami destroyed, Kurara was the only one who could put up a decent fight, but Tsukimi was sure she would not dare. Not when her friends' lives were in danger. Not when Fujiwa could control Haru. A delighted grin spread across her face.

Making her way over to Kurara, the princess smiled down at the girl.

"Surrender."

THIRTY-FOUR

PRINCESS Tsukimi stood like a god overseeing the world. From the waterfall of black hair that fell past her shoulders to the pleats of her hakama, every part of her appearance was cool and composed. Kurara reckoned the princess could stand on the top of a moldering dump and still look as perfect as ever.

Why in the seven hells was she here? Why now of all times? Kurara gritted her teeth and raised her hands in surrender. "I understand."

With a nod from Fujiwa, Haru slowly climbed off her back. Kurara sat up, rubbing the sore spot where Haru's bony knee had dug into her spine.

Princess Tsukimi looked at her as if she were a dog that had just learned a particularly difficult trick. "Good girl," she cooed.

Kurara bristled. "Why are you here?"

"Why else? For you, of course." Tsukimi smiled the way one would gut someone with a knife. Her smile was an act of violence.

Kurara's jaw clenched. She wondered if this was what it was like to argue with a spoiled child; with someone who refused to take no for an answer despite the fact that what they wanted was impossible.

"You're not a Crafter. We can't form a bond."

Tsukimi smirked. "Nothing is impossible for me. A century ago, people would say it is impossible to fly, and yet look how far we've come. There are no impossibilities in this world, only problems that do not yet have solutions."

It was not arrogance; Kurara could hear it in the princess's tone. She really believed that the world would bend to her will. What must it be like, Kurara wondered, to live such a privileged life? To hold such unwavering confidence that even the laws of nature would change for you?

"But you don't even *need* a shikigami! You have so many people who are already loyal to you. Fujiwa. The military. All the servants and soldiers who would run to the ends of the empire for you. Surely you have more than enough people to worship you!"

"Let me ask you something," said Tsukimi. "Before this Himura fellow sold you out, if I'd asked you, would you have said that he was loyal to you?"

Kurara lowered her gaze. She would have. Perhaps loyalty was not the right word, but she had not expected his betrayal—that was what had made it hurt all the more.

"As long as there is free will, there exists the possibility of betrayal. But you shikigami are different."

270

"If you want something that won't disobey you, go and buy a hammer! Shikigami aren't tools. We were once human too!"

"Oh, I know," said Tsukimi. "But what of it? Do you think having a soul makes you special? There are millions of humans in the world. Roaches breeding roaches. Why should being human, why should having a soul, mean anything?"

Kurara could only stare at the princess, flabbergasted. "Because, as fellow humans, it's wrong to—"

"Let me tell you something. Humans kill humans every day. Humans rob and beat and enslave other humans every day. You say shikigami are mistreated. I say I'm just treating them as I would any normal human. Isn't that fair? Isn't that the equality you want? What more could you ask for?"

"I . . . No, that's—"

Wrong, Kurara wanted to protest, but she could not explain why. Tsukimi was better with words, twisting everything Kurara said to fit her own point of view.

Frustration and anger bit at Kurara's thoughts. Every time she tried to object, the princess spat her own arguments back at her. There was no point in trying to explain how truly awful Tsukimi's views were, how wrong she was about the value of life—of freedom. There was no persuading a person like the princess.

All she could do was stand and seethe.

She turned to glance at Tomoe and Sayo, who stood with their hands up and Fujiwa's ofuda daggers pointed straight at their throats.

"Don't worry about us, Kurara! Just run!" shouted Tomoe.

"Uh-uh." Tsukimi tutted. "Did I say that you could

271

speak?" She nodded to Fujiwa, who plunged a paper dagger into Tomoe's shoulder.

The girl's body jerked with pain, but she bit her lip so that she would not scream. Sayo, on the other hand, could not keep quiet.

"Let go of her, you worm! May your bones lie rotting in the earth for eternity!" She struggled against the paper ropes holding her in place as she threatened to call down every god and demon she knew to come and smite them all.

"Quiet! Or I'll put another dagger into your friend here!" snapped Fujiwa.

Sayo clamped her mouth shut, but her eyes burned with a hatred Kurara had never seen before.

A loud bang suddenly echoed through the cavern. Something struck the ceiling, and a ridge of stalactites above their heads started to shake.

"Run!" a voice shouted from above as pieces of the cavernous ceiling began to fall.

The princess did not flinch. She did not move at all. Before she could be buried beneath the rocks, Fujiwa knocked them away with his ofuda.

"Mr. Himura!" Haru's eyes lit up.

Everyone turned just in time to see Himura jump down from his perch above one of the torii gates. He landed in the water, close to the remains of the monkey shikigami's body, and snatched up the core. Holding an ofuda knife to the wet ball of paper, he yelled at the princess. "Surrender now, or I will break this core open!"

Tsukimi turned to him, coolly. "You. Himura, wasn't it? Didn't you betray your comrade? Didn't you sell her to

272

me? What do you think you're doing—trying to save her now? What could you possibly hope to achieve with this foolishness?"

Himura met Tsukimi's gaze with a hard look of his own. "Do you know what will happen if I crack this open here? Leave now or else!"

"Mr. Himura, what are you doing?" Sayo hissed, but she looked relieved to see him nonetheless.

Kurara's feelings were far more conflicted. Had Himura been following her? She was glad he was here to help, but she also wished he had just stayed away. A dozen contrary thoughts spiraled through her as she watched the princess take a cautious step toward him.

"Watch out!" Kurara shouted as she suddenly noticed Ruki sneaking up on Himura, taking silent steps across the rubble behind him.

The tiger lunged, forcing Himura to dodge. As he did so, Fujiwa and the bald Crafter ganged up on him from opposite sides.

Before either of them could strike, Himura lifted the paper knife above his head and brought it down upon the core.

THIRTY-FIVE

IT was only a small puncture, yet it sounded as though Himura had cracked through the crust of the earth. There was a low hissing as black smoke spewed out from the needle-thin hole. It hovered in the air, forming something almost human-looking.

A shadow stood in front of her.

The creature was a mass of hands. It had no eyes or mouth. Even its head was simply a collection of fingers, overlapping to create a squashed sphere of a skull. Where its legs should have been was a pair of arms, upside down, its hands taking the place of feet. More arms wrapped around each other to form a torso. The moment Kurara laid her eyes on it, she felt something tremble through her gut. A stomach-churning cocktail of revulsion, fear and pity.

"Banri?"

No, Banri was dead, and the thing that had come out of

its core had disappeared. This was . . . this was whatever had lived inside that monkey's core.

In the distance, Kurara heard shouts of alarm, the pattering of quick footsteps—people retreating. Before she could even think of running, the shadow lurched forward—and entered her chest.

Kurara staggered forward as liquid fire ran through her veins. Pain brought her to her knees. Kurara's teeth clenched together so hard she thought they might crack. Every breath was like swallowing knives. Like burning to death and freezing alive all at once. As if something was trying to tear her core from her body.

Someone screamed right next to Kurara. She clapped her hands over her ears to block out the sound, but the voice was ringing inside her skull.

"All that lives shall die!" Men dragged a struggling boy in ragged clothes to the center of the circle where a large bonfire waited. *"As cicadas at the end of summer, as mayflies before the autumn moon, all that lives shall die, and be reborn!"*

In the next moment, Kurara found herself ejected from the memory. She staggered back, blinking as she remembered where she was.

Before she could make any sense out of what was happening, the shadowy monster began to grow in size. Darkness gathered around it like a brewing storm.

"What in the seven hells is that?" Himura swore.

"Don't tell me you cracked the core open without knowing what it would do?" Kurara wheezed as she clutched at her chest.

"Your friend Haru said—" Himura began, but whatever

275

he was about to say was lost as Ruki roared and leapt away from the shadow reaching out for it.

Fujiwa removed the ropes from Tomoe and Sayo in order to gather all his ofuda together. He brought down a rain of paper arrows over the disfigured monster, but they did nothing more than fly straight through the creature's smoke-like body.

"Don't let it touch you!" Haru shouted at Sayo and Tomoe, who were staring at the growing monstrosity in horror. "If it touches you, you'll—"

He did not get to finish his sentence. The moment he spoke, the shadowy thing lunged at Fujiwa. Ruki yanked its master out of the way and the shadow swerved around to hit the other Crafter in the chest. He screamed and clawed at his skin until he bled. His eyes bulged and his mouth began to froth before he collapsed onto the ground, completely still.

Kurara stared at the body in horror.

"Go!" Himura shouted at her. "Run! I'll take care of everything!"

"Let's go!" Kurara grabbed Haru by the wrist. If she could get Haru away from Fujiwa before the man realized what was happening, he would not be able to use Haru against her. While Fujiwa was distracted, Kurara pulled Haru toward Tomoe and Sayo. The girls sprang into action.

"Come on!" Sayo pushed Tomoe toward the tunnels as well and the four of them raced across the cavern toward the exit.

Just as they reached the end of the cavern, Ruki jumped in front of them, blocking their way.

"Move!" Kurara wrapped a long chain of ofuda around

the tiger's front paw and yanked it with all the force her mind could muster.

The shikigami cried in surprise as it lost its balance. It only took a second for Ruki to correct its stumble, but that was all the time Kurara needed. Taking Haru by the hand once more, she fled from the cavern and into the dark tunnels leading farther underground.

The passageways were narrow warrens that snaked around each other in an impossible labyrinth. Soft blue lights from luminous fungi dotted the path, but Kurara could feel the paper in the rock walls leading away from the lights, and into pitch-black darkness.

"Rara, do you know where you're going?" Haru shouted as he was pulled along in her vice-like grip.

She didn't, but there was no time to care about that. She knew they had to get away.

Pounding footsteps echoed after them. There was not a moment to waste.

The tunnel opened up into wide, uneven caves filled with shallow water. Sayo and Tomoe ran a few paces ahead, barely visible in the gloom. Just as Kurara was about to catch up, she heard Tomoe shout, "Wait! This way is a dead end too!"

The girls stood before a large chasm. On the other side was nothing but a steep wall of sheer rock. Below, soft lights glimmered, though Kurara could not tell if they were from the mushrooms that dotted the caves, man-made lanterns, or the lights of deep-sea fish shining up from beneath the water.

"What do we do now?" demanded Sayo. It was a long way down.

"What else?" cried Tomoe. "We turn back!"

Kurara was about to do just that when a paper spear struck the ground in front of her.

"Do not move!" shouted Fujiwa.

Upon his orders, Haru stiffened, but Kurara just grabbed him by the shoulder and shoved him over the edge of the chasm.

"Jump!" she yelled to the others.

"Oh, no way! Not this! Noooo!" Tomoe shrieked, but it was too late. Sayo tackled them both over the edge and they all fell together.

The wind knocked the breath from Kurara's lungs. She had plenty of experience falling through the sky, but each time she had barely managed to keep injuries to a minimum as she plummeted, face first, toward the ground. If only she could fly like Himura could. Or at least fall with grace.

Himura. She had left Himura.

There was no time to decide whether she felt guilty. It was too dark to tell where the bottom of the chasm was, but Kurara did not think she was going to enjoy finding out.

"Rara!" shouted Haru. "Remember the snail!"

That was right. She had built a paper body around herself once, she could do it again. Although it would not be quite as simple as the paper snail she had created under Haru's instructions, she was confident in the theory. Her left arm snapped off and crumbled away. With a flick of her other hand, her ofuda whirled around her limbs, clothing her in paper. Pieces of ofuda folded together around her arms to form heavy sleeves that billowed into wings. With the rest of her ofuda, she made paper ropes that she wrapped around Haru and the others.

Kurara flapped her sleeve-wings. It was not flying so much as controlled falling. Her arms strained to hold the weight of three other people as she waved them furiously, slowing down the speed of their descent.

It was difficult. It was exhausting. For every beat of her wings, Kurara felt her body jolt in a sickening motion that made her stomach clench. She gritted her teeth until they were close enough to the bottom to just about make out the ground.

With a heave of relief, Kurara released her ofuda and they fell the rest of the way, tumbling over each other as they fell onto a pile of . . . something.

Bruised and aching, Kurara lay still for a minute with her ofuda scattered around her, trying to catch her breath. At the bottom of the chasm, the ground was covered in broken statues. Empty faces stared at her with blank eyes. Bits of bird wings and the tails of what could either be dragons or snakes carpeted the ground.

She sat up with a start, gathering her ofuda back into her arm. For a moment those eyes and severed heads looked so real she thought that they might be pieces of dead shikigami, but they were statues. Just statues.

With a loud curse, Sayo and the others picked themselves up. They dusted themselves off, running their hands over their bodies as if amazed that they were still alive.

"Are you all right?" Kurara turned to Haru. He looked a little woozy. She knew that being around Fujiwa, under the influence of the Crafter's orders, exhausted him.

"I'm fine. Did we lose Fujiwa?" asked Haru.

Kurara nodded. "For now, at least."

THIRTY-SIX

THE monstrosity that had emerged from the shikigami's core was nothing like what Himura imagined a soul would look like. Its mere presence made the hairs on the back of his neck stand up. It was a black, viscous ooze. A living darkness made of a thousand hands. A violent, thrashing shadow that that seemed to seek only destruction.

Was that really what dwelled inside all shikigami? Inside all Crafters? All human beings? When flesh and paper were burned away, and only the essence of a person was left, was that what humanity was truly like on the inside?

I love you, Master. Akane's voice rang through his head, haunting, always haunting him.

Everything happened too fast. After the monster killed the other Crafter, after the man hit the ground and his crow shikigami fled, the cavern devolved into more chaos. The shadowy creature reached for him, its limbs like the tendrils of some monster from the depths. Himura jumped out of the way just as a white spear launched toward him, shot from Fujiwa's hand. He didn't know if it was aimed at him or the creature, but it missed them both—barely grazing his cheek. A thin line of blood dribbled down to his neck where it had nicked him.

Without warning, Fujiwa called the spear back to his hand and launched himself at Himura. He swung his spear with such force that he felt the wind whistling against the blade, but before it reached Himura, the weapon crumbled.

He did not have to look far to discover why Fujiwa had pulled back his ofuda. On the other side of the cavern, Kurara had disappeared into the tunnels.

"Fujiwa, go after the children. Leave this one to me!" Princess Tsukimi called.

The Crafter nodded. "Ruki, stay here and protect Her Highness!" he shouted as he raced after Kurara and the others.

The moment he spoke, Ruki turned toward Himura with a menacing growl, but Himura was not interested in attacking the princess. He had to stop Fujiwa; had to buy Kurara enough time to run.

He made a break for the tunnel, but before he could make it, he felt something enter his chest like a blade of ice.

He had been so focused on avoiding Ruki and chasing after Fujiwa, he had not noticed the shadowy creature moving toward him until it was too late.

A searing cold set his nerves aflame. It felt as though the very blood inside him had frozen. Himura did not realize he was screaming until the inside of his throat became ragged and sore. Voices flitted through his head like flies inside a rotten melon.

All that lives . . . all that lives shall die . . . May you be worthy . . . worthy of your name . . .

Someone was screaming, crying inside Himura's mind. Or maybe that was his own voice echoing back at him.

"Look out!" Something—someone—yanked him backward with such force that he felt the cold lift before it could reach his heart.

Himura's vision was red. When he breathed, there was only agony. His legs were like noodles. Suddenly unable to hold up his own weight, his body tipped backward.

He was falling forever, down, down into an endless void.

Himura's vision swam. Someone was playing the taiko drums against his skull. For a moment, all he could feel was a throbbing pain in his head.

When he tried to stand, his muscles screamed in protest. Ignoring them, he stumbled to his feet. As soon as he was upright the memories hit him like a levistone cannon. He winced. Gingerly touching the back of his head, he blanched as he felt a throbbing lump at the back of his skull. Just what had happened? He remembered fighting, remembered helping Kurara and the others escape, and then . . .

"Are you awake yet? How long do you intend to sleep?"

Himura jerked at the sound of a voice echoing inside his head. Hastily, he scrubbed his eyes and blinked until his vision came back into focus.

Mana was wrapped around the bottom of a stalactite hanging from the ceiling. Its head was level with Himura's as its scales coiled around the shard of rock.

"What are you doing here?" Himura could not help the words that tumbled out of his mouth. He blamed it on his throbbing head.

"Hmph! Master Oda did not say I could not follow you." Mana slipped from the stalactite to slither closer. *"My orders are to find Crafters and persuade them to return with me to my master. Which I am doing. You are a Crafter. I have found you. And now I will persuade you to come back to my master. Would you like to see the Grave-keeper?"*

"No, thank you," said Himura, dryly. Given how badly the first time had gone, he did not hold much hope in a second visit.

Taking a few pieces of ofuda from his bracelet, he made some paper bandages to wrap around his head while he glanced around the ruins. The cavern was empty and everyone had gone.

"What happened? Kurara and the others, the shadowy thing, Princess Tsukimi—!"

"Calm yourself," said Mana. *"As far as I know, the girl and her friends escaped. The princess went after them. And as for the monster you unleashed . . . it has wandered off."*

"You . . . Did you save me?" Himura stared at the snake in wonder.

The shikigami did not look as smug as Himura expected. *"If it had touched your heart, you would be dead. I merely pulled you back before that. Poor Zagi. Of all Master's shikigami, Zagi spent the longest time away from home. I think that affected its*

283

mind a lot. Even with a bond, Zagi was always a little unhinged. Still, it did not deserve this fate." Mana shook its head.

"That thing . . ."

"You know that shikigami are created from the souls of Crafters, do you not? Inside their cores, they are harmless, but unleashed upon the world like this . . . it is like destroying a wasps' nest without killing the wasps first. They wish to return to the warmth and safety of their cores, but they cannot, and that turns them rabid. The dead do not belong in the world of the living."

"And that *thing* is inside you? Inside all shikigami?" cried Himura. Was it inside Kurara and Haru too? Was this their soul laid bare?

"Hmph! They only turn out that way because they are forced to abide in the world of the living, in the filth and pollution of this impure world. Even the purest of monks would become twisted and corrupt!"

Himura ran a hand through his hair. Everything was a mess. Everything he had tried to achieve had ended in failure, and he was tired. He should not have let Ruki and that damn Fujiwa beat him. He should have been able to protect himself.

"Oh, cease your self-pity!" Mana snapped, as if reading his mind. *"The shikigami children escaped and the princess and her Crafters went after them. If you wish to atone by protecting that girl, then you better get a move on."*

"But I cracked open that shikigami's core. I killed it. I knew that opening the core would do something and I did it anyway, just to help Kurara." Not that she would thank him for it. If anything, she was probably angrier at him than before. Once again, he had used a shikigami's life to farther his own ends.

"*Yes, you killed another shikigami.*" Mana did not pull any punches. "*If not for you, Master Oda could have retrieved Zagi's core. What you did was awful, but what is done is done. The question is: what will you do from now on?*"

"I need to go. I need to catch up with Kurara."

She would hate him for it, of course, but Himura was fine with that. Kurara could hate him all she liked, but he would protect her. After all, she was still his student. Besides, he needed to return to the *Orihime* in time for the hunt.

He missed the crew. The thought unsettled him.

"*Then I will come with you and continue to pester you.*"

Himura stared down in shock as Mana slithered up his body and coiled itself around his waist.

"What are you doing?" He tried to prise the snake off, but Mana moved to his shoulder and clung to his arm.

"*Lending you my aid, what else?*"

"Why? What do you want from me? A bond?" Himura did not think he could bear to create another one, but at the same time, Mana was whip-smart with a twisted sense of humor that Himura found himself actually liking. If he was honest, he wanted Mana to come with him, not because the snake was magically compelled to do so, but because Mana had chosen to stay by his side of its own free will.

"*Bond?*" snorted Mana. "*How ridiculous! I told you; I am fulfilling my master's orders. Would you like to meet the Grave-keeper?*"

"No," said Himura, emphatically.

"*A pity.*" Mana sniffed. "*I shall ask you again tomorrow.*"

285

Himura understood what the snake was doing; he had just never seen a shikigami do it before. Mana had no choice but to obey its master's orders, but it was fulfilling Oda's commands in a way that let it accompany Himura. "Will you be all right?" Himura ignored how strange it felt to ask after a shikigami's well-being.

"What a ridiculous question!" the snake snapped. *"Of course I will be all right! Now stop flapping your gums and let us move!"*

Something inside Himura seemed to unfurl. He did not have a name for the feeling, but he could describe the symptoms: how his pulse quickened, the way his stomach flipped and his breath seemed to catch in his throat.

"Why are you doing this?"

"Because you are a fool."

Himura supposed that was true enough. After all, he had betrayed Kurara and lost Akane. His parents had insisted that their ancestors were people full of greatness, but all he had learned was that they were monsters who had sacrificed each other and fought one another to their very own downfall.

Mana flicked its tongue out in the equivalent of a grin. *"And I am very fond of fools."*

Interlude

No matter how much you feed it
That howling part of you
Is always hungry

—From *Conversations with Yōkai*
(banned by the Patriots Office)

Princess Tsukimi stood on the edge of the chasm, looking down into the unending darkness. She noticed Fujiwa and Ruki skirting around her, watching her with caution. After the shadowy thing had killed Himura, it had drifted elsewhere, phasing through the cavern's walls.

It had been disgusting. Abhorrent. Like something that had crawled its way out of the wasteland of Yomi.

Just like Ugetsu had described, it would make for an excellent weapon. This was why Tsukimi liked shikigami: they were always so full of interesting new uses.

"There's a soul," she murmured as she replayed back everything that had happened in the last hour since meeting Kurara.

"Your Highness?" Fujiwa peered at her with concern.

A bright grin split Tsukimi's face. "I knew I was on the right track! I knew shikigami had souls within them, but Kurara has confirmed it!" She had suspected something of the sort when Ugetsu had described the monster to her, but after seeing it she was sure that she was right. The experiments in her workshop, the orphans and annoying maids she had sacrificed for her research, had not been in vain after all. She had been close to the right formula, so close.

What else did she need? How did one bind a soul to a core? Was the way she drew the sacrificial circle correct? Was she burning her sacrifices correctly? Kurara and Haru seemed to know. Tsukimi would ask them.

She just had to make those shikigami children hers first.

Tossing her head back, the princess gave a howling laugh. Did no one else see how the world bent to her wishes? She wanted the shikigami children. She wanted to know how to make shikigami—real shikigami that would obey a Crafter, and finally, one that would obey her. She wanted to know more about the shadowy creature that emerged from the broken core.

In capturing those shikigami children, she could learn everything. The world had conspired so that, in chasing after one desire, all her other desires would be granted as well. Was that not evidence that the very universe was on her side? Was that not undeniable proof that she was someone special?

Despite the lack of light, Tsukimi took a step toward the rim of the rocky ledge and leaned over into the chasm below.

"And you're sure they jumped down there?"

"Certain," said Fujiwa. "Your Highness, please step away from the edge."

Tsukimi did no such thing. She leaned farther, squinting down at the last place her prey had been spotted. She could not see the bottom of the chasm, though she supposed that did not matter to someone who could control paper.

Her hands curled into fists. Whoever said jealousy was an ugly emotion had never seen how well she could wear it.

No, there was no need for envy. The world would eventually give her what she wanted. All she had to do was be patient and follow her desires, and she would be rewarded with a shikigami of her own and the powers that should have been hers by birthright: the gifts that her Crafter mother had failed to pass on to her.

"Your Imperial Highness?" said Fujiwa.

Contrary to the way the Crafter skirted around her, Princess Tsukimi was not angry. No, Tsukimi enjoyed a good hunt; the thrill of outsmarting and eventually cornering her prey was all the more satisfying when they struggled.

Fujiwa watched her with a hesitant look. "Your Imperial Highness, if I may, Goro is dead and his shikigami has disappeared. Perhaps it is best we withdraw and—"

Princess Tsukimi suppressed a sigh. Really, it wasn't Fujiwa's fault he was so dim. She loved Crafters, but some really did have paper for brains.

"Withdraw? Fujiwa, do you doubt your ability to protect me?"

The Crafter gave her a terrified smile. "No, Your Highness, not at all."

Tsukimi grinned. "Then let us be off."

A hunt was no fun without a little bloodshed.

THIRTY-SEVEN

A S soon as everyone gathered themselves, Tomoe grabbed Kurara by the shoulders and pulled her into a bone-crushing hug.

"Kurara! Bloody skies, thank goodness you're here! Just look at you—all not dead and everything!"

The moment she got over her surprise, Kurara relaxed into Tomoe's embrace. It really was good to see Tomoe and Sayo again. After she had woken up in Kazami, so much had happened she had not had time to truly think of her friends. Being with them now made her realize how much she had missed their company.

"Hey, don't I get a hug too?" Haru smiled sheepishly.

"No," growled Sayo.

"You're bleeding." Kurara noticed the damp red patch seeping across Tomoe's kimono.

"I am, aren't I? I think I might be a little giddy too. Not

sure if that's the relief or the blood loss." There was a slight tinge of hysteria to Tomoe's laughter.

Sayo tore off the hem of her skirt to use as a bandage. With deft fingers, she wrapped Tomoe's bleeding shoulder.

"Keep some pressure on the wound. If you pass out, we'll have to carry you like a sack of rice. And these two will probably drop you."

"It's good to see you too, Sayo," said Kurara. Sayo sighed and rolled her eyes, which was as close to affection as anyone aside from Tomoe could get from her.

"Come on," she said. "Let's move before Fujiwa catches up with us."

They all began to make their way over the mound of statues littering the chasm floor. The huge pile of broken marble and stone created a small mound that led upward to the only passage out of the chasm that Kurara could see.

Tomoe grunted as they staggered up the mound of crumbling statues. She was doing her best not to show how much her injury was slowing her down, but every time they stopped, she slumped against Sayo, who hovered besides her like a mother hen. "So, are we going to talk about what in the blue skies all that was? Especially that smoke monster. It killed that Crafter when it touched him, but you were fine."

No, Kurara thought, she had not been fine. Just like when that thing inside Banri's core had touched her, she had seen glimpses of a shikigami's memory.

"Before we talk about that, first tell us how you ended up in Princess Tsukimi's clutches," said Haru.

Sayo recounted everything that had happened after

291

the *Kuroi Kame* was destroyed—how they had washed up somewhere and encountered Zagi, the large monkey shikigami that had led them to Kazami, and how they had been captured by Princess Tsukimi.

"The princess brought us with her as hostages to use against you. Though she didn't know you would be at Kazami." Sayo swore as several bits of broken statue slipped beneath her feet, tumbling down to the bottom of the chasm where they crashed to the ground with a resounding echo.

The higher they climbed, the steeper the incline. Kurara felt guilty for making Tomoe stagger after her, but they could not afford to linger here. They were almost at the top of the stone heap. If she squinted, Kurara could see the small tunnel above them. Once they reached the very top of the mound, they could finally get out of this creepy place.

It was Haru's turn to share the story of Banri's demise and meeting Oda, and the truth about shikigami and what—who—they were. Kurara could not help but feel guilty as she listened to Haru recount everything she had told him. Banri was still out there. Or rather, Banri's soul was still out there, wandering the coast where the shikigami had died. Was it frightened? Was it in pain? She shuddered to think that kind, shy Banri could still be suffering long after its body had been destroyed.

Tomoe and Sayo were silent as they climbed. The fact that shikigami were human seemed to affect them, though Kurara suspected that it would not stop them from hunting—the shikigami they targeted would hurt and kill people if they were allowed to roam free—though perhaps the next time they dealt with one, they would be just that little bit gentler.

Kurara took over the story, telling them about Himura and Akane.

Saying it made it feel all the more real. She wished she at least had some incense to light for Akane, some wine with which to toast the shikigami's passing. She supposed most people did not mourn when a shikigami died, and that itself left a bitter feeling inside her chest.

"Akane?" Tomoe's voice shook. "I can't believe it. I know he betrayed you, but to let Akane die . . . I never thought Himura would go that far."

"Even so, he is a member of the *Orihime*. We shouldn't have left him," said Sayo.

"If you want to go back and get him, be my guest," snapped Kurara.

To her surprise, Sayo clamped her mouth shut.

Once they reached the top, Kurara hauled herself into the tunnel and crawled through the passage until it opened up into another series of caves. She lifted a hand to the wall. Embedded in the rock, she felt the presence of paper guiding her through the dark. "Follow me. I'll lead the way," she said.

They plunged into the pitch black tunnels. Soon . . . Soon Kurara would come face to face with Suzaku, and then she would find out the truth. The weight of the future and the freedom of all shikigami relied on this meeting. With each step forward, she felt the crushing pressure of responsibility bear down on her shoulders. "When we reach the Grand Stream, let me talk to Suzaku for a bit," she said.

She could not see Tomoe and Sayo's expressions in the dark, but she noticed them pause before they replied.

"If it attacks us, we're fighting back," said Sayo, which was as good an agreement as she was going to get.

"Everyone knows Suzaku is mad," said Tomoe. "Or at least half-mad. I don't know if it'll tell you anything useful."

Kurara knew that. Maybe when she reached the Grand Stream, Suzaku would do nothing but ramble and screech. Perhaps the shikigami would not remember her at all. Or maybe it would only want to peck her eyes out, but she had to try to speak to it. The shikigami was the only one that might know something about the Star Seed.

They kept a brisk pace, conscious that Ruki and Fujiwa might come crashing through the tunnels right behind them at any moment. After what felt like hours of walking, the tunnels opened up into another vast cave full of paper-like buildings and bridges. Stone lanterns lined the way from the front of the cavern, across a wide white bridge and beneath a rotting torii gate covered in mushrooms that bunched together like clouds.

Kurara traced the path as it snaked past tall pagodas and lotus-shaped fountains, all of them covered in the same cloud-like fungi that flung their spores into the air. She brushed them from her clothes as the path wound upward. When she looked at the crumbling buildings around her, Kurara remembered the scorch marks and bone fragments in the last ruins. She remembered the shikigami symbol hidden beneath the ground. Though she did not feel any paper hidden beneath her feet here, a shudder ran up her body.

"Kazami is a place of misery and death," Oda had said.

Suddenly, she heard Tomoe shout, "Aha, look at this!"

As they came to the edge of the cavern, a set of double doors loomed over them, blocking the way forward.

Tomoe prepared to brace her good shoulder against one side of the door. "Sayo, I'm going to need you to push with me."

Before Sayo could take up position on the other side, Kurara's ofuda unravelled and slammed against the stone.

The doors flew open upon impact.

"Oh, right. I forgot you could do that," muttered Tomoe.

Kurara did her best not to smirk.

Clutching her shoulder, Tomoe hobbled through the door. On the other side was an unlit passage slowly sloping upward. It was too dark to tell what was on the other side. There were only rocks and dirt and shadows as far as Kurara could see. She stretched out her hand; there was no paper in the walls. She would have to walk through this tunnel without a guide.

She handed Sayo the map of Kazami. After a quick look, Sayo nodded. "This tunnel should take us up and out into the center of the Grand Stream."

"Say, when we reach the Grand Stream, the *Orihime* will be there, won't it?" Tomoe peered uncertainly into the dark.

"Here's hoping," said Sayo.

"What do you mean 'here's hoping'?" cried Tomoe. "You're supposed to say yes! 'Yes, Tomoe, they will definitely be there because the *Orihime* is amazing and nothing can stand in the crew's way'!"

Sayo scowled at her. "Well, excuse me for being realistic."

"Quiet!" hissed Kurara. She raised a hand to her ear. "I hear something."

Everyone stopped to listen to a high-pitched whistle in the distance. A howl muffled by layers of rock and dirt.

"Is that . . . the wind?"

A gentle draft played with the ends of her hair. The Grand Stream had to be close. Kurara clenched her hands into fists. A thousand worries she had never let herself dwell on suddenly crowded her thoughts. All this time she had been heading toward Suzaku, certain that if she met with the shikigami, she would learn about the Star Seed, but what if that was wrong? What if Suzaku didn't know anything? What if Haru and Oda's suspicions were right and there was no Star Seed?

"Come on." Sayo nudged her. "Let's go. Back to the sky."

Kurara nodded. It was too late to back out now.

THIRTY-EIGHT

THE walls of the tunnel seemed to grow narrower as they walked. The ceiling felt as though it was slowly crushing them as the ground sloped upward. By the time Kurara saw a square of light shining in the distance, she was crawling on her hands and knees.

A swift breeze blew through the passage, bringing with it the smell of fresh grass. This was it: the way back to the surface. Kurara crawled forward, hardly caring for her sore knees or the dirt catching beneath her nails, until she reached the end of the tunnel.

For a moment, the light was so blinding that Kurara saw nothing but white. It was only when her vision returned that she found herself at the edge of a large impact crater, staring across the land at the trees and lakes contained within it.

She quickly stumbled to her feet. The ground around her curved like a bowl, the tall rock walls arcing upward toward the clouds. There were several tunnels around the edges of the crater leading back down into Kazami, but Kurara's gaze was not fixed on the outskirts but upon the center of the crater, where the water had collected to form a series of small lakes and ponds that glittered in the sunlight. Trees awash with vibrant emerald leaves bent their branches low to touch the water's surface.

The wind howled louder than before. People often said that the only calm part of a hurricane was its center, but Kurara had not believed them until now. A blustering storm swirled around the outside, forming an impassable barrier of wind, but within the crater the air was perfectly still.

Somewhere in the distance, hidden by the whirling gales, Suzaku beat its white wings. The sound vibrated through the air like a thundering drum. Kurara could see neither the bird nor the *Orihime*, but surely they were out there somewhere, behind the curtain of wind.

"Do you smell that?" Tomoe lifted a sleeve to cover her face and nose.

Kurara sniffed. She caught the scent of grass and sunbaked earth, but nothing more. They were certainly not unpleasant smells, at least not to her, but perhaps a Sorabito thought differently.

"Blood." Tomoe grimaced. "It's faint, but it's still there. The smell of blood and wet earth. Of levistone."

No matter how hard she tried, Kurara could not catch the scent Tomoe described, but when she squinted at the crater walls, she did notice thin blue lines glowing softly through the rock.

Levistone veins.

"Never mind that. Where's the *Orihime*?" Sayo desperately scanned the sky for a glimpse of their airship, but Kurara was looking for something else.

"Suzaku!" Kurara screamed up at the blustery sky. "Suzaku, I'm here!"

Her eyes were watering as she stared up at the hurricane. Bits of tree and rock and what looked like the remains of airships that had been ripped apart by the winds swirled through the clouds.

"Suzaku!" Kurara shouted until her throat burned. Would it recognize her voice? Would it still be angry at . . . whatever it was she had done? Or had the shikigami forgotten her?

Just then, a white blur swooped through the whirling storm. If she squinted, Kurara could just about make out a trail of long tail feathers streaming behind it like banners torn in the wind.

The next thing she knew, a sudden quake shook the ground beneath her feet as Suzaku landed on the edge of the crater. When it came to a stop, the winds around it began to die down, dropping trees and rocks and bits of broken ships to the ground. Debris fell both inside and outside the crater, causing the earth to shake each time. At last, Suzaku came to perch on the edge of the crater wall, its talons biting into the rock as it stared down at her through a single, beady white eye.

"Aki, there you are." The phoenix sounded just as furious as it had in her dreams.

It had not forgotten her at all.

"Uh, Kurara, maybe this is a bad idea!" Tomoe tugged at her sleeve, but Kurara did not move. She stared right back at Suzaku as the giant phoenix stretched its long, swan-like neck toward her.

The shikigami was large enough to swallow her whole. Just one jab of its beak could create chasms in the ground. Its wings spread like a fan, creating an impenetrable curtain of paper feathers.

Kurara had no idea what to say. "Hello" might be a good start, but she doubted Suzaku would appreciate it, and "Hi, I don't actually remember why you're angry at me" would probably only anger it even more.

Without warning, Suzaku flapped its wings. Kurara acted on instinct, her arm unfurling into a hardened shield that protected her and the others from the sudden blast of wind. Though she had strengthened her ofuda, the gale still ripped apart the corners of her paper, and tore the nearby trees from the ground.

"Aki!" screeched Suzaku.

In hindsight, she probably should have practiced what she wanted to say before coming here. Kurara had no idea how to calm the enraged shikigami, but she did know that she—or Aki, rather—had probably hurt it. When someone was hurt, there was only one thing anyone could say to them.

"Suzaku, I'm sorry." She took a cautious step forward. "I did something awful to you, didn't I? Well, I'm sorry for what I did. And I'm also sorry because I can't remember it."

The phoenix lifted its head to the sky and let out a piercing screech that seemed to make the very air around them tremble. Kurara and the others slapped their hands over their ears as the sound slammed into them as hard as a punch.

"I know that saying sorry might not mean anything to you, but if you can tell me what I did, maybe I can fix things!" She would do anything if Suzaku would just calm down and *talk* to her.

"What you did to me? To us, to us, to all of us! Eternity is the bladed edge of a knife! The present only cuts us deeper!" the bird screeched at her.

"It's not making any sense! The thing's stark raving mad!" snapped Sayo.

Kurara pulled the girl back before she could spring into an attack. They could still reason with Suzaku. At least, she hoped they could.

"Where is the Star Seed?" she yelled up at the towering shikigami.

"How dare you! How dare you!" Suzaku was not listening. The phoenix was so caught up in its rage, it could only glower and scream. Kurara wanted to be patient. She wanted to be understanding, but frustration was beginning to claw at her throat. She wanted answers, not this rambling nonsense.

"Suzaku," she said, as slowly and calmly as she could. "There's a ship coming to hunt you. I'm trying to find a way for shikigami to have their freedom, for them to live without worrying about bonds or losing their minds! If you don't tell me what happened to the Star Seed, then I can't protect you."

The phoenix screeched. *"You had the Star Seed! It was given to you so that* you *might protect it!"*

That was the last thing Kurara wanted to hear. She didn't have it! Had she lost it? Had it been destroyed?

"Then what happened? After you gave the Seed to me, what happened?"

"The past shall catch up with you all. There is no escape!"

"Suzaku, concentrate!" snapped Kurara. "What happened to the Star Seed?"

"The Star Seed is where you left it!"

"And where is that? Please! I don't remember!"

"It's gone mad! Either that or it's lying to you, Rara!" cried Haru. "There is no Star Seed. It doesn't exist!"

Suzaku reared back, enraged. *"Liar? The only liar here is Aki! Traitor and murderer!"*

Kurara's core dropped into her stomach. Liar? Murderer?

"Have you forgotten how we were made, Aki? Have you forgotten what you did to us?"

Kurara sucked in a sharp breath. Us. It kept calling itself "us."

Suzaku screeched. *"We, the people of Kazami, are eternal! We remember, though other shikigami forget! We were human and we remember what you did to us!"*

The shikigami's words thundered through Kurara like a storm. She clutched her head and tried to remember just what it was talking about. What had she done? No, whatever happened wasn't her fault. It was Aki. What had Aki done?

There had been a fire in Kazami. There were bones scattered along the ruins. A shikigami circle etched into the ground. Fire, but no ash. Bones, but no ash. Scorch marks upon the ruins, but no ash!

Kurara clutched her head as a dozen voices screamed in her ears.

"This is the only way to keep the Star Seed safe!"

"Are you insane? I didn't agree to this! None of us agreed to it!"

"Please, Lady Aki, you promised us an honorable death!"

Flames flickered at the back of her mind. Kurara remembered . . . she remembered a fire.

There had been a fire in Kazami.

An eight-pointed star within a circle used to create shikigami.

Someone must have used the ashes from that fire. No, not just "someone." Aki. Her. Kurara.

She had created a shikigami from the people of Kazami.

She had created Suzaku.

"No, no, that's impossible!" she groaned as she clutched her head. It felt as though her skull was going to split in two. "No, I came to Kazami to help the people, not kill them! I didn't kill them! I didn't kill anyone!"

Distantly, she was aware of Haru and the others shouting her name. She could hear the worry in their tone, but their voices were so very distant, as if they were calling from somewhere far below the ocean's surface.

Kurara squeezed her eyes shut and fell to her knees as the pain became blinding. In her mind's eye, she could see the caverns of Kazami before they had become ruins—the bell towers standing tall, the buildings as white as paper, and the stairs neatly carved out of the rock leading upward, past magnificent statues of shikigami to neat bridges that arched over the water. She saw a man. She saw herself. She . . . She . . .

She remembered.

———————o———————

"Take it, Lady Aki! It will be safer in your hands. This is the last one, and I want you to have it."

The Crafter placed something the size of a pine cone in her hand.

A Star Seed. The last one.

Kurara blinked, and suddenly she was standing in one of Kazami's many caves. Some of the buildings had crumbled and others were covered in cracks. In the distance, she heard the sound of men screaming, of blades clashing against blades, and the heat of battle.

"It's too late, they have us surrounded! If they capture us, they'll turn us into shikigami!"

"They're collapsing the tunnels! They're blocking our way out!"

Kurara's fingers tightened around the Star Seed. "I won't let that happen! I promise you, I will lead you all to an honorable death!" she heard herself say. She had meant it. At the time, she had meant it, but as her surroundings flickered and changed once more, she knew it was a lie.

When she blinked again, Kazami was in ruins and they were overrun. Most of the tunnels leading back to the surface were blocked, and the few that remained were occupied by the enemy. They were trapped and outnumbered, their men and women ragged from the constant fighting, and hope was dwindling fast.

Still, Kurara clutched the Star Seed to her chest. Even if Kazami fell, she had to protect the Seed at all costs. She needed a hiding place. She needed a weapon.

They're all going to die anyway. If the enemy catches them, their only fate is to become shikigami. I have to do what must be done.

———o———

Kurara emerged from the depths of her mind, wide-eyed and gasping for breath.

Echoes of long-dead voices haunted her. Shaking off the last dregs of her memories, she stumbled back onto her shaky feet and stared at Suzaku.

She remembered setting up a shikigami circle in one of Kazami's main caves, remembered telling the people of the village to lure the enemies to them, remembered promising them a glorious last stand that people would speak about for eternity.

The phoenix glared back at her, coldly. *"You remember. Now you know your guilt! Liar and traitor! Murderer!"*

Without realizing it, Kurara clutched her hand to her chest. "You . . . You were all going to be turned into shikigami anyway! At least I was able to use your life for something noble! Something worthwhile!" she cried.

"Use us," Suzaku hissed. *"Yes, use us. Use us, use us, use us, like tools! Like all the other Crafters do!"*

Kurara flinched, but she did not dare look away from Suzaku. There was no way she could bring herself to glance at Haru and the others, to see the judgment on their faces.

"If I hadn't done anything, the Star Seed would have been destroyed! It was for the greater good!"

"The greater good!" scoffed Suzaku. *"It was for yourself! Aki, you selfish monster, if you wanted us to have our freedom, why didn't you plant the Seed? Why did you hide it away for all these years? Why did you continue to allow shikigami to be born and destroyed without doing anything? Why? WHY DID YOU RUN AWAY?"*

Kurara fought back the tears stinging her eyes.

Everything that Suzaku said was true, wasn't it? She had run away, forgotten everything important just because it hurt, and lived a normal life on the *Midori*.

"Do you know what it is like inside our body? Inside our head? My core—our core—is naught but a dozen squirming souls writing and screaming for control. Not only did you betray us, look what you have done! A shikigami with multiple souls— an abomination that only one such as you could dream up!"

She did not want to hear anymore. The more Suzaku spoke, the more she remembered. She had been desperate— there had been no time for her to make several shikigami, not with enemy Crafters on their way to steal the Star Seed.

"The Seed. Where is it now?" Kurara remembered holding it, remembered keeping it safe against her chest as the fire raged on. That was where her memory ended. What had happened to the Seed afterward?

Suzaku screeched as it flapped its wings. Another blast of wind tore through the rest of the trees and ripped loose boulders from the crater walls. *"Traitor! The people of Kazami trusted you to keep it safe and yet—and yet! We remember, though other shikigami forget! For eternity! Eternity! If you want the Seed, take it! It's right where you left it! Here, inside our core!"*

"What?"

She had put the Seed inside Suzaku's core when she had made the shikigami? Horror cut deep. So that was why Suzaku was so furious with her. All this time, she had been disgusted at Himura's actions and shocked at Oda's ploys, when she was ten times worse than the both of them.

"Take it if you can, Aki!" Suzaku screamed. *"Rip out my heart and take it!"*

Kurara thought of the bones they had found in the inner caves, the scorch marks on the buildings, the symbol carved into the ground with paper. Killing people. Burning them. Turning the very humans who had given her the Seed into a shikigami . . . She could not imagine any version of herself doing something so cruel.

If she wanted the Seed back, she would have to destroy Suzaku. Once the core was gone, there was no way to bring a shikigami back. She did not want to kill anyone. Yet she had already killed so many.

"Rara."

She jumped at the weight of Haru's hand on her shoulder. She had almost forgotten that he had been here the whole time, listening. Kurara was too afraid to look at him. She had not told him what she had done when she had asked Haru to erase her memories, leaving him only to guess that her failure to protect the Star Trees had been too much to bear. Surely, he must hate her now that he knew the truth.

"Rara, you can give up if you want to. Even if Suzaku is telling the truth, even if the Star Seed is real and is inside its core, you don't have to do anything about it." Haru's voice was soft. Understanding. With an unshakable kindness that made her want to cry.

Kurara shook her head, but the moment she opened her mouth, a loud shot rang out across the crater. In the blink of an eye, a white harpoon buried itself in Suzaku's chest.

The phoenix staggered, eyes widening in surprise, but it did not fall. The shikigami was far too big to be taken down by a single paper harpoon.

The weapon yanked itself free and disintegrated into

a hundred tiny squares of paper. Kurara followed the trail of ofuda as they whirled past her and toward the crater walls.

Toward the princess and her imperial Crafter.

Tsukimi's eyes narrowed as she stared back at Kurara.

"Poor girl," she purred sweetly, even as her eyes shone with malevolence. "Don't you know there's no point reasoning with beasts?"

THIRTY-NINE

"DO you want it?" Tsukimi smiled at her—the grin of a woman who enjoyed playing with her food. She did not look angry at all that Kurara and Haru had escaped. In fact, her face was flushed from the thrill of the chase. "Do you want that creature's core? I'll get it for you. I'll give you anything you want. If you join me."

Kurara said nothing. She could not bring herself to speak, too shocked by Suzaku's words to say or do anything. Had she really put the Seed inside Suzaku's core? Had she really turned the people of Kazami into a shikigami, forcing all those souls to coexist inside a single body?

She had killed those people. Everyone in Kazami was dead because of her. She had created Suzaku and put the Seed in its core to stop anyone from finding it ever again.

Haru had told her that the two of them had fought hard to protect the Star Trees and grant shikigami their freedom.

Perhaps that had been true at the beginning, but as time went on, Aki began to care less about freedom and more about punishment.

"If you were still Aki, you would agree that Crafters deserve to be punished!" Oda had snarled at her. *"Isn't this divine punishment?"* Haru had asked.

Kurara could trace the circle of Aki's thoughts. If Crafters were bad people and shikigami, were just Crafters, then all of them were just as rotten as each other. It was cruel. It was illogical. It was a snake eating its own tail. Where did the blame end? Aki had not considered, as Kurara did, that once someone became a shikigami, they were a different person. Aki had been too frustrated, too angry. She had simply wanted everyone to suffer.

Who are you? she wanted to ask her past self. She felt like a stranger in her own body. No matter how hard she tried, Kurara just could not picture a version of herself who had thought those things, a past self who had prioritized her own rage over the freedom of the shikigami. She thought about Akane and Banri and Mana, about all the shikigami she had met. Kurara did not know what they had been like as Crafters, but she did not care. They deserved their freedom.

She stared at the crater walls in shock. Suzaku flapped its wings, trying to dislodge the spear that had missed its core but remained embedded in its chest. The force of its wings blew boulders across the ground like tumbleweeds. The wind howled. Clouds as large as cumulus whales swirled around the crater, and the sky was gray with the threat of rain.

"Try to take it if you wish! We shall destroy you all!"

On Princess Tsukimi's command, Fujiwa readied another spear.

Kurara snapped out of her thoughts.

"I told you that nothing you do will make me obey you! I don't want anything to do with *you!*" she hissed.

"You disappoint me." Tsukimi looked truly mournful. "It seems the only use I'll have for you is as an empty core that I can crack open and study."

"You can do that and it still won't make you a Crafter. You can study me all you like and you'll still never have a shikigami!" Kurara gathered her ofuda around her, ready to strike.

The whirling hurricane of paper did not deter the princess. Tsukimi merely adjusted her grip on the hilt of her katana. "Oh, I will. I told you before: there are no impossibilities in this world, only problems that do not yet have solutions. And I am very good at finding solutions."

"Then find a solution to this!" Kurara's ofuda surged toward the princess like a swarm of angry wasps. Fujiwa extended a wall of paper between them, blocking the blow. When Kurara drew back her ofuda to prepare for a second strike, he flung a paper spear at her.

Kurara knocked his weapon out of the air just as Princess Tsukimi drew her pistol and fired. There was no time to dodge the bullet, but Kurara knew the trick behind Tsukimi's gun. She had fallen for it once before; she was not going to do so again.

Though the bullet seemed to fly straight toward her, Kurara was ready. Her paper arm grew into a claw. She anticipated the way the bullet would swerve around her back and spun around, deflecting the shot with a piece of hardened paper.

Ruki flung itself at her. The sight of the giant shikigami barreling toward her at full speed was a lot like standing in the path of an avalanche, but Kurara held her ground. As the shikigami lunged for her, Kurara tossed a handful of ofuda into the air. The paper floated in midair, folding and hardening into a sword. The tip of the blade pierced its body, tearing a deep gouge along its forehead.

Ruki howled. A blow like that would have killed a normal tiger, but Kurara had missed its core, leaving only a hollow gash in the middle of its forehead.

"Ruki, deal with the Sorabito children instead!" Fujiwa ordered as he flung spear after spear of ofuda at Kurara. "Haru, stop the girl and pull out her core!"

"Of course, Master!" Despite how awful Fujiwa's commands were, Haru chirped cheerfully and caught the large paper ōdachi that Fujiwa threw to him.

The sword was easily as long as Haru's arm, but he swung it as if it weighed no more than a feather. As Kurara blocked one of his blows, she felt the force of the strike vibrate up her arm.

"Haru, stop!" She parried left, trying to avoid hurting Haru while also avoiding his sword.

"Why don't you stop, Rara!" Haru shot right back at her. The white edge of his blade glinted in the sun as it arced through the air. "Think about it! Why not give the core to Princess Tsukimi? Isn't that what your ship was going to do anyway?"

Their blades clashed once more. Kurara noticed Ruki leap toward Tomoe and Sayo. The girls scattered like sparrows. They flitted around the tiger, avoiding its claws by a hair's breadth that would have made Kurara's core jump to her throat if she was not so distracted trying to keep her own attackers at bay.

With a flick of his hand, Fujiwa sent a dozen paper spears flying toward her. Kurara was too busy dealing with Haru to dodge, but before his ofuda could hit their target, Suzaku stabbed its beak between them, blocking the attack and leaving a huge hole in the ground as it reared back. How fitting that a shikigami created by shikigami was far stronger than anything a regular Crafter had created. Suzaku was power incarnate.

"Aki, come! Either you kill us or we shall destroy you!" Suzaku spread its wings wide as if to embrace her.

Kurara gritted her teeth together. If she cracked open Suzaku's core, if she *killed* Suzaku and took the Seed, she could save so many other shikigami—but wouldn't that make her just like those Crafters from long ago? Those despicable people who had no qualms about killing a shikigami as long as it farthered their own goals?

"I wouldn't if I were you," said Princess Tsukimi, coolly. "You heard the beast. It's not a normal shikigami. Inside that core there are hundreds, perhaps thousands, of writhing little souls. If you crack it open, what do you think will happen?"

As much as Kurara hated to admit it, the princess was right. The thing that had come from Banri's core, from Zagi's core—those unleashed souls—had been terrifying. How many souls were inside Suzaku? Kurara imagined unleashing a whole army of those things on the world and shuddered. A shikigami's core was strong; it would not rot on its own. The only way to safely deal with it would be to burn it, like one burned a shikigami, but doing so would burn the Seed inside it too.

How was she going to get the Seed out without causing a calamity?

Fujiwa opened his mouth to bark another order at Haru, but his words were drowned out by a sudden thunderous boom. Cannonballs streaked through the sky like comets, some striking Suzaku's chest and neck while others fell into the crater in a cloud of dirt.

"There it is! The *Orihime*!" Tomoe suddenly pointed to the sky.

"Where?" Sayo craned her neck up.

"There!" Tomoe gestured to a white dot above them.

Kurara could not help but glance at the sky for just a moment. There was indeed a ship bearing down upon them, but it did not look like the *Orihime*. As it came closer, Kurara could make out its white hull and sleek curves. Gold lettering across the side proclaimed the ship's name as the *Hotei*.

"That's an imperial ship!" cried Sayo.

Once the ship was directly above Suzaku, the bottom of the *Hotei* opened, and a large barrel of something tumbled out of the sky. When the canisters hit, they burst open, drenching the phoenix in a strange, bluish liquid that smelled suspiciously of blood and earth.

Kurara had spent enough time in the *Orihime*'s engine room to recognize the smell.

Liquid levistone.

Cannon fire stormed the sky. Flaming cannonballs hurtled toward them, striking the ground at random in a shower of dirt and flames.

"Holy skies, where are they aiming?" Tomoe screeched as a fiery cannonball landed mere feet away, sending a shower of soil over her head.

Both Haru and Kurara leapt out of the way as another struck close by, but Suzaku was not as lucky. The bird was a larger target, and as Suzaku caught alight, the flames licked along its wings and down its back. Wreathed in fire, it almost looked like an actual phoenix.

"Idiots!" cried Sayo. "They'll burn the whole shikigami and the core with it!"

Even Princess Tsukimi and Fujiwa seemed outraged by the ship's sudden appearance. If the ship was trying to avoid hitting the princess, they were certainly not doing a good job; cannon fire continued to rain all around them.

Screeching in anger, Suzaku rose into the air.

Kurara knew she had to do something and fast. She could either give up on ever getting the Star Seed or she could destroy Suzaku's body, take its core and run, but she had to make a choice and make it now. If she dithered any longer, they would all burn to a crisp.

What was the right thing to do?

Using her ofuda as a springboard, Kurara launched herself into the air. With a snap of her fingers, her ofuda swirled into a tail that flared outward across the ground. Paper bound to her legs, forming long talons and clothing her in paper feathers. The wings were almost as big as Suzaku's. She was a puppeteer inside a giant paper bird, controlling the wings and tail from within.

With a flap of feathers, she took off.

FORTY

FLYING was not as easy as birds made it seem. Though she was not as large as Suzaku, Kurara kept tipping to one side as she flew. Every time she tried to turn, her body wobbled and canted too far.

She flapped her wings and shot through the heart of a cloud, feeling the icy droplets run down her face. Higher and higher she soared until she thought she might touch the sun and swallow the stars. The rush of air seared through her lungs. Her paper feathers whistled through the wind.

It was exhilarating. It was exhausting.

"Suzaku!" she tried to shout over the cacophony of sounds, but the shikigami only screamed and writhed in the air as the flames climbed up its body ever higher and cannon fire erupted all around.

Kurara gritted her teeth and tried to close the distance between them as her mind raced. Would she really crack open Suzaku's core? Would she really kill Suzaku? And what about the things that would be unleashed when she did? They would spread across the country. They would kill people. Was Kurara prepared to shoulder the responsibility of that?

Haru had once asked her: *"Knowing what they used to be, do you really think shikigami deserve freedom? Isn't this just karma for what they did as humans? Isn't this divine punishment?"*

If Kurara let the Seed burn away with Suzaku, nothing would change. The world would continue as it had always done.

Was that so bad?

What was the right thing to do?

No, what did she *want* to do? Haru had asked her that question before. He had told her to forget what was right or wrong, forget her duties and responsibilities. What did she want?

When Kurara asked herself that question, there was no doubt in her mind.

She wanted only to give the shikigami their freedom.

The white airship battled against the winds that grew as Suzaku flapped its wings. From her position, Kurara looked down onto the ship's deck to see soldiers rushing to regain control.

Straining her mind and body to its limits, she chased after Suzaku as it began to circle around the crater. Cannonballs streaked past her as she veered and dived out of the way. As she finally got closer, she released the ofuda around her, letting her wings crumble away.

As Kurara fell, she pulled her ofuda together to form

317

a long spear almost as large as Suzaku itself. It hung in the sky like a weapon wielded by an invisible god. Then, without warning, it shot toward Suzaku, impaling the shikigami through its chest.

Suzaku hit the ground with a resounding crash. It lay there, motionless and burning, for several terrible minutes before it slowly hauled itself up on trembling wings. Everyone froze as they watched the shikigami drag itself to the lake.

"*We are the people of Kazami,*" it groaned.

With Kurara's spear still embedded in its body, the shikigami's movements were slow and torturous. The sound of crackling flames and the smell of smoke filled the crater.

The shikigami collapsed into the lake. Streams of water shot into the air, steam rising with a hiss as the flames were doused. Suzaku lay on its back, unmoving, scorched and sodden and half-dead.

When Kurara dropped back down to earth, she landed on the phoenix's chest.

"I'm sorry," she whispered.

"*Aki!*" Suzaku screamed.

"My. Name. Is. Kurara!"

She clenched her teeth together and pulled the spear out of Suzaku's chest. As the flames crept closer to her, she stood up, rammed her arm through the gaping hole that her weapon had left, and pulled out Suzaku's core.

FORTY-ONE

HIMURA wished that he could go back in time and punch whoever had the bright idea to build Kazami underground. No, it was not the underground part that bothered him. Despite the darkness and general gloom of the interlocking caves, there were just enough mushrooms and paper guide-stones for him to make his way without stubbing his toe or bumping his head against a low ceiling. It was the tunnels. Whoever had dug them had done so like a child putting pen to paper and just scribbling all over the empty space.

The result was a confusing mess of narrow, winding passages that looped back on themselves several times; paths that led down other paths that knotted together in a huge ring; tunnels that ended in empty caves; and caverns that seemed to promise a way forward only to suddenly end.

Mana clung to his shoulders as Himura pushed his

way through underground chambers filled with statues of shikigami. Each one had a small stone plaque with a name carved onto it. Himura wondered if these statues represented actual, real-life shikigami that had once existed.

As he traveled farther, the number of homes and storehouses thinned until he was sure that the remaining caverns were used only for trapping unsuspecting intruders and leading them to their grisly deaths.

It was only thanks to the snake's warnings that Himura avoided spring snares and pits full of spikes. There was no way an ordinary human would be able to pass through the caves. Even if they managed to avoid the traps, there were wide chasms and caves where one could only advance with the use of ofuda.

Himura stopped dead as another tunnel opened up into a grotto filled with water. Dark shapes flickered beneath the surface. Light seeped through the cracks in the ceiling, illuminating large spires of rock and mineral deposits that poked out from the underground lake.

"Ugh, water! Do not let my scales get wet!" Mana climbed to the top of his head.

For a moment, Himura wondered what he was doing allowing Mana to hang so very close to his neck. It would not take much for the shikigami to squeeze the air from his throat.

"What are you waiting for? You must cross the water to reach the Grand Stream."

Himura jolted into action. His paper bracelet unraveled, forming a sturdy boat that he used to push himself across the lake.

At first, the trip seemed simple enough. The boat easily cut through the water, and the creatures beneath the surface let him pass without a fuss. It was only when he was halfway across the lake that he heard a strange creaking sound, then the whoosh of something flying through the air.

"Look out!" cried Mana as a log, tied to two pieces of rope, dropped from the ceiling and swung toward him.

Himura ducked, but the bottom of the log caught Mana and knocked the snake into the water. The shikigami sank with a splash.

"Mana!" Himura plunged an arm into the lake and fumbled blindly for the snake.

Something wrapped around his wrist, squeezing hard. Himura held his breath and hoped that was the shikigami and not some deep-sea monster as he leaned back and hauled the thing out of the water. To his relief, a soggy but otherwise uninjured Mana fell back into the boat.

"Oh, cease your fretting! I was not even in there long!" the snake snapped as Himura quickly bundled the shikigami inside his kimono, hoping to dry out its paper scales. Long-term exposure to water could be just as damaging as fire.

Himura did not know what to do with his concern. He had never worried about a shikigami before. Was he only feeling that way because he knew that there was a soul inside Mana's core? If Akane were still here, if it had been Akane who had fallen into the water, would he feel the same way?

"Why are you helping me?"

"I told you, I am fond of fools."

Himura pulled a face. Why though? What was good about him? Himura could only see his arrogance, his bullheaded pride, the shameful need to feel special that he had mistaken for a love of knowledge. Didn't Mana see that too? Of course not; if the snake did there was no way it would stay with him—but if it didn't realize just who Himura was by now, then when would it? When would Mana's cackling laughter turn vicious? When would the snake leave him?

"I want to . . . apologize for the things I said to you before," he said. "I didn't understand anything about shikigami. You were right about why I was so obsessed with the past. In the end, I didn't understand anything at all."

"*I accept your apology. You should not feel ashamed. Children must be allowed to make mistakes in order to grow.*"

Deadly mistakes, thought Himura. Akane had paid for his stupidity with its life. How could anyone forgive him after that? How could he forgive himself?

"I'm not a child."

"*All humans are children to me. By the time you figure out what is really important, you've already wasted half your life. Really, I pity you humans. And I envy you.*"

Himura said nothing. He did not want to think about how much time he had wasted chasing after the past, or how many years he had spent believing incorrect things about shikigami. He only knew what he wanted and what he had to do now.

The log trap swung back and forward for a bit before losing momentum and hanging, perfectly still, on its ropes above the middle of the lake. Himura made sure to avoid it as he pushed the boat the rest of the way to the other end of the cavern.

"I hear something." He hauled both himself and Mana

onto dry land. His ofuda turned back into the bracelet around his wrist as he tipped his head back to look at the ceiling. There was a distant whistling sound coming from somewhere up above.

"That would be the howl of the Grand Stream," said Mana. *"We should be close."*

Himura made his way through another narrow passage and into a large cave filled with paper. Next to the tunnel from which he had just emerged, there were three other entrances, revealing alternative paths that all led to this single point. On the other side of the cave, there was only one way out. Sunlight streamed through the exit. As Himura approached, the whistling sound stopped.

"This must be it."

"You're not going anywhere without me." Mana coiled itself around his arm.

Himura flashed the snake a grateful smile. He had never thought a day would come when he would be grateful to a shikigami but now, as he made his way into the sunlight, he was glad that he was not alone.

FORTY-TWO

THE paper strings binding the sphere to Suzaku's body snapped. One last, dying screech pierced the heavens as its body disintegrated, sending a tidal wave of paper washing over the ground. The deluge swept Kurara across the crater and into a shallow lake several feet away from Suzaku's remains.

Her ears were ringing. Covered in dirt and soaked to the bone, she blinked back the water stinging her eyes and crawled toward the shore.

The world tipped to one side. Everything was muffled and blurry. The core! Where was the core? Her hands scrabbled blindly through the dirt. She had not just killed Suzaku only to lose the Seed again. It had to be here somewhere!

As her hearing returned and her vision cleared, Kurara glanced at her new surroundings. The scene inside the crater had descended into mayhem. Sayo and Tomoe were barely able to dodge Fujiwa's attacks while cannon fire from the *Hotei* continued to bombard the ground. The levistone in the rock walls exploded and burned, spreading flames across the grass that turned the trees to matchsticks.

Kurara slapped a hand over her nose and mouth to stop herself from inhaling the smoke. Suzaku's core was nowhere to be seen. As she stumbled toward the ashy remains of Suzaku's body, she spotted a skinny figure standing in the middle of a shallow pond.

Haru was as dirty as the rest of them. The shelling from the cannonballs had thrown dirt all over his head and shoulders, catching in his thick tousle of black curls. His clothes were ripped and wet, but in his hand he held a white ball covered with red patterns.

Suzaku's core.

"Haru!" barked Fujiwa.

Haru jerked to attention, and Kurara felt her stomach drop. Fujiwa was still Haru's master. He could order Haru to do whatever he wanted.

Princess Tsukimi must have realized this at the same time Kurara did, because her smile morphed into a grin of vicious triumph.

She opened her mouth, but whatever she was going to say was drowned out as a loud rumble split apart the sky. When Kurara looked up, she could see the hull of that large, white imperial airship bearing down upon her. It landed in the middle of the crater, coming to a stop with a thud that shook the ground.

"All right, all right, let's break it up, shall we?"

Kurara could only gape up at the man leaning over the

deck of the white ship. He was unmistakably a groundling: dressed in a fancier version of the military uniform she had often seen when she was a servant on the *Midori*. A general perhaps? There was no doubt that the man was someone of important rank—he had that air about him, that aura of easy charisma that often accompanied those with status and power.

Princess Tsukimi looked absolutely livid.

"Ugetsu!"

"Aren't you going to ask me what I'm doing here, dear sister? You know I worry about you when we're apart," the man called down.

"Don't get in my way!" shrieked Tsukimi.

"And not a single word of thanks for saving you! Dearest sister, do we need another lesson in gratitude?"

Kurara swallowed around the hard lump in her throat. *This* was Prince Ugetsu? Why was he here of all places? From the look on Tsukimi's face, she was *not* happy to see him. Did that mean that Kurara could consider him an ally?

"Where's the *Orihime*?" cried Sayo, her expression aghast.

Neither the prince nor the princess paid her any mind. It was as if the world only contained the two of them. Princess Tsukimi glared at her brother. She looked two seconds away from ripping him apart.

"Why are you here?" she demanded.

"Haven't you heard the news? No, of course you haven't, dear sister. You're too busy chasing shikigami and crawling through dirt to pay attention to matters of the empire."

"What news?"

The man smiled. "Sohma—or rather, the Sorabito—have declared war against the empire."

———————o———————

"*What?*" Kurara's disbelief was echoed by everyone present. Only Princess Tsukimi looked completely unfazed.

"So, they've decided to doom themselves. Then why is there a Sorabito right next to you?"

Kurara jerked her head back to peer at the deck. Sure enough, there was another man standing next to Prince Ugetsu. He was a sticklike figure with a head that looked like an egg balancing upon a twig. There was something in his face that was strangely familiar. She felt as though she had seen him before, though she could not pinpoint where.

At least, not until Tomoe gave an incredulous cry: "Father?"

Kurara turned to stare at her friend. Yes, that's why the man's face looked familiar, she could see it now. They had the same nose, the same sharp, cunning eyes.

"There is a Sorabito with me because I've decided to take their side against the Emperor," said Ugetsu.

"Those sky rats?" Princess Tsukimi looked utterly aghast, as if the thought of siding with Sorabito was no better than siding with a pack of animals.

"I told you that Father has no plans to give either of us the throne. Frankly, I grow tired of waiting. If he won't decide an heir, then I'll take the throne for myself." Ugetsu turned to the others. "Don't be scared, children. You heard me, did you not? I'm on your side."

"Where's the *Orihime*?" asked Sayo, again.

"Is that the name of your ship? I'm afraid I don't know. Why don't you come on board and we'll discuss this? I swear I will ensure your safety."

Sayo and Tomoe didn't say anything; nor did they move when the Imperial Prince extended a hand toward them. Ugetsu did not seem deterred by this, though.

"You there." He turned to address Kurara. "I saw you fighting. You're the shikigami girl my sister has been making herself a fool over."

Kurara swallowed. How did he know that she was a shikigami? She opened her mouth to reply, but no sound came out.

"That core in your friend's hand belonged to the shikigami known as Suzaku, did it not? Give it here. That's a dangerous item. It should be in the hands of the military," said Ugetsu.

Kurara glanced at Haru, who still clutched Suzaku's core tight.

"Don't do anything rash now. Tomoe, tell your friend to do as Prince Ugetsu asks," said Tomoe's father.

Tomoe jerked at the sudden sound of her father's voice. Balling her hands into fists, she shouted back, "And what are you doing standing next to a groundling? And the prince of the empire, no less! Aren't you disgusted with yourself?"

"Children, children, the adults are making important decisions that don't concern you. Let us take you back to where you belong. You can continue your life as usual while we take care of everything else," said Ugetsu.

Kurara should have known that the moment Princess

Tsukimi was no longer part of the conversation, she would try something. While Kurara's attention was on Prince Ugetsu, Tsukimi turned to Haru.

"Give me the core!" she cried, and Fujiwa repeated the order, compelling Haru to obey.

"Haru, don't!" Kurara screamed, but she knew that no matter how loud she yelled, she could not change what was about to happen. She gathered up the ofuda that had fallen when Suzaku had barreled into her and aimed a long paper rope at Haru, hoping to catch him and reel him toward her like a fish, but Fujiwa blocked her shot.

"Rara, do you want the core, or do you actually want the Seed inside? There might be nothing in here at all," Haru said, as if he had not heard Fujiwa.

Fujiwa gave him a baffled look and barked the same order once more, but again Haru did not seem to hear him.

"No, it's in there. The Star Seed does exist. I remember. I . . . I . . ." Kurara stuttered.

"You and I once thought the same way. Crafters learned how to create shikigami, and then used that knowledge to control and enslave others. A way to kill. A way to wage war." Haru's fingers curled around the core. "Crafters. Shikigami. They're all the same. Crafters treat shikigami like dirt, and then they die or become shikigami themselves. That's righteous punishment, isn't it? Those Crafters deserve to know what it's like to be treated like a tool. Why should people like that be given their freedom?"

His words struck her harder than a cannonball. Kurara took a step back. When their eyes met, she saw not the bliss of obedience but a fierce anger swimming in his gaze.

329

"That's not true. Maybe Aki thought like that, but not me. Some Crafters were innocent when they were caught and turned into shikigami—and even if they weren't, even if all the people who were turned into shikigami were horrible people, once they become shikigami they're no longer the same. They're different people with no memories of the past. Why should they be punished for what they did in another life?"

Haru's expression was a complicated web of emotion. Kurara could not tell if he was testing her or if he really believed the things he said.

The smallest of smiles tugged at the corners of Haru's lips. "I'm on your side, Rara. I'm *always* on your side. Whatever you decide, I'll agree with it. Do you want the Seed or not?"

Kurara sucked in a deep breath. She wanted the Star Seed, of course she did. But did she want it enough to live with the consequences of retrieving it? Did she care about freeing the shikigami more than she cared about the damage that unleashing all the souls trapped in Suzaku's core would do?

If only there was an easy answer. She could have spent an eternity mulling over the question, but that was time she did not have. Regret could come later. For now, she went with her gut.

"I want the Seed, Haru," said Kurara.

"Did you not hear me? Haru! Give the princess the core!" Fujiwa stared at Haru in confusion and frustration.

Haru smiled. "No."

Kurara's stomach did a flip. It was not that Haru had not heard Fujiwa the first time; he was ignoring him. But that was impossible. Shikigami could not disobey the Crafter they had a blood bond with. They could not ignore their master.

"Impossible! You cannot say no to me!" Fujiwa's shock mirrored her own.

"Well, I'm special, aren't I?" Haru continued to back away as Fujiwa advanced.

Tsukimi's grin widened, but there was nothing humorous about the look in her eye. She stared at Haru the way a cat assessed its prey.

"No, someone . . . someone used their blood to create a new bond with you. They wrote over Fujiwa's bond with their own blood. Who was it? Who had the gall?"

Himura! Kurara's stomach flipped at the very thought. It had to be Himura; they had not run into any other Crafter besides him. But how? *When?*

Then she remembered. While she had followed Oda into the woman's home, Haru had been alone with Himura. Well, Mana had been there as well, but Kurara had no way of knowing if the snake had stuck around.

"Haru, if Himura forced you into a bond . . ." She would kill him. She would rip his heart out of his chest. She was so furious with Himura that for a moment she completely forgot that Haru had fooled her, too, while he had pretended to be under Fujiwa's control.

"Don't blame him, Rara. I *asked* to bond with Himura," said Haru. "So that Fujiwa couldn't use me against you. So that I could do this!"

Crouching down, he dropped the core between his feet and picked up a large rock. Raising it above his head, he brought it down on the core with a crack that seemed to split the world in two.

The agony was a familiar one. Kurara screamed as

331

invisible hands tried to rip out her ribcage. Her vision flickered, the sight of the crater overlapping with something else—somewhere else. Her surroundings disappeared. Suddenly, she was standing in the middle of a cave somewhere as people chanted around her.

All that lives shall die.

As Kurara yanked herself out of the memory—a memory that was not hers—another creature passed through her. She screamed as more memories assaulted her vision. The pain was excruciating.

From now on, your name is . . .

When she blinked, she saw a pair of twins holding each other's hands. The enemy had them surrounded. There was no way out. The sounds of battle raged on in the distance. How strange it was to know with such certainty that you were going to die.

May you be worthy . . .

A man dressed like a samurai looked across the battlefield at the oncoming wave of soldiers as fire raged around him. He was bleeding; he was going to die whether the flames took him or not. He smirked as the fire grew. At the very least, he would take the enemy with him.

May you be worthy of your name.

With one last, desperate gasp, she tried to fight off the heavy hands dragging her into a memory that did not belong to her, but it was no good.

Before the darkness could pull her under, she was blind-sided by a rush of paper crashing into her body with the force of a speeding train. A pair of strong hands wrapped around her, and someone yanked her free from the shadows.

Interlude

Brother did not die
Our people do not know death
We are eternal
And I will see you again
Though you wear another name

—Written by a Crafter of Unknown Origin
(from the personal library
of the Imperial Princess)

A dark shadow rippled out from inside the core, then another and another, each emerging like a monstrous newborn: a writhing mass of smoky limbs and tangled mouths that made no sound. Shadowy, humanoid shapes dispersed in every direction. Some disappeared over the rock walls while others swirled around the crater.

Ugetsu reeled back as he stared up at the blackened sky. His hands gripped the side of the airship, and his face was pale with fear. In Nessai, he had talked so loftily about learning

333

more about these strange shadows, about using them as a weapon, but in the end he was just like their father: a coward who could not understand the intricate wonders of shikigami.

From below, Tsukimi stared at the swirling darkness that rushed around her. This was something even more terrifying than the shikigami. A weapon that could be used to expand the empire, to remove her father from power, to get her anything she wanted—if only she could control it.

Something with too many arms dived straight for her. Tsukimi barely managed to avoid its knife-like hands. She jumped back as several more monsters advanced. Her gaze darted from one creature to the next as they swirled like sharks around their prey.

"Ugetsu, let us on!" If she could fly away, she might just be able to lose these monsters.

Her brother tore his eyes away from the swarm of shadows to peer down at her. The Sorabito behind him whispered something in his ear, something Tsukimi could not catch, but when Ugetsu nodded, the engines of the *Hotei* came to life and the airship began to rise.

A ragged scream tore Tsukimi's attention away from her brother. She turned her head only to find herself face-to-face with a pair of misshapen heads that dangled down from the broken stick of its neck. On crooked, spiderlike legs, the monster lunged for her.

"Your Highness! Ruki, get Her Highness out of here!" Fujiwa dived for her, pushing her out of the way just in time. The smoke creature leapt forward and entered through his ribcage. Fujiwa clutched his chest with a gasp.

 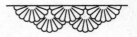

It felt as though all of time stopped. Ruki howled in horror. A choked gasp escaped Fujiwa's lips. His eyes rolled back as he fell. His body hit the ground where he lay, unmoving.

Princess Tsukimi did not have time to fully process Fujiwa's death before she was suddenly hoisted off her feet. Ruki grabbed the back of her kimono in its mouth and lifted her up.

"What is the meaning of this?" she spluttered. "Let me go!"

While she struggled against the shikigami's hold, Ugetsu and his pet Sorabito retreated into the depths of the airship.

"Ugetsu!" she screamed. "Ugetsu!"

Her body swayed as Ruki climbed up the rock walls and carried her over the lip of the crater. The barren ground below stretched out like the cold, gray skin of some giant, dead beast. This was alien territory. A landscape that was meant to be part of their country and yet looked eerily like the wastelands of Yomi. Without the constant winds of the Grand Stream, there was no dust or sand to obscure how bleak the surroundings truly were. The trees were thin and cracked, the ground as dry as a tinderbox, and the rocks like jagged bones. Even the sky was an off-putting pale gray. The color of a fresh corpse.

As the *Hotei* took flight, Ruki bounded down the other side of the crater and away from what had once been the Grand Stream. Once they were far enough away, Ruki spat her out of its mouth.

"Go!" it bellowed. *"Go quickly, before I lose myself!"*

Tsukimi staggered to her feet, bewildered and furious. Dirt clung to her hair and clothes. She clenched her teeth together. "How dare you . . ."

Ruki growled. *"Master ordered me to take you away. Master Fujiwa was loyal to you. He wished you to be safe. Now he is dead, I am no longer bound by his orders. The only reason I do not tear you limb from limb is out of respect for my former master. Go now, before I cannot stop myself!"*

Running away was something a coward did. Tsukimi would not humiliate herself by running. She stood tall, her hands balled into fists. As she glared back at the shikigami, a storm of shadowy creatures whirled around the crater and spilled over the top of the rock walls.

They were heading toward the nearest town.

Her hands shook. Not only had she not captured the shikigami children, Tsukimi had lost all her imperial Crafters, she no longer had her airship, and now there was news of a war. Why was everything falling apart? Why could she not control paper? Why could she not bond with a shikigami? She was the princess, was she not? She could have anything she wanted.

Tsukimi grabbed the shikigami by its paper fur. The only reason it she was able to yank the tiger toward her was because Ruki put up no resistance, but Tsukimi was not going to dwell on that.

"Listen, you overgrown cat!" she hissed. "I am the Imperial Princess of the Empire of Mikoshima; you will *not* leave me here!"

Ruki's marble-white eyes flashed with anger. It jerked out of her grasp. *I have watched you for many years, and I know this—you are neither as talented nor as intelligent as you think you are.*

"You may know more than anyone else about shikigami, and your experiments may be impressive, but that is only because you have access to books no one else has—anyone with the same resources and enough determination could achieve what you have. Your father does not keep the throne from you and your brother because he enjoys your petty squabbles but because neither of you are fit to rule! You are nothing but a child!"

No one had ever spoken to her like that before. Tsukimi fought the urge to rip the shikigami apart with her bare hands. What did a mere beast know about power or talent? She was the Imperial Princess, and she was more fit to rule the empire than her oaf of a brother or her dullard father.

"If that's what you believe then let us make a bet." Tsukimi drew her gun from its holster. "If I can defeat you in combat, you must obey me and assist me in my goals until the day your madness takes you."

"And if I win?"

"Then you may tear my body to shreds."

Ruki lowered its head level with the princess. Its unblinking marble eyes betrayed no emotion, but it sounded rather amused when it said, *"Very well! I shall relish the sensation of your flesh between my jaws!"*

FORTY-THREE

KURARA did not realize that she was back inside the tunnels beneath the Grand Stream until she was thrown onto her hands and knees. Spluttering like a swimmer surging up from beneath the sea, a barrage of angry voices thundered over her.

"What in the blue skies were you thinking? You could have killed us all!"

"I only did as I was asked!"

"We almost died!"

"Oh, cease your prattling! You have all your limbs, have you not?"

Confused and disoriented, Kurara stumbled to her feet only to find everyone had stopped arguing in favor of staring at her.

"Kuraraaaaaa!"

"T–Tomoe?" Kurara hardly had time to blink. Relief

caught in her throat and tied her tongue in knots. There was Tomoe, her hair and face covered with dirt but otherwise whole and uninjured, with Sayo trailing across the crater behind her like a grumpy baby chick. She was so glad they were all right.

She was so glad they were here.

"By the blue skies, Kurara, no one from the *Orihime* is going to believe the last few hours we just lived through! I can hardly believe we're alive. *Are* we alive? Gods, we're not actually dead, are we?"

Kurara swayed on her two feet. She was not entirely sure what had just happened.

"I pulled all of you into the tunnels." Himura approached her with Mana wrapped around his shoulders. Their faces were illuminated by the soft glow of the luminous fungi. "I used my ofuda to carry us all underground." He offered her a hand to steady herself.

Kurara did not take it. Something in his expression shifted. When Himura spoke, there was nothing but steely determination in his tone.

"As far as I know, Prince Ugetsu and Princess Tsukimi have also fled from the crater. We should move as well. Those shadowy things are spreading across the land. I don't know where they will go, but we should probably not stay here."

So it was Himura who had helped her. Kurara squeezed the bridge of her nose, feeling an awful pain building up at the back of her eyes, when a sudden realization struck her.

"Wait! What about the Seed? Where's the Star Seed?"

She remembered Haru cracking open Suzaku's core,

remembered the shadowy creatures that had emerged and then—

Nothing. She could not remember what had happened next, only the pain.

Kurara drew a sharp breath. If she had not put the Seed in Suzaku's core, the shikigami would still be alive. There would not be a dozen or more monsters roaming the land. If she had never turned the people of Kazami into a shikigami, they would not have had to live for centuries fighting off the pain of being a creature with too many souls in one body, or the madness of being a shikigami without a bond. If she had not asked Haru for the Star Seed, he would not have cracked open the core.

If she had lost the Star Seed, if it had been destroyed, then everything she had done would have been for nothing. What was the point of everything, what was the meaning in all the pain she had inflicted, if she did not have the Seed?

"I have it." Haru stepped forward, holding out his palm. Sure enough, lying inside the flat of his hand was a small white object in the shape of an eight-pointed star. It did not look like any seed Kurara had ever seen before.

"Haru," Kurara clenched her teeth together. "That's a rock."

"This is what was inside Suzaku's core," said Haru. "Honestly, I still can't believe it's real."

"But it's a rock." Despair crept around the edges of Kurara's core. How was some stupid rock supposed to help her?

Haru nodded. "I told you before that Star Trees were no ordinary trees. They didn't produce fruits or seeds, but . . .

do you remember the old lullaby? *A dying star fell from the heavens, and from that star grew a tree.* I think that perhaps the term 'Star Seed' is just another name for the dying stars that fell from the sky and turned into Star Trees."

That made sense. Perhaps that was why both Oda and Haru had insisted that the Star Seed was not real. It wasn't actually a seed. *A dying star fell from the heavens. And from that star grew a tree.* Kurara felt the tension in her chest ease. It had not been a fairy tale. The key to the shikigami's freedom was right here.

"So you're gonna plant a rock?" Tomoe cocked an eyebrow.

Well, when said out loud, it did sound ridiculous, but Kurara reckoned it was as good an idea as any.

"Give it here, Haru." She held out her hand.

"Do you really want it, Rara? I asked you before why you thought it was your responsibility to free the shikigami. It's not too late to change your mind. You could do anything you want. We could go exploring. Or we could find our old village and live there in peace for the rest of our lives."

Kurara's arm ached from how long she had held out her hand. Exhaustion threatened to creep through her body, but she kept her palm open, her fingers outstretched, and waited. Despite the secrets and the disagreements, she knew Haru. She knew him the way the moon knew its orbit, the way birds knew how to fly, or stars to burn. She knew that he always had her best interests at heart.

"Aki wanted to protect the Star Trees," she said. "But after failing so many times, she grew angry and bitter. She stopped caring about shikigami. If shikigami were just Crafters that had been sacrificed and Crafters were all bad people, then what was the point in trying to save the shikigami? That's what she thought.

"Something's been bothering me though. If Aki wanted to, she could have just destroyed the Seed, but she didn't. She didn't because I think, deep down, a part of her still felt the way I do now—that no matter who a shikigami was in their past life or what they did, when they're reborn they shouldn't have to carry those mistakes with them."

Kurara took another step forward, her arm still extended.

"So, yes, Haru, I want the Star Seed," she said.

He smiled at her as if no one else existed in that moment. Yes, no matter who else they met during their long lives, it had always been the two of them, hadn't it? From the moment of their creation, they had been inseparable.

"Did you know that names are important for shikigami?" said Haru. "They represent the wishes and hopes people have for them."

"I know. Shikigami are not the people they were in their previous life. That's why they're given new names. It's a new start." Kurara thought about the glimpse of Banri's memory that she had seen, of the flashes of other Crafters becoming shikigami.

May you be worthy of your name, they had said.

Haru ran a hand through his hair, pushing it out of his eyes. "Did you know that I gave you your new name?"

Kurara looked at him in surprise.

"Ku. Ra. Ra. It means—"

"Joy," she said. "And suffering."

"It means 'may your happiness be greater than your sorrow.' That was my wish for you."

342

Haru dropped the Star Seed into her palm.

"May you be worthy of your name."

———————o———————

When the others found another way back to the surface, they emerged several miles from the crater where they had fought the princess and Suzaku. The shadow creatures were gone, as was any sign of the Imperial Prince and Princess.

It was quiet without the howling winds. Too quiet. The sun had set and the stars emerged to wreath the night's sky, but even the gentle glow of starlight could not change just how barren the land looked.

"Well, this has been nothing but one nightmare after another," said Sayo. "And out of all that, we didn't even get Suzaku's core."

"We're alive, that's good, right? Right?" Tomoe gave Sayo a small shove. "And now we can return home. To the *Orihime*."

"Where is the *Orihime*?"

"Sola-Ea. The plan was to stop at the sky city of Sola-Ea for repairs before heading on to the Grand Stream. If war was suddenly announced, they were probably held up there, unable to leave," said Himura. Kurara could not get used to the sight of him with Mana draped over his shoulder. She wanted to snatch the shikigami away.

"War . . ." she muttered.

It felt as though she had been underground for a hundred years, only to emerge to find the world was completely different. Sure, the empire waged plenty of wars, but they were always overseas. Elsewhere. This was different. The sky cities hovered above Mikoshima. There were Sorabito living on the ground and groundlings who had made their homes in the skies.

War, thought Kurara, was completely ridiculous.

"Kurara," said Himura, his expression solemn. "What are you planning to do now?"

"I'm not sure." Kurara could not think straight, her mind too caught up with thoughts of war and the shadowy creatures that had escaped Suzaku's core.

Himura nodded, as if he understood everything that was going through her head right now.

"Whatever you decide to do, take me with you."

"You expect me to agree to that?" She wanted to remain angry at him for what he had done to her and Haru, for Akane's death, but she did not think she had the right to judge him anymore, not after learning about Suzaku.

Himura looked chastised, yet still he insisted. "Take me with you. I want to . . . learn more about shikigami. Not how to make them. I mean, I want to learn about how they live. What their hopes and dreams are. I want to get to know them."

As people, he didn't say, but his thoughts were betrayed by the way his ofuda flitted nervously around him.

"And I will come with you." Mana brushed its tail against the side of Himura's cheek. *"By the way, are you interested in seeing the Grave-keeper?"*

Himura chuckled, though Kurara did not understand what was so funny.

"You and Mana . . ." She eyed him with suspicion.

"We don't have a bond," said Himura.

344

No, but you bonded with Haru. You made yourself his master. Kurara held back a bitter retort.

"What will happen to those shadow things now?" asked Haru.

Kurara didn't want to know. She couldn't bear to think about what she'd set loose. Would they disappear eventually? Or would they wander across the country, bringing death and destruction wherever they went?

"There is nothing we can do about them now," said Mana. *"They will roam the land, attracted to the light, searching for life, and will kill all they encounter."*

"But there must be some way of stopping them. Like how hunters stop shikigami that have lost their minds."

Mana's silence was not comforting. Kurara glanced over to where Sayo and Tomoe had been having a whispered conversation of their own. As their eyes met, Sayo peeled away from Tomoe's side to stand by the fire, her features softened by the flickering firelight.

"Tomoe and I will return to the skies. We'll head to Sola-Ea and meet up with the *Orihime*. You have other business to attend to, don't you?"

It was a goodbye. Sayo did not ask her to come with them and Kurara did not push. Perhaps, long ago, she would have been hurt by that—didn't Sayo want her to return to the *Orihime*? Did she think that she would be a burden to the ship?—but now she understood that their paths were simply taking them in different directions. Sayo and Tomoe's priorities would always be with the ship first and foremost, but Kurara's goals were leading her away from the sky. There was a Star Tree to plant, and shikigami that needed to be protected.

345

"You'll be out of a job soon," she said, half-jokingly. "Once this tree is grown, there won't be any more wild shikigami. They won't lose their minds, and there will be no need for hunters."

Sayo smirked. "I've always thought I'd make a good merchant."

"We need to find somewhere safe to plant this Seed," said Haru. "But in the meantime, shikigami will still die. Shikigami will still lose their minds and be hunted; they'll still be used as tools by heartless Crafters—and if there truly is going to be a war, things will just get worse for the shikigami."

"Now that both Princess Tsukimi and Prince Ugetsu have seen what comes out from a broken core, I don't doubt they'll try to use that knowledge to their advantage," Himura added.

Kurara stared at her hands, one as white as snow and as light as paper, yet capable of slitting throats and punching through wood. When she looked toward the sky, she thought about all the people she had met, about how far she had come to get here. There was still so much to do.

"Then we'd better get a move on," she said.

GLOSSARY OF TERMS

Crafters – People who can control paper at will.

Hakama – Clothing tied around the waist that falls to the ankles.

Haori – A traditional jacket worn over a kimono.

Katana – A type of sword with a curved, single-edged blade, wielded with two hands.

Kimono – Clothing made from straight cuts. Wraps around the body and must be tied and folded securely in place.

Kitsune – Fox yōkai known for their intelligence and cunning. They appear in mythology both as faithful guardians and as tricksters.

Ko – The common currency of Mikoshima.

Kohane – A common type of aircraft used for transport, fighting and scouting.

Menko – A game played by two or more players using cards with images printed on one or both sides. The aim is to try to flip the opponent's card by throwing your own at it.

Mochi – A snack made from glutinous rice, which is pounded into a paste and molded into various shapes.

Obi – A sash worn with a kimono.

Ōdachi – A type of sword, longer and larger than a katana.

Ofuda – Paper used by Crafters. Though traditionally one should write a blessing or prayer onto ofuda, many Crafters these days skip this step.

Okayu – Savory rice porridge, also known as congee.

Oni – A fierce type of yōkai with horns protruding from their head. They are commonly depicted with red or blue skin (though other colors of oni exist) and are often compared to ogres or demons.

Qipak – A type of aircraft typically used for short flights. It resembles a small fishing boat with wings.

Shakujo – A staff with metal rings hanging from the top.

Shikigami – Creatures made from paper. A Crafter can bind a shikigami to their will with a blood bond. Without a master, shikigami eventually become violent.

Shoji – Traditional sliding doors made by placing paper across or between wooden frames.

Sorabito – Literally: Sky People. A group of people who are born on one of the seven sky cities. Considered second-class citizens by the empire.

Suzaku – The name given to a famous shikigami that dwells in Southern Mikoshima. It is known for destroying any airships that approach it.

Tanto – A short sword usually compared to a knife or a dagger.

Tatami – A type of mat made from woven rushes and other materials.

Yōkai – Supernatural, spiritlike creatures.

Yomi – The underworld.

PLACES

Grand Stream – An area of Southern Mikoshima cut off by fierce winds. Rumor has it that these winds are caused by the beat of the shikigami Suzaku's wings.

The *Hotei* – Prince Ugetsu's imperial airship.

The *Jurojin* – An airship made by Sorabito craftsman, taken by the Emperor and gifted to Princess Tsukimi.

Kazami – An underground settlement created by Crafters during the Great War. Built to purposefully confuse invaders with long, labyrinthine tunnels.

The *Kuroi Kame* – A merchant ship that operates across Mikoshima. Its crew can often be found drinking and gambling at Nessai Harbor.

The *Midori* – A floating restaurant made of banquet halls and private rooms built by groundlings. The place where Haru and Kurara worked before it was destroyed.

Nessai Harbor – A port town in Eastern Mikoshima. It was constructed from the remains of a failed sky city.

The *Orihime* – A Sorabito ship dedicated to hunting shikigami. A place Kurara once considered home.

Sola-Ea – One of the seven sky cities belonging to the Sorabito.

Sola-Il – The first sky city ever built. It is considered the Sorabito's founding city.

ACKNOWLEDGMENTS

When asked to provide an acknowledgment, my first thought was, "Oh no, I'm going to forget someone!" Therefore, before the caffeine-induced fog takes me, I would like to thank the following:

Once again, a huge thank you to my agent, Lina Langlee, for continuing to champion my work. You are truly worth your weight in gold! Thank you to my tireless editor, Gráinne Clear, who I'm sure has had enough of my shenanigans and weird tangents. Thank you for wrangling all my flights of fancy into line and getting me to deliver on time. Anyone who says you can't herd cats has clearly never met Gráinne. My thanks also go to Amir Zand for the amazing cover art, Ben Norland, Rosi Crawley, Rebecca Oram, Jackie Atta-Hayford, Denise Johnstone-Burt, Jo Humphreys-Davies, Jenny Bish, Rebecca J. Hall, and all the good folks at Walker Books for their hard work and passion.

A huge, huge thank you to Nikoo Saeki once again for being such an amazing first reader. Your comments are so unbelievably helpful, I don't think all the gold in the world could make it up to you. Thank you once again to my friends David, Dane, Kimiko, Maria, Monika, and Chloe for lending me a figurative shoulder to cry on whenever I needed it and for your constant reassurances that everything would be OK. It won't be, but I appreciate your lies.

Of course, I would be remiss not to mention the authors of the 22 Debuts group. Your support, advice and morale boosts were so invaluable, I don't think it's an exaggeration to say I wouldn't have finished this book without you all cheering me on. Also, a million thank yous to the teachers and librarians who have read and recommended *Rebel Skies* to their students. It warms my heart to see young people falling in love with books.

Lastly, but by no means least, many thanks to you, the person reading this book. Without you, there would be no *Rebel Fire*. Thank you for coming along with me into this world, for spending time with the characters, and walking their journeys with them.